What Readers Are Saying

"Full of richly drawn characters who will tug at your heartstrings, *Child of Grace* explores a serious topic in a delightful, intelligent way."
   —Deborah Raney, author of *Beneath a Southern Sky* and *A Vow to Cherish*

"Lori Copeland has long been a master of the romance genre, and *Child of Grace* moves her front and center to the woman's-fiction arena."
                              —Colleen Coble, romance author

"*Child of Grace* is thought provoking, richly woven, and guaranteed to touch your heart."
                       —Kathleen Morgan, author of *Lady of Light*

"*Child of Grace* delivers laughter, the light and love of God and, as promised by the title, grace, grace, and more grace. You'll be glad you spent time in Cullen's Corner."
              —Lisa E. Samson, best-selling author of *The Church Ladies*

"Lori Copeland skillfully invites your heart to journey inward and examine itself. This town and its events will linger in your mind long after you close the cover."
                         —Kristin Billerbeck, romance author

child of grace

child of Grace

LORI COPELAND

Tyndale House Publishers, Inc., Wheaton, Illinois

Visit Tyndale's exciting Web site at www.tyndale.com

Edited by Diane Eble

Designed by Jacqueline L. Noe

Unless otherwise indicated, all Scripture quotations are taken from the *Holy Bible*, New Living Translation, copyright © 1996. Used by permission of Tyndale House Publishers, Inc., Wheaton, Illinois 60189. All rights reserved.

Scripture quotations are taken from the *Holy Bible*, King James Version.

Scripture quotations marked NRSV are taken from the New Revised Standard Version of the Bible, copyright © 1989 by the Division of Christian Education of the National Council of the Churches of Christ in the United States of America, and are used by permission. All rights reserved.

Library of Congress Cataloging-in-Publication Data

Copeland, Lori.
   Child of grace / Lori Copeland.
     p. cm.
   ISBN 0-8423-4260-5 (sc)
    1. Acquaintance rape—Fiction. 2. Pregnant women—Fiction. I. Title.

PS3553.O6336 C48 2001
813'.54—dc21   2001017146

Printed in the United States of America

06 05 04 03 02 01
9 8 7 6 5 4 3 2 1

To my sons:
Lance Randall, Richard Loren,
and Russell Dean Copeland

And my grandsons:
James Randall, Joseph Lance,
Joshua Daniel, and Russell Gage Copeland

My granddaughter:
Audrey Loren

Thank you, Father, for allowing me to be there for
the first smile, the first tooth, the first step. . . .

May my children walk beside You in green meadows.

I have called you by name, you are mine.

—Isaiah 43:1, NRSV

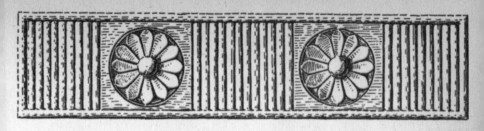

PROLOGUE

Now, here's the thing, folks. When we're young and full of hopes, it's easy to think that we know everything. At seventeen or eighteen—fresh out of high school—we have the world at our fingertips. No more rules; we're free to make our own, and most often do—with tragic consequences.

Which one of us hasn't assumed that we're invincible, that bad things happen only to other people? A plane crash, an automobile accident, death, divorce, rape, or abortion can't touch us because . . . well, because it doesn't, or it hasn't to most of us, so we conclude in our naïveté, it likely won't.

We and we alone control our life.

Most people can't pinpoint the hour or moment their life actually changed. I'm lucky because I can. (Or maybe that's not so lucky.) June twentieth. Nine o'clock in the evening. I even know the weather that night: muggy and unseasonably warm for North Carolina. While it all seems a long time ago, time is irrelevant.

Yet because I do know the day my life took a different course, I am filled with awe at God's power to change a person on the inside. I'm not without occasional doubts, but I have a lasting conviction that he is alive and working in my life.

I listen to the soft sounds of my sleeping infant. The scent of baby powder fills my senses, and I'm almost heady with joy as I gently tuck a lightweight blanket around the source of my happiness. I marvel at the tiny fist clenched almost combatively as if she knows . . . as though she's smarter than we are and knows life is precious, however it's given to us.

But for now, this blissfully quiet time while my child sleeps, I tiptoe around the cradle for fear of disturbing her. For the moment, everything is right in her world and I am deeply thankful. I know that won't always be the case. There will be death and sorrow and decisions—some made right and some made wrong. And happiness: incredible moments when life is so full, so good we're frightened, knowing that change is coming.

My daughter isn't invincible, though she doesn't know that yet. Her life might not be altered as dramatically as mine was that night in June, but it will change. Innocence will fall away, and the world will intrude as sure as wrinkles.

But for now, my child sleeps in grace.

Everything is right in my world: I am equally yoked to a man whom I love, I know God's love, and God has enabled me to accomplish much in my life. The recent birth of this child ranks right up there with feeding the multitudes with five loaves and two fish, for this precious, squeaky, six-pound-three-ounce bundle of joy is truly a miracle.

"Little but scrappy," my husband likes to brag. I laugh at his pride—as if I weren't experiencing my share of maternal bliss, gooing and cooing like a fool.

Ah, blessed quietness. I retreat to the front porch and sit down in the old swing with a cold glass of iced tea and the newest issue of *Parents*. Cullen's Corner is settling comfortably into afternoon like an old lady in her rocking chair. The melodic hum of lawn mowers does little to affect the stolen moment. Resting my eyes, I smell the sweetness of blooming honey-suckle mingling with Grams's old climbing roses and reflect on my accomplishments, none of which I can claim the slightest credit for. It's all God's hand.

Sitting here in the gentle breeze, I relax in his love and wonder at his unending grace. I think of the psalms that speak of God's mighty deeds and of passing the stories of God's goodness down through the generations.

I once read about a woman who longed to sit around a cooking fire with other women and share stories about the lives, loves, and passions of other generations. There are too few cooking fires to connect our lives, and maybe that's one of the problems with life nowadays. With no fires, there's nothing we share. In sharing the past we can learn how to prevent life from being harder than it has to be.

I want you to learn how to avoid some of the mistakes we all make! Perhaps hearing my story will help you to understand the depths of grace that is our heritage.

My story isn't particularly pleasant, but knowing it will help you understand the consequences of decisions. As a wonderfully wise old woman used to tell me, "Life's made up of the good and the bad, and the sooner you accept that, the happier your life will be. It's our decisions that make the difference." I have to admit, I've found that to be mostly true. Good and bad: that's life. It's our decisions that make the difference.

My story. Let's see . . . I suppose if I were to light the campfire between us, I'd begin with the day Eva Jean Roberts came back to Cullen's Corner, full of pride and determination. Oh my, what a choice that turned out to be. . . .

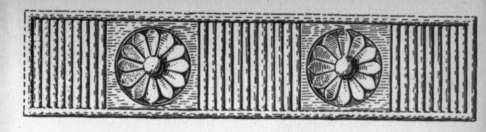

CHAPTER ONE

Cullen's Corner, North Carolina, is not now or ever was the center of the universe. And it didn't claim to be. Most maps left blank the space between Mistler's Point to the west and Garden Grove to the east. Local and state maps sold at the annual Onion Days Festival put the tiniest black dot along Highway 22E to pinpoint the sleepy burg. Population at last census: 423.

In spite of its size, remarkable things happen in Cullen's Corner. Like I said, there are the annual Onion Days Festival in July and the Thanksgiving Turkey Trot and canned food harvest in November. The highlight of every year, "A Cullen's Corner Christmas"—an original work written by Ferris Knob, the local newspaper editor—is performed each year by members of the First Full Baptist Evangelical Church of Christ. This church is the only church in Cullen's Corner, a conglomeration of three denominations that joined together when they realized that dividing the body of Christ severely hampered the prospect of a full cast for the Christmas pageant.

Cullen's Corner might be small, but it has its share of bad weather. Hurricanes from the Atlantic and a sporadic tornado occasionally wreak havoc in the quiet Carolina nook, but the town stands firm, picks up the pieces when Mother Nature deals a bad hand, and thanks the Lord when clouds move on and the sun comes out.

Neighborhood children play in yards, on porches, and sometimes in the middle of the street with little interference. The two stoplights at the edges of town work nearly all the time. When they don't, hardly anyone but passers-through notice.

At one of these lights, one sultry Wednesday evening in mid-June, as folks were sitting on porches to talk politics, baseball, and quilting, Eva Jean Roberts—E. J. to friends—stopped for a red light. The rented Ford carried just about everything that E. J. could throw into a suitcase in fifteen minutes: a toothbrush, four and a half pairs of socks in various colors, three shirts, three pairs of slacks, and five shoes. Neatly tucked in the side pocket was a small tube of Kilgore's Simply Fabulous Hair Foam, guaranteed to make your hair, well, simply fabulous. It was E. J.'s favorite product partially because she used it every day and mostly because she owned half of Kilgore's Kosmetics, such as the company was. At the time she pulled into town, the red ink overrode the pride of partial ownership.

Cell phone crammed to her ear, E. J. concluded the thirty-sixth business call of the day and depressed the button. Stress lay unkindly on her features. Normally a pretty woman, tonight E. J. looked as if she'd been pulled through a knothole backwards.

The light changed, and she took her foot off the brake. The blue Alamo bumper sticker on the rental drew a fair share of attention from children chasing fireflies in the fading twilight. The luminescent bugs lit the faces of small children who held them close in their hands or trapped them in Ball jars to show their parents, who had done the same thing for their parents before. E. J. had performed the same ritual growing up in Cullen's Corner: chasing the flying critters, capturing them, taking them to Grams and, occasionally, when she happened to be around, proudly showing her catch to Mommy.

Oh, Cullen's Corner attracted its fair share of tourists pulling off the highway at the local Conoco for gas, candy bars, and bathroom breaks. Folks stopped, but usually not this early in the season.

People born in Cullen's Corner tend, like Newton's First Law of Motion, to remain inert—to live, work, breathe, marry, and die right here in the Corner. Those who do leave tend to keep going, with no inclination to look back.

E. J. belonged to the latter. None of the end-of-the-day wearies lounging on their porches or in swings drinking tea or telling stories on front stoops and porches that June evening would have known that the prodigal daughter had returned. E. J. hadn't realized it herself, even though she found herself sitting in front of the house of her own firefly-chasing, porch-swinging childhood, listening to the car ticking a slow death.

She beeped the horn. No one appeared at the door. A second later she caught a glimpse of something big and orange approaching on the left. She jumped, and the seat belt caught her arm hard enough to leave a mark.

Unsnapping the harness, she spotted a large orange ball of fur coming at her with an old lady's face on top. The face was Grams's, and the cat was Albert.

Cora Roberts owned one cat at a time, and when it died of old age or was mercilessly flattened by an unsuspecting motorist, she would drive to Raleigh's animal shelter and get another one. She named each feline according to its personality. Georgie had been a Siamese named for E. J.'s great-aunt Georgia because, as Grams claimed, anyone could see that the cat looked exactly like Georgia. Ralph was a hyperactive tabby with a fur ball problem. Awful retching sounds in the night would be a precursor of presents in the hall and on the stairs the following morning.

Grams's animated face beamed as she pumped Albert's paw up and down in a furry welcome.

E. J. found the strength to open the door and step into the humid Carolina twilight.

"E. J.! As I live and breathe—what in the world are you doing here?" E. J. braced for the hug. Grams was a hugger, one of those touchy-feely kind of people who drive you nuts. "Albert and I stepped over to Edna Davenport's, and I said, 'I'll be if that don't look like my Eva Jean,' and Edna said, 'Now, Cora, you know that isn't her! She's in LA!' But it is and here you are." Grams swooped down on her, unseating the cat.

Albert sprang off her shoulder, scurrying for cover. Folks, hugs were not on that cat's list of favorites. Albert figured there were plenty of other things to do besides being squashed between two emotional women.

"How are you?" The hug unsettled E. J.'s footing, and she fell against the hood of the car. Cora Roberts was a five-foot-one bundle of energy with impish blue eyes and snow-white hair whacked short like a boy's. The faint scent of Cashmere Bouquet clung to her dress, and E. J. experienced a sentimental tug—something she hated.

"Let me look at you." Grams thrust E. J. at arm's length, her observant eyes skimming over her, head to foot. "You're still the prettiest girl Cullen's Corner ever produced, excluding me, of course." She giggled and her features softened with concern. "Have you been sick?"

"No. Why?"

"You're skinny as a rail. Don't they feed you in LA?"

Relief flooded E. J. and she unconsciously smoothed her tousled hair.

"Oh, listen to your ol' Grams. Here you are, a big success in the cosmetics world taking time to visit your grandmother, and I'm standing in the street yapping. You must be starved."

E. J. turned to see the neighbors lining the porches of Peach Street, trying to see what all the fuss was about. The summer evening carried Grams's voice for blocks, challenged only by katydids and jar flies.

Gabe Faulkner, Cora's neighbor for thirty-one years, got up from his porch swing and descended the stairs next door. Folks in Cullen's Corner said the only sign that the town barber was getting older, like everyone else, was the hair that was graying nicely at his temples. Gabe had seen the events of nearly half a century and had held up well. He had seen and lived his share of trouble, and he understood and accepted it as an inevitable part of life. Not always pleasant, seldom invited, but at Gabe's age, anticipated.

"Well, Eva Jean. I thought that was you," he said, approaching the car. "It's been a long time."

E. J. smiled. "Yes, I'm afraid it has been." She stuck out her hand, and they shook.

Gabe appraised her warmly, and she wondered how she had almost caught up with him in age. When she was little, he'd seemed old; right now he looked a youngish middle age, no worse for wear.

"I was sorry to hear about Nell. I meant to send flowers. . . ."

Nell Faulkner had died three years ago. Grams had written how lonely Gabe was, wandering around his empty house like a lost soul. The Faulkners had had a good marriage, and Gabe wasn't adjusting to the loss well, Grams had told E. J.

"But you did. You sent them with Cora's." His expression clouded at the memory of Nell's funeral. "They were real pretty. Daisies were her favorite flower."

E. J. sent Grams an appreciative look, but Cora had already started up the sidewalk with E. J.'s small overnight case.

Gabe didn't seem in any hurry to leave. The widower seldom had anywhere pressing to go. He broke off a few dead blooms from Grams's climbing American Beauty, reluctant, it seemed to E. J., to leave. "What brings you back to Cullen's Corner? It's been what . . . ?"

"Eighteen years."

Gabe shook his head. "Eighteen years. Where does the time go?" He broke off a rose and handed it to her. "Cora tells me that you're a big-time corporate woman now. Making . . . what is it . . . hairspray?"

"That and other things." The rose scent turned E. J.'s stomach. "Kilgore's Kosmetics has a wide selection of women's hair care products."

"Spoken like a true businesswoman." He smiled that easy smile E. J. remembered from years past.

Grams returned to take E. J.'s hand and lead her into the

house. Gabe excused himself, claiming he wanted to do some wash before he went to bed.

"Poor thing," Cora whispered. "I wish he'd get over Nell's death."

"Death's not easy," E. J. murmured, thinking of her boss, Isabel Kilgore, who had lost her son recently.

Very little in Grams's house had changed in eighteen years, including the cabbage-rose couch in the living room and the Pennsylvania hutch in the dining room that most antique dealers would give their eyeteeth to own. Even the woven fabric rugs still covered the hardwood by the door and in the hallway. Stairs to the right took infrequent visitors to guest rooms as meticulous as the downstairs, dusted weekly and given clean linen once a month.

Albert squeezed through the doorway and loped through the living room and into the kitchen.

"Why, Albert, you're right! Where are my manners?" Grams turned to E. J. "I'll fix you a bite to eat. Fried a chicken for lunch, and I happen to have a bowl of that potato salad you love. How does that sound?"

Fifteen-year-old E. J. answered from nowhere. "Potato salad? Wonderful, Grams."

E. J. breathed deeply of familiar kitchen smells: fresh bread, fried chicken, and Johnson's floor wax. She automatically took the chair closest to the door, the one she had so often occupied as a child so she could dart outside after dinner to play in the few precious hours before bath and bedtime. But she wasn't a child any longer, and she wouldn't be going outside to play after supper.

Drawing a deep breath, she quietly said, "I'm sorry I came unannounced . . . I needed to get away for a while."

Grams sensed E. J. had troubles on her mind that day; why else would she come home after so many years? Grams opened the refrigerator and pulled leftover chicken from the second shelf, peeling plastic wrap off an old glass plate. She didn't interrupt; Grams was like that. She let a body speak his piece, then made her observations. Reaching for a jar of bread-and-butter pickles, she smiled. "You don't need an excuse to come home, Eva Jean. Haven't seen enough of you these past few years."

"I'm sorry, Grams . . . I know I haven't kept in touch like I should." E. J. watched the cat lope out of the room.

Grams merely smiled, spearing a couple of sweet pickles on the plate. A tendril of gray hair stuck to her forehead and she brushed it away.

"Honey, I know you're busy. I'm not too old to remember when there weren't enough hours in the day. Why, I can't imagine what your life must be like—traveling, selling, meeting interesting people. I'm not surprised that you can't make it back here more often. How are things going in your life, hon?"

Now, honestly? It would have been easier on E. J. if Grams wasn't so nice, but she was, and E. J. was clearly in the wrong for having neglected her all these years. E. J. attempted a smile, but it died before it could reach her cheeks. Taking a deep breath, she dropped her face to her hands.

"It's not going so well, Grams. The company—" Before she could explain, a wail erupted from the living room. The women started and Grams dropped the fork, splattering pickle juice on the linoleum.

"That Albert! Isn't happy inside or outside. Just like a man. Can't make up his mind about a thing." Grams winked at E. J. and bent over to clean up the mess. "You don't mind letting him out for me, do you?"

E. J. got up, went to the living room, and unlatched the screen door. Albert stood on the threshold—body out, tail in—taking his sweet old time leaving. Nudging him with her toe, she herded him out and shut the door.

Grams put the finishing touches on the plate. Three pieces of cold chicken mounded against a pile of potato salad looked to be more than a "bite to eat."

Grams beamed. "Eat up!"

"Really, Grams, it's too much. Half a sandwich and a glass of water would be fine."

Grams shook her head. "Nonsense. You've got to be starving after driving all the way here from California."

"I didn't drive. I flew in to Raleigh this morning and rented a car."

Grams gave her that intentional look that said, "You have that kind of money to burn, do you? My, my."

"And you just got here? Goodness gracious, it doesn't take but thirty or forty minutes to get from Raleigh to here, does it? Are they working on those roads again? Always tearing something up in the name of progress." She shook her head disapprovingly, biting into a pickle.

"No, the roads were fine. I had business to attend to before I drove here." E. J. hated lying. Though she did fly into Raleigh on business, it was a trip she didn't really have to make. Her real business in Raleigh was that appointment, which wasn't until Friday. She'd driven for hours trying to get the nerve to come home.

She picked up a drumstick, then set it back on the plate. Tiny drops of condensation chased each other down a glass of lemonade.

Grams sank into a chair opposite her and pulled a Snoopy fan with an insurance advertisement on it from the pocket of her housedress. Box fans swirled hot air in the stifling kitchen, and E. J. felt faint. She stared sickly at the mound of chicken. She'd eaten nothing since the dry airline bagel early that morning. Picking up the fork, she speared a potato, and it dropped to the Formica before making it to her mouth.

Grams was instantly there with a napkin. "Don't worry, hon. I got it."

She dropped back to the chair and resumed fanning.

They chatted while E. J. tried to eat. Grams wanted to know all about life in LA, and E. J. answered between bites of potato salad. Yes, it was always sunny there—almost. No, not everyone got mugged going to work every day. Yes, there was smog. No, she didn't know any movie stars. No, she didn't mind living in a big city.

"And your company?" Grams leaned closer. "Making lots of dough?"

E. J. stopped chewing. Reaching for the lemonade, she took a drink.

"Actually, no. Profits are down this quarter. If we don't find something new, and soon, I don't know what's going to happen. The old products are outdated, and the research department can't seem to come up with anything new and exciting."

"Well, you're a smart girl," Grams said. "You'll think of something." That was Grams: simple. If only life were that way.

She got up and went to the phone.

"I can't wait to call the girls in my bridge group and tell them you're home. You'll have to visit Maggie and Jerry. Sue Henning will be tickled to death to hear from you. Asked me just last month when I thought—"

"Grams, please." E. J. closed her eyes. "Don't make a fuss. I simply want to . . ." She paused, wondering what it was she simply wanted. She simply wanted her old life back. Busy executive, carefree loner. "I want to rest for a few days. So please, don't be making plans for me. I'll only be here until Sunday."

"Oh. Well, if that's as long as you can stay, that's as long as you can stay." She replaced the rotary phone in its cradle. "We'll enjoy the time together, regardless."

E. J. finished the meal in silence, and the two women retired to the living room. E. J. avoided mentioning the real reason for the visit, and Grams continued to assume it was for rest.

Friends, it's called miscommunication, and in this case, it was premeditated on E. J.'s part, but that's the way it was. E. J. was not exactly in touch with the best parts of herself when she arrived in Cullen's Corner.

The hall clock struck ten, and Grams eased out of her chair and stretched.

"My lands, look at the time. I'd love to stay up and talk all night, honey, but it's an hour past bedtime for me and Mr. Albert." Albert had since decided that inside was better, and the decision had worn him out. He stretched wearily along the back of the sofa, flicking his tail.

"I'm a little tired, too." Ten o'clock in North Carolina meant seven o'clock in California. E. J. had never gone to bed at ten o'clock in her entire life. But lately she could barely hold her eyes open past eight-thirty.

"Breakfast at seven," Grams called, hoisting the sleeping cat into her arms. "Do you want Mr. Albert to wake you?"

"No, thanks. I brought my travel alarm."

"Are you sure? Mr. Albert is a whole lot friendlier."

E. J. looked at the cat, who scowled at her with sleepy eyes. "I'll pass on that one, Grams." The farther away E. J. was from anything feline, the better.

"Okay, then. Nighty-night."

"Good night."

Grams climbed the stairs. E. J. sat for a moment listening to the sounds drifting through the open window. Crickets, singing tree frogs. By now North Carolina's nightlife was almost as deafening as LA's traffic.

Upstairs, the light was already on and the bedcovers pulled back in her old room. Grams had left everything the same, right down to the handmade quilt on the bed.

Pictures of E. J. at various ages sat about the room: a smiling E. J. with a missing tooth; E. J. and her brother, Chris, with a cat whose name she couldn't remember; E. J. dressed for prom. Nostalgia settled over her like a pall. Sitting down on the squeaking bed, she gazed around the room, allowing memories to slowly come back, permitting painful ones to surface. Grams bustled around next door, getting ready for bed.

A soft knock a moment later interrupted E. J.'s reverie. Grams poked her head in. "Do you need anything, honey? There are fresh towels in the bathroom."

"Thanks, Grams. I'm okay."

What a lie. What a terrible, unforgivable lie. She wasn't okay, and right now it didn't seem that she'd ever be.

The old lady smiled and hurried into the room to give E. J. a quick good-night squeeze. "It's good to have you home, Eva Jean."

"It's good to be home." E. J. squeezed back.

At least that wasn't a lie; she was improving.

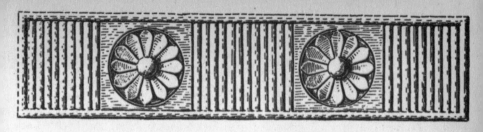

CHAPTER TWO

L ife's the oddest thing, isn't it? When a person has the most on his mind, nature has a way of stepping in. E. J. slept like a baby her first night back in her old bed. Grams's house smelled familiar, of sun-dried sheets and the faint scent of cedar coming from the closet. Normal scents.

Scents that sent her sprinting out of bed and straight for the toilet the next morning.

Cora glanced her way as E. J. streaked past, frowning while she stored a batch of freshly laundered towels in the hall closet. E. J. slunk out of the bathroom minutes later, holding her side.

"Eva Jean, you poor thing. I knew I should have cooked that chicken longer." She handed E. J. a pink bottle. "A little Pepto-Bismol will fix you right up."

That pink goop wouldn't fix what ailed her, but E. J. took the medicine and headed back to the bathroom. Grams shook her head and swiped a hand across her forehead to smooth back a stray hair. The phone rang, overriding the retching sounds coming from the bathroom.

Maggie Markus's cheery voice greeted Cora when she answered.

"Hi, Cora. Gabe said E. J.'s back. Can you put her on the line?"

Now, folks, news travels faster than a wish in Cullen's Corner. Too fast, some folks say, though town gossip Lucy Mitchell contends it doesn't travel fast enough. Cora had kept her promise; she hadn't mentioned a word about E. J.'s coming home, although it nearly killed her. But that sort of news leaks out. Barbers, unlike grandmothers, are as good as town reporters and generally more accurate.

"Myrna told me that Tim told her that Gabe says Eva Jean showed up around eight last night."

"She did," Cora confirmed, "but she's not feeling so good this morning, Maggie. Something must have been wrong with the chicken last night."

"Oh—that's a shame."

It was a shame because Cora's fried chicken was the talk of Cullen's Corner and to Cora's knowledge had never made anyone sick, excluding Newt Lewis at last year's Fourth of July celebration. But that wasn't Cora's fault. Newt had made a pig of himself.

Cora stretched the phone cord across the room to open the refrigerator door and take out the suspicious poultry. Lifting the plastic cover, she sniffed. Smelled all right to her.

"Funny. Doesn't smell bad."

"Well, maybe I'll drop by later when I get the kids up and dressed. I can't wait to see her again."

"That'd be fine," Cora said, dumping the chicken into the disposal. "She took some Pepto-Bismol, and I expect she'll be feeling her oats in a while."

Cora knew getting loose from Maggie wasn't easy. Oh, she was a nice girl and could single-handedly keep her entire brood headed in the same direction, but she was as yappy as a gelded terrier. A body couldn't get free once she got to talking.

A pale E. J. came downstairs a few minutes later. Grams hung up the phone, worry dotting her features. "Goodness, Eva Jean, you look as white as a sheet."

"I feel like a sheet."

Grams glanced at the disposal and slid the teakettle on the burner.

"Well, sit down before you fall down. I'd fix you breakfast, but my hair appointment is at nine and if I miss it, it'll be next week before I can get back." She patted her coif. "And that could get ugly."

Food was the last thing on E. J.'s mind that morning. She stared at the ceramic napkin holder with a pink pineapple on it and shuddered at the thought of anything remotely related to food. The scent of the roses stuck in a bud vase beside the napkins turned her stomach. She clasped her lips tighter to ward off a new assault.

"Fry yourself a couple of eggs and some bacon, hon. You're too thin." Grams patted E. J.'s shoulder.

A few minutes later Cora's Monte Carlo chugged off down the street. Pulling a slip of paper from her pocket, E. J. reached for the phone and dialed the number of the Raleigh clinic.

The phone rang three times before a pert woman with a Mickey Mouse voice answered. At Disney World she would be cute; to someone sick as a dog, it was disconcerting.

"Winston Health Center. Can I help you?"

"I need to verify an appointment."

"With what doctor?"

"I don't know. I don't live here." E. J. started to sweat. In LA she would be lightly perspiring—delicately warm and femininely misted. But this wasn't LA; it was Cullen's Corner, and she was just plain sweating. Lying never came naturally to her, and she didn't like it; it felt unnatural.

"Your name?"

"Smith, Laura Smith."

"Smith . . ."

"Look, I'm pregnant. . . ."

"Dr. Sojo is our obstetrician."

E. J. leaned against the wall and flicked the phone cord at Albert, who promptly jumped up on the counter. The cat crept along the Formica, looking for treats.

"I don't need an obstetrician."

Lori Copeland

Confirming the appointment wasn't hard, but could she actually go through with it? What choice did she have?

Albert viewed her coldly when she flicked him with the cord again.

"The family planning clinic?" the receptionist suggested.

"Okay. Family planning."

"I'll transfer you."

The euphemism changed the focus for better. Planning. That was what she was doing. Taking control of her life again.

A series of short clicks brought a Muzak version of "Muskrat Love" to the line. Albert glanced at the door and jumped to the floor, skittering off into the hallway.

"I swear, I'd forget my head if it wasn't glued on."

E. J. whirled at the sound of Grams's voice behind her. At the other end of the line another receptionist with a normal tone of voice interrupted "Muskrat Love." E. J. slammed the receiver back into place.

Grams frowned. "Who were you talking to?"

"No one." E. J. casually poured a glass of juice as Cora proceeded to search for whatever it was she'd forgotten. "An office."

"What office? Yours?"

"No." She sipped the juice. Why lie? Grams would eventually know what she'd done. As painful as it might be, she might as well tell the truth.

"A doctor."

"Oh, honey. Are you that sick?"

Now, Cora Roberts didn't upset easily. She'd been around long enough to know upset stomachs were as common as brown beans, but no one in her house was going to lack medical attention if they needed it. "Dr. Strobel's number is on the icebox. I'll give him a quick call and see if he can get you in this morning."

"You don't have to do that."

She waved E. J.'s protests aside with a smile. "No trouble at all. He'd be happy to see you."

Dropping to all fours, Grams fished around under the living room sofa and came out with a small black-leather

14

change purse. "That Albert. I should have known he'd be the culprit. It was in my purse the last I saw it." She mumbled something about a "naughty" cat and placed the call to the doctor.

"Eleven. Well . . . if that's the best you can do, Louise." She hung up the phone. "Louise said she'd work you in at eleven." She dropped a kiss on E. J.'s forehead and continued to the garage.

The Monte Carlo backfired. E. J. glanced at the phone as the car's roar faded in the distance. Now what?

Sighing, she turned back to Albert, who flexed a nimble paw and concentrated on digging out some bit of imaginary dirt from between his toes. Sinking to a kitchen chair, E. J. admitted what she had known all along.

"I can't tell her." She might have imagined she could calmly drop a bombshell, but now she knew she couldn't. Not this way, not out of the clear blue. She'd have to find a way to break the news of her impending procedure over supper tonight.

Albert met her heartsick gaze with one that clearly said he'd like to sympathize, but he couldn't, being neutered and all.

E. J. picked up the phone again. Why was it so hard to make a simple phone call? Because she knew it wasn't a simple phone call. She was about to do something that would change her life. But what choice did she have? Her life had already been changed, and it wasn't her own doing. She had to finish what someone else had started. Dr. Strobel could give her something for morning sickness, tide her over until the appointment.

E. J. started when a knock sounded at the door a few moments later. Dropping the receiver back into place again, she went to unlatch the screen door. Maggie Markus barged in, grinning from ear to ear. Two younger versions of Jerry Markus clung to her skirt, each trying to hide from the other. The youngest was carrying a bottle, trailing sticky milk on the floor. E. J.'s head pounded at the commotion. By the size of Maggie's stomach, the next was due any day.

"E. J.!" Maggie screeched, latching onto E. J.'s neck affectionately. "Cora told me you were under the weather, but I couldn't wait to see you. I thought I'd run over for a minute and see if there's anything I can do to help."

Locked in a tight embrace, E. J. helplessly patted Maggie's back while Maggie hugged. There's nothing like high school acquaintances to make you realize how long you've been away. Maggie was two years E. J.'s junior, and the girls hadn't kept the same company. E. J. was the achiever, the one "most likely to succeed." She had been editor of the Cullen High newspaper, *The Cullen Corner Caw*. Well liked and sought after by boys, Maggie had been the head cheerleader for the Cullen Crusaders. Jerry Markus had been the most popular boy—a quarterback and basketball all-star in school. His graduation ring had dangled from a gold chain around Maggie's neck. Maggie would hang on him at halftime while E. J. watched from the stands in her band uniform, glasses fogged from the overheated gymnasium or crowded stands.

E. J. had made good grades; Maggie had terrible grades. E. J. wore braces and glasses; Maggie wore darling skirts and blouses with trendy name tags. Sometimes E. J. would bump into Miss Congeniality in the hallway or while Maggie merrily skipped along Boy-Ain't-Life-Grand Street on her way to baton, gymnastics, or dance lessons.

"Maggie Sloan," E. J. said lamely. "How in the world are you?"

"Maggie Markus," she corrected, winking. "I married Jerry. I know, I'm not wearing a ring, but this heat has my fingers swollen like pork sausages."

The older child made a break for the back bedroom where Grams kept the toys—toys E. J. had played with as a child. The younger child trounced along behind, dripping milk on the rug.

Maggie lumbered into the front room and dumped a diaper bag, purse, and baby bottle on the sofa. She stretched her back, and Albert stretched with her. Loosening a rubber band, she adjusted her short blonde ponytail.

"Gosh," she mumbled around the band in her mouth, "it's gub to see yew." She wound the rubber band in her hair and tightened it by pulling hair in opposite directions. "How long has it been? Fifteen years?"

"Eighteen," E. J. corrected.

"No way! We're that old!" She giggled, and laugh lines burrowed into her flawless complexion.

"Too old," E. J. said with a sigh. Right now she felt every day of her thirty-five years.

"Are you married? Any kids?"

E. J. knew that Maggie knew she wasn't married. Cora had kept the whole town informed of E. J.'s inability to find a suitable mate. And as for children . . .

She rearranged the sofa pillows. "Neither. My job keeps me pretty busy."

"Cora said you were the president of some big corporation in LA."

"I co-own a small company, nothing big."

"Gosh. All that business stuff." Maggie circled her head with her finger and rolled her eyes. "Flies right out."

"Looks like you've been rather busy yourself." E. J. tried not to stare at Maggie's girth, but found it impossible. Maggie must be miserable.

"Number four," Maggie said, rubbing her belly proudly. "Due around the end of the month, but if I know this one, it'll be early. Jerry says I have a sense about these things. Predicted the other three to the day.

"Pete is at his Meemaw's helping weed the garden." Maggie grinned. "As much as a six-year-old can help."

E. J. motioned to a chair and was about to ask her to sit down, but Maggie had already planted herself with a groan. Knees spread, she positioned a pillow to support her back.

"You're getting a late start, aren't you?" Maggie remarked.

Now, in Cullen's Corner, when you were talking about getting married or having babies, doing either after the age of thirty was getting a late start. Times hadn't changed.

E. J. shrugged. "I—"

A bang from the hallway alerted the women that the children were on their way back to the living room, toys clacking behind them.

Maggie paid no attention to the noise.

"I've been doing my share to populate the world. There were a few false alarms." Maggie's top lip disappeared in thought. "Miscarried twice. Shortly after I lost number two, Jerry's dad passed away and Jerry took over the feed store. He wanted to be sure we were ready before we started adding to the Markus clan." She grinned adoringly at her brood. "The wait was worth it."

Having children had never been E. J.'s main goal in life. Yet, who knows, maybe if things were different . . . she dismissed the thought.

"Of course, Jerry wants six when it's all said and done," Maggie continued, obviously pleased with her childbearing capacity. "A couple more and the family will be complete."

Maggie's older girl pounded a wooden truck on the hardwood floor, and the youngest searched under the couch, grasping Albert by the tail and sending him into a yowling fit. Maggie plucked the youngest up and out of the way when Albert retaliated. The banging and yelling didn't seem to faze her, but it was getting to E. J. The older one ceased banging the toy truck against the floor and got up to run around in circles. E. J. breathed silent thanks and glanced through the doorway at the cat clock hanging over the kitchen stove. Ten-fifteen. She had to be at Dr. Strobel's in forty-five minutes.

"Boy or girl?" she asked, warding off the inevitable question about why she was here. Her mind scrambled for a plausible excuse to escape without having to tell an outright lie.

"We didn't want to know this time—either one is fine. Jerry said we maybe ought to find out before we paint the nursery again but I said, who cares? Paint's cheap. Last time, they told us Emma was going to be a boy, and, well, as you can see—" she rolled the toddler onto her back and cooed— "she's a girl. Yes, she is. Yes, she is." She took the child's hand and pretended to gobble it affectionately. "And we wuv her, yes, we do."

The chubby girl rolled and wrestled and giggled until Maggie set her down on the floor and she took off in hot pursuit of the cat.

"Speaking of kids," Maggie said, frowning, "whatever happened to your brother? Chris, isn't it?"

"Oh, he's here and there." E. J.'s laugh sounded hollow, even to her. Chris was another subject she didn't care to address.

"Do the two of you talk much?" Maggie drifted off before E. J. could elaborate. "I always wanted a brother. My sister is fun, but a brother would have been nice. I'm glad the girls have Pete to look after them once they start school."

E. J. thought she was about to execute the perfect getaway, but as her lips were forming the excuse, Bea banged Emma in the head with a toy truck. E. J. caught her breath as Emma's face turned bright red and a lump instantly puffed up where the truck hit. The child let out a bloodcurdling yell.

"Oh, honey pie, come here," Maggie cooed. "Bea, Bea, that wasn't a nice thing to do to your baby sister." Sticking out her tongue, Bea darted for E. J.'s lap.

E. J. became lost in the fray. With a crying child on each woman's lap, conversation halted. Maggie rubbed the plump knot, quietly shushing the injured child.

Bea nestled snugly in E. J.'s lap and whimpered. E. J. sat dazed for a moment, listening to the little girl's sobs. Big soggy blue eyes met hers. A tear plopped, making a wet stain on her sleeve. Snot began running from one nostril. Maggie handed her a tissue, and E. J. gently dabbed Bea's nose. When the girls had been sufficiently comforted, Maggie smiled and set Emma back down on the floor.

"So what's LA like? Is everyone tan? Does everyone really drive convertibles, like in the movies?"

E. J. winced as Bea slid off her lap and onto her bare toe. "No, Maggie, nothing like that. It's large and noisy, but it has marvelous restaurants and wonderful shopping."

E. J.'s LA loft was less than posh, and the company's earnings were less than glamorous. The past few years' profits were down. Right now Kilgore's Kosmetics was hurting.

"I'd love to go to California someday. Jerry promised to take me there on a second honeymoon as soon as this one's weaned from the breast." She patted her circular belly again.

"But I don't expect to go. Last month the car needed a new transmission and the pump went out on the washing machine. We had to dig into our savings to replace them."

Well, depleting a savings account would depress most folks, but not Maggie Markus. On the contrary, the harried mother seemed almost chipper. But then Maggie had found the secret to true happiness, and it had nothing to do with fanciful trips.

Would that we were all so lucky.

Silence fell between the two women. E. J. stared longingly at the cat clock, hoping Maggie would notice, but she didn't.

"Oh, before I forget. I was on my way to Jill Bentley's. You remember Jill?"

A bulb went off in E. J.'s head. Jill Barton. She'd married Jack Bentley. Jack and Jill had been inseparable in high school, but when an invitation to Jill's wedding had come, E. J. had conveniently misplaced it.

"Yeah, I remember her. Played tuba. Jack Bentley. Married Jack Bentley a few years ago?"

"Yep. Anyway, Jack was killed in a tractor accident almost two years ago. They'd been married five years with no children, bless their hearts. Now Jill has ovarian cancer. They diagnosed it last year, and the women in the church have been trying to help her since she's been on chemo. We take turns cleaning and cheering her up." She leaned in closer. "She's housebound." Her nose wrinkled. "Not doing very good."

"That's too bad." Jill had always been in the library when E. J. stayed after school to work on a book report.

"The doctors say she's got a chance, but who knows? She looks awful."

E. J. shifted in her chair, absently wiping nonexistent dust from an end table. In view of Jill's illness, her problems were small.

"Maybe you'd like to help while you're here. We need someone to take Jill her Tuesday night meal. You and Cora could whip something up."

"I'm sorry. I'm leaving Sunday."

Maggie's face fell. "But you just got here."

"Sorry." E. J. smiled. Once the procedure was over, she'd return to LA. Isabel and Brian were unhappy she had taken a few days off.

"Well, maybe you could stop by and say hi. She'd be tickled to see you."

E. J. rose, hoping Maggie would take the hint. This time, she did.

"Oh, look at the time!" She yelled for the kids, who were backing Albert into a corner of the kitchen. "Gotta run. Jill will wonder what's happened to me."

"Thanks for stopping by. Tell Jill hi for me." E. J. forced yet another smile. If Maggie didn't leave soon she was going to scream. How did she stand the constant noise and demands on her time?

"Well, you stop by anytime you like. The house is always unlocked and I'm usually somewhere in the neighborhood."

"I'm leaving Sunday," E. J. reminded.

Maggie slung the diaper bag over one shoulder and, with a friendly wave, herded the kids out the door. E. J. watched the noisy procession, wondering how Maggie handled so many kids.

"And there she was on my doorstep," Cora said. "Well, not really on my doorstep, but in her rented car out front."

"Did she say why she's here?" Gabe trimmed Cora's hair and applied a gel.

"Not yet. There has to be a reason, though. She hasn't been home in years, not even for Christmas."

Now you see, Cora had never understood E. J.'s absence, just accepted it. That's what grandmothers do. But the holidays were never the same without E. J.

"My lands." Roberta Knots shook her head, thumbing through a copy of *Good Housekeeping*. "And now she's back with no notice at all?"

"Not even a call from the airport. I could have gone and gotten her. . . ."

"Cora Roberts, listen to you. You could no more find your way around Raleigh than you could in New York City. Your eyes are worse than mine."

Cora stiffened at the accusation. Gabe grinned and snapped the cape from around Cora's neck.

"First of all, I can see fine, Roberta. Shows what little you know. I could buzz around Raleigh all day and never miss a sight. Secondly, I don't see you tooling around town much these days. And thirdly, Cullen's Corner is E. J.'s home. She doesn't need an excuse to visit."

"Of course not! I merely meant . . ."

"Ladies," Gabe reprimanded, shooing Cora out of the chair. "Am I going to have to have you locked up for disorderly conduct?"

Cora chuckled. "You do that, and I'll never bake you another elderberry pie as long as I live, Gabe Faulkner."

Throwing his hands up in mock surrender, he motioned for Roberta to take the chair. "Okay, no law enforcement. But, ladies, duke it out outside the shop. I've got a reputation to maintain."

Ah, friends and neighbors. Relationships as comfortable as old shoes. The three dissolved into good-natured laughter, and Eva Jean was forgotten for the moment. Why E. J. came home didn't matter; Cullen's Corner was glad to have one of its own home again, for whatever reason.

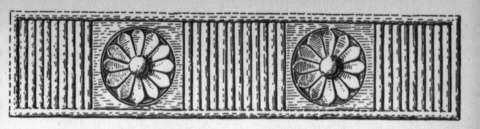

CHAPTER THREE

I s Gus out of the office this morning?" E. J. asked, frowning at the handsome young physician who'd breezed through the doorway. He picked up a chart and briefly scanned it.

"Dad? He's most likely on the golf course this morning. He retired two years ago. I took over his practice."

Wonderful, E. J. thought, pulling the sheet tighter to her chest. Grams hadn't written her about that. Seeing old Doc Strobel was like visiting family; she wasn't prepared to face a tanned, bicepted hunk reeking of Preferred Stock.

He took a pen from his coat pocket with one hand and extended the other. "Dan Strobel. You're Cora's granddaughter."

E. J. shook his hand. "Yes."

"And you do know this isn't food poisoning."

"Yes, I know."

He flashed a disarming grin. "Only seven months to go, but it'll get easier." After the brief examination, he scribbled a few notes on her chart.

E. J. tightened the sheet. She knew she wasn't suffering from food poisoning, not by a long shot. Patient-doctor confidentiality aside, by coming to him she was running the risk of Grams finding out about the pregnancy. One more day wouldn't kill her, but even a few hours' relief from this awful sickness was worth a trip to the doctor. Or was something else going on here? She wasn't thinking about canceling that appointment. . . . She shook the thought away.

"So, morning sickness isn't fatal?"

"No, only feels that way." He smiled, but a physician wearing Birkenstock shoes didn't comfort E. J. "Actually, the second trimester is the easiest. The nausea should be easing before long—unless you're one of those unfortunate souls who's sick the whole nine months."

E. J. winced. "Perish the thought."

She avoided his scrutiny. Many things puzzled her—the swelling, the nausea—but after tomorrow, questions would be unnecessary.

"You can get dressed now. I'll be back in a few minutes." He left with the nurse trailing behind, and E. J. shimmied into her clothes. He returned shortly, flashing her an engaging smile. "Let's set up another appointment for a couple of months from now. I'll schedule an ultrasound and we'll see how the little tyke's doing." He clipped his pen to his coat pocket and closed the chart.

"That won't be necessary. I'll be going back to LA Sunday afternoon."

His smile faltered.

"If you could give me something for the nausea . . ."

"Yes, I can give you something. It doesn't work like magic—often takes a few doses to be effective, and it doesn't work on everybody."

E. J.'s heart sank. If it wouldn't help right away, why was she here? She only needed something for the next day.

Dr. Strobel was looking at her intently. She squirmed under his gaze. His left brow rose.

"Do you have any questions about the pregnancy or delivery? First child—you must be curious."

E. J. forced a smile. Her voice sounded hollow. "Not really.

Maggie Markus filled me in." Rather, her frantic lifestyle had educated E. J.

"Maggie?"

"She told me all I need to know."

The doctor opened up the chart again. "Ms. Roberts, can I ask you a few personal questions?"

She shifted on the table. "Is it necessary?"

Questions were not good. Not at this point in E. J.'s life. Questions meant there had to be answers about paternity, and she certainly wasn't about to reveal the whole gruesome story to a stranger.

"If you don't mind."

The office chair rolled back as he sat down and straightened his tie. Without looking up he began taking notes.

"You seem to be worried about something. Is it your age?"

"Excuse me?" E. J. leaned closer. Her age? Granted, she wasn't in her twenties, but thirty-five wasn't over the hill. Plenty of women E. J.'s age waited to start a family—career, education, all sorts of considerations delayed the process.

"I don't mean to be insulting. Many women your age wonder if there will be extra complications with labor and delivery. Then there's the issue of responsibility of raising a child in a one-parent household." He glanced back at her chart, apparently to double-check her marital status.

E. J. shook her head. She hadn't thought about risks; actually, she hadn't thought about anything but amending a terrible injustice.

"I hadn't really thought about it—"

"Because those certainly are valid concerns." He absently twisted his wedding ring. "Not that you need to worry about them."

"I'm not worried. I'm more concerned about my options."

He pivoted in his chair to look at her. "Like C-section or natural birth? We won't know about that for a few months."

A trickle of sweat rolled down her back, even though the room was as cold as a meat locker. She cleared her throat.

"No. Other options."

The doctor clicked his pen on the desk, refusing to look up. "Terminating the fetus?" He fell silent, then said, "That's a serious matter with sometimes severe physical and psychological repercussions."

E. J. pressed her lips together. She should just leave. But she didn't have the nerve.

"Do you know what the procedure involves?" He turned to an illustration in a thick flip chart of pink sketches.

"That isn't necessary." E. J. averted her eyes. She knew the procedure—the possible repercussions. At least she thought she did. Truth is, she hadn't allowed herself to think too much about that side of it. Either way, she would be taking a risk. At least with this option she could try to put her past behind her.

He pointed to the parts of the chart, explaining abortion in excruciating detail. The room began to expand and contract with her breathing. For a moment she felt faint.

"We don't perform the procedure here. You'd have to go to Raleigh."

"I know. I'm aware of that." The way he referred to it as a "procedure" made it seem technical, mechanical, like getting fired or assembling a lawn mower.

He moved to steady her arm. "Of course, it's your decision. I can't tell you what to do, but I want you to be knowledgeable about the process."

A tight knot formed in her throat, and she forced back tears. "It's my life."

His eyes lifted to hers, and compassion shone in their depths. "Well, actually it's two lives, but your decision. And a tough one," he conceded. "But we all have to make them, Ms. Roberts."

She closed her eyes. "I'll be returning to LA shortly."

"I'm sorry to hear that." He closed the chart. "I'm sure Cora's enjoying your visit."

E. J. summoned the courage to look at him. "You aren't allowed to say anything to her about my condition, are you?"

Crossing his arms, he shook his head. "I wouldn't, regardless. You're a grown woman, not a child."

She stared at the floor. "But you don't believe in abortion."

"You're not paying me to share my beliefs. Now go home and get some rest." He tapped her knee lightly and helped her down from the table. "I'll give you something for that morning sickness."

Emerging from the drugstore, E. J. wandered past local shops and insurance agencies. She paused to stare in the window of the small café on the corner.

The window reflected Edison's Bank on the opposite street corner. Grams wrote that it had been sold to a large conglomerate. E. J.'s mother had briefly worked as a teller at Edison's, then as a waitress at the corner café. No job met her expectations, but then motherhood couldn't either.

E. J. glanced up to see Maggie and her troop coming out of the feed store.

"Eva Jean! Hi!" Maggie waved when she caught sight of her. The children waved. The youngest one threw a toy in the street, and a bicyclist swerved to miss it, jumping the curb and hitting a garbage can. E. J. started across the street in the opposite direction.

"Hey, wait! I need to ask you something!"

E. J. paused and waited for the family to catch up.

Breathless, Maggie approached, her face flushed with heat. "Jerry's usually home by six. How about supper at my house tonight around seven?" The hassled mother snatched a child back from the curb.

"Oh, Maggie." The last thing E. J. needed was a dose of family fun. Not now—not today. "Thanks, but I'm a little tired. I need to check in with my office and then I think I'll take a hot bath and turn in early."

"On your vacation? Look, you'll only be here for a few days— you can't waste your time sitting around Cora's. I make these to-die-for enchiladas you simply have to eat to believe. Hot and spicy—they're killers."

E. J. winced at the thought. Her stomach did a high dive. "Thanks, but Grams will probably . . . "

"Cora's invited! And so is Gabe. We'll make it a coming-home party."

Cornered, E. J. heard herself agreeing to come, though she couldn't imagine why. Enchiladas? She'd die on the spot.

"Fantastic!" Maggie exclaimed, dragging a child to safety. She eyed the prescription tucked in E. J.'s purse and frowned. "Nothing's wrong, is it?"

E. J. glanced at her purse and tucked the brown vial farther inside. "No, a little upset stomach. Nothing, really."

"That's a relief. Maybe I should make mashed potatoes and oatmeal." Maggie laughed.

"Listen, Maggie—I'm not feeling well so don't count on me tonight, okay?"

"Sure—but the medicine will hopefully fix you right up." She turned to look in the window of the diner, tucking a stray lock of hair behind her ear. "Hey, didn't your mom used to work here?"

"Yeah, for a few months." E. J. had been young, only four when Marlene—she could never think of her as "Mom"—had gone to work. There must have been excitement in the young woman's voice when she told Grams she'd gotten a job. Grams had argued that she couldn't keep up her grades and hold down a job, but Marlene won out. Grams had been right. She hadn't kept up her grades, but by then it was a moot point. Shortly after the discussion, Marlene took up with a corru-gated-siding salesman and dumped school, even though she was about to graduate.

"I can still remember how my sister talked about your mother's milk shakes," Maggie said. "She made shakes extra special for kids. Put in a little extra chocolate and two cherries instead of one." Maggie stared at her own reflection in the glass. "You know, Jerry and I had our first date here. We come here every year on our anniversary and order a milk shake, but my sister always said the place was never the same once your mother left."

"So, seven o'clock?" E. J. said, turning away. She didn't really know how good her mother's shakes were. Marlene had never made one for her. "I'll try to make it."

"Seven it is," Maggie said, pulling a child from a trash receptacle. "Come hungry!"

"Right!" E. J. said good-bye and turned to leave. Enchiladas? Did she have a death wish? Looks like she got that medication from Doc Strobel just in time.

It had better work.

When E. J. let herself into the house later, she paused, viewing signs of a recent scuffle: an overturned kitchen chair, the tea roses knocked over, and the plastic tablecloth still damp. There was a note taped to the refrigerator: *Taken Albert to the vet for his shots.*

E. J. stepped to the phone and made a quick call to her office in LA.

"E. J.? When are you coming back?" Brian demanded. "The mock-ups for the new product line are due next week." Brian was head of marketing, high-strung, running on caffeine and cigarettes.

"Late Sunday night. I need a few more days to wrap up some personal business."

"Well, hurry up. We need you. Isabel's fit to be tied."

E. J. said good-bye and hung up the phone, leaning her head against the cool wall. It wasn't as if she took time off frequently. This was the first time in four years she'd used personal time. Surely Kilgore's could do without her for another few days.

Sidestepping an overturned tricycle, E. J. crossed the street and climbed the concrete stairs to Maggie's porch at a quarter to seven that evening. Pausing, she took a moist wipe out of her pocket. Humidity was thick enough to slice, and she experienced a wave of dizziness. Dabbing at the pools on her neck and cheeks, she closed her eyes, then took a deep breath and rang the bell. Sounds of running feet erupted, and a scuffle could be heard on the other side of the door.

Her gaze traveled over the littered porch. Evidence of family life abounded. Abandoned muddy sneakers, a half-empty glass of grape Kool-Aid sitting on the railing, mashed Froot Loops ground into the concrete. Flies were having a field day with a partially eaten Popsicle. The door swung open, and the elfin face of Jerry in a miniature body greeted her.

"You must be Pete," she offered, summoning a tentative smile and praying he would unlatch the screen door and let her into the air-conditioned house.

She cleared her throat. "May I come in?"

"You havta say the magic word."

E. J. shifted. Great. Guessing games. "Please?"

"Noooo."

"May I?"

He flashed her a grin, revealing holes where several teeth should have been. "That's two words, silly."

"Chocolate."

"Uh-uh."

"Bluebird."

He rolled his eyes. "That's two words."

"No, it's not. It's one. It sounds like two."

"Still not it." The child shifted from one foot to the other, obviously excited and pleased that he'd gotten a grown-up—and a stranger, no less—to play his game.

"Pete!" A male voice called from down the hall. The boy's head snapped around to look. "Let her in this minute! She doesn't want to play your game."

The boy turned back to E. J. and whispered, "The word was *baby*. Like my mom's going to have."

Entrance gained, although through a third party, E. J. stepped into the cool hallway.

"BeaBeaaaaaa." Pete disappeared into the den.

"E. J." A slightly paunchy Jerry turned the corner, holding a dish towel. He opened his arms to greet her. "You're right on time. Cora is setting the table."

E. J. could hear the two women talking in the kitchen, children running and laughing. She hesitantly moved into his embrace, which smelled faintly of sweat, charcoal, and Old Spice.

"How you doing, Jerry?"

"Couldn't be better. Let me look at the prettiest girl out of Cullen High." He inspected her at arm's length. Jerry, although a bit heavier, had gotten no less handsome. Friendly blue eyes twinkled out from under his perfect head of red hair. He'd always pretended to be a ladies' man, but everyone knew his heart belonged to Maggie.

"I heard that, Jerry Markus!" Maggie chided from the kitchen.

Jerry fetched his wife and led her into the living room, stepping over toys that he quickly kicked aside.

"It's never straightened up for long around here. Pete!" The boy appeared from the den. "Pick up this mess."

The child obediently stooped to gather an armload of Hot Wheels when the doorbell pealed. He jumped to answer it. In the hallway they heard him ask, "What's the magic word?" and Gabe answer, "Bulldog." Jerry rolled his eyes and went to corral his son.

E. J. followed a toy truck convoy into the kitchen, where she found Grams taking a dish towel to the silverware, blowing and rubbing off spots. Maggie lumbered around the room, rubbing her back and shooing the girls away from a huge chocolate cake. The room was pure Maggie—disorganized and welcoming.

"There's the sleepyhead!" Grams said, giving E. J. a quick squeeze. "Have a good nap, hon?"

"Great . . . thanks. I meant to come early, but I overslept."

Maggie laughed and handed her a bowl of greens. "What's a vacation for? You can finish the salad."

E. J. searched a drawer for a paring knife. "Grams telling you how to run your kitchen?"

"Helpful advice," Cora corrected. "Can cure any vice."

"Or take the spots off silver." Maggie snatched the towel away and laid it aside.

Now, folks, most women would be offended if another came in and polished the spots off her silver, but Maggie welcomed the help. Nothing fazed her. Anger was not an emotion she often showed or even felt, and how many of us can say that? Especially with another woman poking around in our kitchen?

"You have a lovely home, Maggie," E. J. said.

"Oh, it's a mess." Maggie put ice and tea into glasses. "I told Jerry this morning that a new dinette is next on our list."

E. J. glanced at the butcher-block table with six mismatched chairs and a high chair. Junk, but Maggie didn't seem to mind. A picture of the Last Supper hung over the scarred table.

"Those enchiladas smell good."

"Well, thank goodness you've got your appetite back. Did E. J. tell you I about killed her?" Cora asked Maggie.

"Really, Grams," E. J. protested.

"Got a hold of some bad fryers . . . didn't affect anyone but E. J." Grams leaned over to hug her. "I'm really sorry, hon. Maggie said the doctor gave you something."

"Yep. It should do the trick."

Gabe and Jerry came into the kitchen. E. J. met the widower's eyes and smiled.

"From my garden." He handed Maggie a bouquet of fresh-cut summer flowers.

"They're beautiful!" Maggie gasped, trying to hug him, but her stomach got in the way.

A fray started in the hallway and the two oldest children, with a mutt dog leading the pack, flew through the kitchen, disrupting chairs and knocking into the table. Dishes rattled. In a split second, they were gone, but the noise remained. Shrieks, yelps, and dog barks bounced off the walls and tile floor. Jerry went to quiet them as Maggie moved a casserole from the oven to the table.

"I'll just put these flowers in the sink. Jerry can get a vase when he comes back." She winced, her hand going to her back. "Uh-oh. I need to sit down."

Cora glanced up. "What's wrong? You look a little peaked."

"Nothing . . . the baby's particularly heavy today."

E. J.'s hand unconsciously moved to cover her own stomach.

Jerry returned with children, concern shading his face. "What's wrong, Mag?"

"Nothing . . . really. Let's eat." Everyone sat down.

"Would you say grace, Cora?"

"Certainly, but why don't we ask E. J. to bless the food?" Grams smiled. "Go ahead, honey. I remember you used to love to say the evening prayer."

Grace? E. J. froze. She hadn't said grace since she'd left Cullen's Corner eighteen years ago. She met Jerry's direct gaze. Hands folded, eyes focused on her, even the children waited quietly and expectantly.

"Why doesn't Gabe say it?"

Cora nudged her leg under the table.

"Or, I could," she recanted, feeling all of twelve. The children bowed their heads and closed their eyes. For a moment, blessed serenity reigned.

"Dear Lord," E. J. began, "thank you for this family and friendship, this beautiful day, and the food we are about to receive. Amen."

And please don't put me through that again, she added respectfully.

Amens were repeated and the feast began. Plates were passed around the table, and Jerry filled them. E. J. groaned at her mammoth portion.

"Now, you're too skinny. You eat up," Jerry admonished. "I like my women with a little meat on them." He winked at Maggie playfully.

E. J. picked at her food while the others visited and ate. Gabe loaded his plate with a second helping. "Maggie, your cooking puts Martha Stewart to shame."

E. J. listened to the playful banter, feeling a sense of belonging. Until that moment, she hadn't realized how much she'd missed family and friends. She had few close acquaintances in LA. Friendship had seemed a luxury her job never allowed.

After dinner, they pored over Maggie's high school yearbook, laughing between coffee and bites of sour cream chocolate cake. E. J. was surprised that she remembered faces, and even occasionally managed to put a name with one.

Finally, the conversation turned exactly where E. J. had feared it would.

"So," Gabe said, leaning back to relax, "Cora says you lead an exciting life. Want to tell us about LA and the big corporate job?"

"That's grandmother talk," E. J. said, feeling her cheeks redden.

"Don't be modest," he chided. "Exactly what is it that you do at Kilgore's Kosmetics?"

"Mostly grunt work. Advertising and a little marketing."

"I thought you were a co-owner," Grams interrupted. "That's not exactly grunt work."

Maggie shifted a sleeping child to her side. "Come on, E. J., tell us what you really do. Give us the lowdown on the cosmetics industry." She glanced at the others. "Kilgore's has one of the finest hair-care product lines around. I love their Tea Tree shampoo!"

"Thanks. It's one of our biggest sellers."

"Wow," Jerry said. "Makes the feed business sound dull."

E. J. laughed. "It's not all that exciting. The glamorous part is exaggerated. Corporate life is pretty routine and demanding."

"God's been good to you." Maggie reached for Jerry's hand. The two exchanged a look that only people in love recognized. "He's been good to all of us."

"Amen to that," Cora seconded. She lifted her coffee cup in a mock toast. Gabe was strangely silent, and eventually conversation dwindled. When they noticed him staring at his half-eaten piece of cake, Maggie said softly, "Something wrong with the cake?"

"No, it's good, Maggie. One of Nell's favorites," he said half to himself. He set the plate aside.

"If I remember correctly, Nelly made very good sour cream chocolate cake," E. J. said quietly.

"Beat mine all to pieces," Maggie offered.

"She was a good cook," Gabe conceded. He leaned over and ruffled the baby's hair, breaking the melancholy.

E. J. glanced at her watch. "Look at the time. I have an appointment in Raleigh tomorrow, and it's going to be a long day, so if you'll excuse me."

"You're leaving so soon?" Maggie shifted the sleeping child to Jerry and got up to walk with her. "Jerry's going to Raleigh tomorrow for the feed-and-weed show. Why don't you ride along and keep him company?"

"Why on earth do you have to go to Raleigh? You're flying out on Sunday, aren't you?" Cora asked, frowning.

"Business, Grams. You know—grunt work." E. J. glanced at Jerry. "I don't know how long I'll be there. I'll take the rental."

"You sure? It wouldn't be any trouble." Jerry absently stroked the sleeping child's hair. "I'd like the company."

"Thanks, anyway. I'll drive myself."

"I wish you didn't have to go so soon," Maggie said. "It's early."

"Sorry. It's been nice." For the first time since she pulled into Cullen's Corner, E. J. meant the nicety she uttered. She'd enjoyed the evening immensely.

"I'll be along in a little while," Cora promised. Maggie walked E. J. to the front door. This time a password wasn't necessary, but a sudden unexpected wave of anxiety stopped her short of leaving.

"Maybe I should stay and help you clean up?" E. J. paused in the doorway.

"Heavens, no. If you stayed, I wouldn't want you slaving in my kitchen. Jerry will help when we get the kids down for the night. How long did you say you were staying?"

"Until Sunday."

"In that case, why don't you come to Bea's birthday party Saturday? Jerry's tied up with deliveries all day—delivery driver is down with a summer bug—I could sure use the help."

"I'd love to, Maggie, but I thought I'd take Grams shopping before I left. Otherwise, I'd help you out."

"Well, if you change your mind, let me know. Jerry will be gone all day tomorrow, so maybe if you get back from Raleigh early enough, we can do something."

"Sure." E. J. felt herself holding on, reluctant to leave and walk home. She'd felt a peace tonight, one she hadn't experienced in weeks. The scent of children was oddly comforting.

"Maggie?"

"Yes?"

"I did have a wonderful time. Thanks for inviting me."

Maggie squeezed her affectionately. "Anytime, babe. Thanks for coming."

Friendship can be so bittersweet. Eighteen years ago Maggie was a young girl, one with whom E. J. had little in common, but today they were women with more in common than E. J. ever dreamed. That's how it is when we get older; friendship becomes dearer, more defined. E. J. wondered now what would have happened if she'd stayed in Cullen's Corner, if she'd never taken her savings from summer jobs, bought an old beat-up VW, and started life anew in LA

Or what would have happened if she'd told Isabel that night that her son was a jerk and she'd rather be horsewhipped than spend an evening in his presence? Jake Kilgore was cocky, spoiled, and accustomed to having his own way; E. J. had known that. But Isabel was a friend, and friends sometimes do things they wouldn't ordinarily do for another.

What would have happened if she hadn't gone to the bathroom that night . . . if she'd looked closer at the drink he'd handed her when she returned?

What if she hadn't drunk a simple Coke?

What if she had suspected he'd laced the drink? What did he use? Rohypnol—known as "roofies" on the street—a potent drug that produces a sedative effect, amnesia, muscle relaxation, and a slowing of psychomotor responses. Or had he used GHB bought off the street prior to the date? She would never know. She'd known nothing about the drug until the day after, when she researched date-rape drugs on the Internet. But she did know that within thirty minutes of drinking that Coke, some drug had rendered her a sitting duck for the evil Jake Kilgore had planned.

Anger flared, and she shoved it back as she crossed the street. All the what-ifs in the world wouldn't change what had happened. Tomorrow would. When tomorrow was over, she told herself, she would be able to forget.

CHAPTER FOUR

Vaulting out of bed Friday morning, E. J. made a beeline for the bathroom, skidding on the woven rug Grams kept next to the bed. If she didn't die from morning sickness, she was going to break a leg on the rug. How long did it take for the Diclectin to kick in?

Five minutes later, she buried her face in her arms, limp from exhaustion. Outside, a thin sun struggled to penetrate a muggy haze. Pulling herself upright, she stared at her mirrored reflection. This would all be over by five o'clock tonight.

Dark-circled eyes reflected back at her. She'd spent a miserable night—hot and sticky and full of awful dreams. In the most severe of them, she watched her mother holding a box of siding and riding away on the back of a motorcycle with a demon-faced man. The face was imprinted on her mind in vivid colors: long graying beard whipping in the wind, skin pockmarked and ruddy. The corrugated-siding salesman.

Across the street, she heard the crying children blubbering good-bye as Jerry Markus's old pickup pulled out of the driveway and roared down the street.

Parting the curtains, she spotted an overripe Maggie holding her back with her right hand and the hand of her youngest with the other. The curtain fell shut. Maggie and her brood. Did E. J. eventually want the same?

An unpleasant smell drifted to her, and she turned around to find Grams standing in the doorway. Her sudden appearance startled E. J., and she sank to the side of the bed.

"Grams! You scared me half to death."

Grams held out a cup of coffee. "Thought you might need something to get your engine started." Her eyes swept E. J.'s state. "You still take cream and sugar, don't you?"

"No coffee—"

Now, in Cora Roberts's house it was unthinkable to start the day without a cup of coffee. The cup was in E. J.'s hand before she could argue. Her stomach gurgled as she stared at the thick, hot liquid and she thought, *This isn't coffee—it's motor oil.* She set the cup on the battered dresser.

"So, what's on your agenda today, Grams?"

"Were Maggie's enchiladas bad, too?"

E. J. stretched up and moved to the window, ignoring the observation. Of course, Grams had heard; the morning sickness disturbed everyone. It was only natural that she would be curious.

"How far along are you, E. J.?"

E. J. shut her eyes. She should have known she'd never be able to fool Grams. And only God knew what had possessed her to come home in the first place. She could have had the procedure in LA. Had she been thinking that normalcy back in her old room would restore her old life? Hours intended to cleanse her thoughts, to restore her life to what it had been before Jake Kilgore? Would it ever be possible for her to return to the young woman who'd had the world by the tail until a rape snatched it away?

"Almost two months."

Oh, how hard those words are to hear for a grandma. This was the child she'd loved and raised and protected with her life. She'd tried with every ounce of wisdom within her to teach E. J. right from wrong. Cora must have thought at this moment that she'd failed. Disappointment registered briefly on her face. But Cora had lived a long time and nothing surprised her anymore. She gestured toward the cup.

"Try it. It helped your mother through morning sickness."

"Coffee?" E. J. glanced up and realized the judgment she'd anticipated wasn't there. Relief flooded her. "It smells horrid."

"Everything will for the next few weeks." Cora came over to sit beside her on the bed. "Try it—you'll feel better once you get it down."

"Getting it down" was a problem, but E. J. lifted the cup, closed her eyes, and drank. Lowering the cup, she faced her grandmother. "I'm sorry, Grams. I didn't want to tell you this way."

Patting her knee, Cora got up. "I'll fix some dry toast."

❀

Cora was puttering around the kitchen, watering plants, when E. J. came downstairs a few minutes later. She didn't stop her busywork, but proceeded into the living room and calmly discussed the pretty oxalis blooms with Albert, who was idly stretched across the back of the sofa, soaking up the warm morning sun.

"Now, Albert, you're going to have to leave my pretties alone, do you hear me, young man? You'll damage this sweet little shamrock plant, and then Mama will be upset with you."

Meowing, the cat inspected the plant and stretched.

E. J. went to the sink and carefully rinsed the cup. Silence hung thick in the sunny nook. E. J. knew discussing her situation with Cora was going to be harder than she thought. The clock ticked away the minutes as E. J. unconsciously ran water, turning the cup over and over beneath the stream.

"You're going to run up the water bill if you keep washing that cup," Grams said, reentering the kitchen.

"I don't want it," E. J. blurted. "I can't stand the thought of it, Grams."

"Oh, Eva Jean."

Well, so much for E. J.'s worry. Like so much of our anxiety, the worst didn't happen. Cora wiped her hands on her skirt, gently took E. J.'s arm, and sat her down at the table. E. J. leaned over and laid her head against Grams's shoulder. The girl was dog weary now, so weary of fighting this alone. What she needed more than anything right now was a dose of Cora's wisdom.

"How could anyone not want a child?" Grams soothed.

"Not his. I hate him." The words came fitfully between ragged sobs.

Cora tenderly drew her to her Cashmere Bouquets–scented breast and held her tightly. "Whose child? Eva Jean, talk to me."

"Oh, Grams. I was raped," E. J. whispered.

Raped. E. J. felt Grams stiffen. Folks, *rape* is such an ugly word. In Grams's day the stigma would have been unthinkable, but she knew it happened far too often in E. J.'s generation.

"I was . . ." The admission was too painful and refused to come out a second time.

"Oh, dear Lord, Eva Jean." Grams shook her head as if to eradicate the hurtful truth.

Sometimes folks need a break from life. E. J. and Cora sat for long moments, grandmother holding granddaughter with unsaid questions and answers festering in their hearts. The doorbell rang, shattering the silence. E. J. started to get up, apparently welcoming the opportunity to postpone the inevitable. Of course, Grams would have to be told the circumstances and how E. J. had decided to handle the problem. E. J.'s appointment wasn't until three, but in order to drive to Raleigh and locate the clinic she'd have to leave soon.

Before E. J. opened the door, she heard Pete Markus babbling. "Momma sent me over," he began excitedly, "to tell you about the baby."

"What about the baby?" Cora asked, getting up from the table. E. J. unlatched the screen and invited the child inside. Pete bounced up and down, out of breath, pointing at his house.

"What about the baby?" Cora repeated.

"It's coming right now."

"What do you mean?" E. J. knelt, taking the boy's hands. "Now?"

"Mommy wants you to come over." He turned heel and ran off, darting across the street without looking. E. J. held her breath until he reached the safety of the yard.

"We'd better go see what's going on," Grams said. E. J. followed her out the door. Entering Maggie's house, they found her on the sofa, trying to quiet the youngest.

"It's started. I should have known when my back hurt so badly last night. Jerry's in Raleigh. We'll have to call the convention center."

Cora knelt and took the toddler from her.

"How far apart are the pains?"

"Five minutes—maybe less. I've probably waited too long to send Pete over."

"I'll call Gabe and have him find Jerry." Grams reached for the phone. Maggie tried to smile at E. J., who was standing shocked at the entrance to the living room.

"Hey, there." She grinned through gritted teeth. "Some vacation, huh?"

"Can I get you anything?"

Now, people, E. J. didn't have the slightest idea of how to help. All she knew about birthing babies involved boiling water and had come from *Andy Griffith* reruns and bad made-for-TV movies.

"I can't have anything but ice chips until the baby comes." Maggie winced. "Which may not be that long."

E. J. glanced at the mantel clock. Eleven o'clock. She should be leaving for her appointment!

Grams came back into the room and helped Maggie off the couch. "Come on. Get your purse. We're heading to the hospital."

"But I have an appointment . . ." E. J. took a step back toward the stairs. If she missed that appointment she'd have to stay longer—there would be more questions, more doubts on her part. . . .

"You'll be right there in Raleigh. We'll get Maggie to the hospital and I'll run you where you need to go."

"But Grams . . ." She couldn't know where E. J. was going! "How . . . ?"

"Where there's two grown women and a van there's a way." Grams shot E. J. a warning. "Now, Maggie, where's your hospital bag? Hurry, we've got a baby to deliver."

"Oh . . ." Maggie moaned.

"Another contraction?" Grams asked expectantly.

"No. The kids. I haven't gotten them dressed yet this morning."

"Can't we take them over to Beatrice's? Jerry's mother would be better off watching the kids than coming to the hospital and getting all upset."

Maggie shook her head. "You know Beatrice, she'd have a fit if we didn't let her go. . . . The kids can come with us."

"Eva Jean, run and get the girls ready. I'll get the car."

E. J. searched the house until she located Bea and Emma playing in a back bedroom littered with Barbie dolls and Barbie clothes.

"Hey, girls. We have to get dressed now."

Emma looked up at her and grinned. Bea kept moving the Barbie doll's arms back and forth. E. J. riffled through half-open dresser drawers, pulling out clothes and looking for a match.

"Where're we going?" Bea asked, putting Barbie in a plastic car with a half-dressed Ken.

"We have to go to Raleigh." E. J. smiled. "Your mom is going to have the baby today."

"Can we get ice cream?" Bea gazed up at her expectantly. Emma got up off the floor, and her diaper fell down around her ankles.

E. J. couldn't promise ice cream. "After the baby is born, we'll ask your momma."

Emma waddled over to E. J., and she wrestled the cloth diaper up into place. Wrinkling her nose, she called over her shoulder, "Bea, get me a clean diaper."

Emma fussed and wouldn't hold still. E. J. chased her around the bed, trying to change the diaper and hold her nose at the same time. Tears smarted her eyes. Good grief. Why were women so crazed about motherhood?

Getting the clean diaper in place, she secured it with a safety pin—hadn't Maggie heard of disposal diapers?—then attempted to even out the other side. Emma stared up at her with solemn blue-eyed fascination. E. J.'s heart turned over. Would the child she carried . . . she had to stop thinking about what was inside her as a child. It was an "it." Jake's it.

"Shoo, you *stink*," E. J. teased affectionately.

"What you want me to do with this?" Bea extended the dirty diaper on the end of a toy popcorn popper.

E. J. eyed the smelly mess. "Where's the closest toxic waste dump?"

Bea frowned. "I don't know what a taxi dump is."

Grinning, E. J. righted Emma and straightened the young girl's T-shirt. She gingerly took the messy diaper and went into the bathroom.

"Momma puts the stinky diapers in the toilet," Bea, who had followed her, offered. E. J. looked at her, then at the diaper, and dropped it into the toilet. She hoped someone would notice it and do whatever the next step was, before flushing. She went back into the bedroom, trailed by Bea and Emma.

"Momma said that the stork would bring the baby here," Bea said. "Why do we have to go and get it?"

"Well, the stork is busy right now delivering other mommas' babies, so we have to help him out and pick it up ourselves."

"Why can't Mr. Bruce bring it when he comes?"

E. J. frowned. "Mr. Bruce?"

"He brings our mail," Bea said, pulling her socks on backwards.

"Oh, well . . . he doesn't have room in his bag for a baby." Emma fussed as E. J. pulled the shirt over her head.

"And what about Bea's birthday party? Do we still get to haf it tomorrow?"

"We'll have to postpone the party until Momma feels better, sweetie."

Both girls fell silent, and in a few minutes they were dressed in randomly colored outfits and ready to go.

Grams had Maggie positioned on the middle seat of the Markuses' minivan. E. J. loaded the kids in the back and turned to see Grams climbing into the driver's seat.

"Grams, maybe I should drive."

Grams turned to look back at her. "Why? What's wrong with me? I can drive her."

"It's forty minutes to Raleigh . . ." Maggie groaned theatrically and winked at E. J. "She needs you back with her. I don't have any experience with childbirth."

Grams shrugged and relinquished the keys.

With everyone safely in the van, E. J. backed out of the garage, barely missing an overturned tricycle.

The noisy trip to Raleigh was utter chaos, with children complaining and Maggie panting and groaning.

"I've got to go to the west woom," Pete chanted ten minutes outside of Cullen's Corner.

"You'll have to hold it," Grams said.

He cupped his britches tightly.

"Where's my Barbie? Where's my Barbie?" Bea broke into tears. "We forgot her. Now she's not going to get any ice cream."

"Jerry!" Maggie wailed. "Where is Jerry?"

E. J. focused on the road and tightened her grip on the steering wheel. Sneaking peeks in the rearview mirror, she saw Emma nodding off in her car seat, oblivious to the din around her.

Thirty minutes later, Maggie's contractions were coming one on top of the other. E. J. nervously wheeled the van into the emergency entrance and leapt out. Two nurses loaded the expectant mother into a wheelchair and whisked her away, while Grams took charge of the children and E. J. parked the van.

When E. J. reached the waiting room, nurses directed her to delivery, one floor up. An orderly greeted her at the elevator with a set of scrubs. Grams, trying to corral the kids, stood beside him.

"That's her. She'll go in with Mrs. Markus."

E. J., stunned, shook her head.

"Eva Jean," Grams said, "you will go in and hold that girl's hand. She needs someone with her, and I have to watch the kids. I've called the convention center and they're paging Jerry, but no telling when he'll get here. Now go on; Maggie needs you."

"I'll watch the kids. . . ." But it was too late. Grams disappeared into the waiting room, and E. J. meekly followed the orderly down the polished hallway, shoving her hair under her paper hat.

Maggie was making big, puffing breaths as she lay on a gurney with monitor cords attached like a spider's legs.

"E. J.!" She latched onto E. J.'s hand, nearly crushing it by the force.

"Are you her sister?" the doctor asked.

"No. A friend."

"Her Lamaze coach?"

"No. Just here to—" A sharp contraction interrupted the questioning. E. J. winced as Maggie squeezed her hand until it was numb.

"Okay, Maggie. It's time," the doctor said. "I want you to sit up and give me a big push."

"Already?" E. J. glanced at the clock. Two-thirty. "Isn't this awfully quick?" According to all the horror stories she'd heard, labor lasted for hours and hours. Sometimes days.

"Not for a fourth one," a starched white nurse from the other side of the gurney said. "We've got to help her get this baby out." They lifted Maggie's back, and the first round of pushing began.

"Eight, nine, ten," the nurse said, and Maggie released her breath. They lowered her back to the bed. Her face was a very unnatural shade of red. E. J. averted her eyes from where the doctor was standing between Maggie's knees.

"Why doesn't this get any easier?" Maggie said through clenched teeth.

"Just a few more pushes and we're done." They leaned her up for the second round, and she strained.

"Nearly there," the doctor said. E. J. concentrated on his lips moving beneath the surgical mask.

The third push started, and before the nurse reached four, a wail erupted. The doctor looked up, grinning. "Congratulations, Maggie. Pete's got some help. The kids have a little brother."

Maggie burst into tears and laughter at the same time. The door opened, and Jerry burst in, still shrugging into green scrubs.

"Honey!" Maggie cried out as he bent to kiss her.

"Sorry, sugar. I came as soon as I got the message." Tears glistened in his eyes.

The doctor held up the baby. "Another son, Jerry."

E. J. stared at the squirming infant, fascinated. The newborn was purple and toothless and screaming at the top of his lungs. The umbilical cord was smattered with blood, and the baby was covered in some kind of white sticky mucus. The room tilted and E. J. grabbed the gurney for support.

"Would you like to cut the cord, Daddy?" the doctor asked. Jerry nodded and the nurse handed him a pair of shiny scissors.

Backing away, E. J. leaned against the wall. She heard the scissors snip, but it was the last sound she heard for a while.

E. J. blinked twice, shielding her eyes against the harsh light. She was lying down. Hospital sounds surrounded her—wheels moving over polished floors, dishes clanking from the dinner cart.

"Is it over?" she moaned and cradled her stomach. She couldn't remember the "procedure," but she was thankful there'd been no pain. A stab of remorse hit her. She'd done it. It was over. Why didn't she feel relieved? Giddy with happiness? Disappointment crushed her. She'd actually done it—why had she done it?

She felt a hand take hers, and she struggled to open her eyes. Grams stood by her bed.

"Grams?" E. J. struggled to sit up. "How did you know?" She felt ashamed, as if somehow she was to blame, yet she hadn't had a choice. Have Jake Kilgore's child? The thought sickened her.

"You fainted."

E. J. realized with errant swiftness that it wasn't over. She hadn't undergone the procedure . . . she was still dressed in scrubs. Maggie. The baby.

"They're beautiful!" Grams said, beaming as if she'd given birth, not Maggie. E. J. sat up slowly, dangling her feet off the gurney.

"They? What are you talking about?"

"Twins!" Grams reported gleefully. "Two perfect little babies. A boy *and* a girl. Maggie and Jerry are beside themselves."

"Twins! How? Maggie didn't know, did she?"

"Apparently one was hiding. Childbirth isn't a perfect science."

E. J. rubbed her head, realizing that she was still in the now empty delivery room.

"What time is it?"

"Close to three. You've been out for fifteen minutes or more."

E. J. bounded off the gurney. "Three o'clock! My appointment!"

"Can't it wait?" Grams asked. "It's just business."

E. J. slumped back to the gurney. *Business,* she thought. *Right.* Grams helped her out of the scrubs, and the two women walked down the hall to the nursery. Approaching the window, E. J. could see three little faces pressed up against the glass on the other side. Pete struggled to hoist Emma up for a closer look.

"Look, Emma! We've got a brother and a sister." Emma wiggled down and scampered to Grams.

"Now you'll have three birthdays to celebrate within a day of each other—Bea's and the new twins'," E. J. pointed out.

Bea jumped up and down. "Yeah!"

The soft light in the nursery illuminated rows of sleeping babies. Two carts closest to the window were the objects of Pete's concentration.

E. J. smiled. The babies stretched and yawned in their sleep. Dressed in pink and blue hats, they looked like toy dolls. A nurse came over and slipped a card in each baby's bassinette.

Sid and Clara Markus.

"How precious," Grams said, grinning from ear to ear as if they were her grandchildren. In a way, folks, they were Cora's grandchildren. She was like a third grandmother to them, baking cookies and taking the Markus children on weekly outings. That's how it was in Cullen's Corner—everyone helping everyone else.

"Come on." Grams pulled E. J. away from the window. Draping her arm around E. J.'s waist, they walked down the hallway to Maggie's room. E. J. waited for Grams to pick up the interrupted thread of conversation regarding her pregnancy. But she didn't. Instead, she squeezed her waist in silent support. Apparently, there'd been enough excitement for one day.

News like E. J.'s could wait for another time.

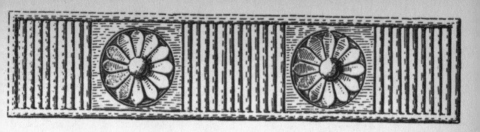

CHAPTER FIVE

Sunday morning, E. J. trailed a string of Citrus Mist across the kitchen countertop. She grimaced, sopping up paint splatters before they hardened. In the process she made an even bigger mess. Rubbing only made it worse. Running a free hand through her hair, she bit her lip. Why couldn't she sit still like an ordinary person? Her life was falling apart, and she was painting the kitchen cabinets. Painting aggravated her back—an old injury she had incurred during her youth. Yet she felt like she was going to jump out of her skin if she didn't keep busy.

She absently wiped her head with the rag she'd used to wipe up the paint, biting back frustration. She'd missed the appointment. The clinic wasn't open on Saturday. She and Grams had spent the day cleaning Maggie's house and watching the kids so that Jerry could spend time with Maggie and the twins.

Around one, Grams had stopped and sat down at Maggie's kitchen table to drink a glass of cold tea. E. J. joined her, heaving a sigh. Kids were messy and noisy and . . . so charming; she'd found herself laughing out loud at Bea's and Emma's antics. They were excited about the new babies and chattered incessantly about how they were going to be "Momma's help-ers" when Maggie came home. E. J. poured a glass of tea, adding a pink packet of sweetener. Grams eyed her silently.

Stirring the brown liquid, E. J. felt her nerves prickle at the scrutiny. "Stop looking at me like that."

"How else would I look at you when you dropped a grenade and haven't revisited the subject? Rape, E. J.? Isn't that some-thing we should discuss?"

"I don't want to talk about the rape, Grams. I've spent two months trying to deal with it, and I'm sick to death of the subject."

"Neither do I—it sounds ugly and devastating, but I think we have to, hon." Her eyes settled softly on the grieving woman. "Oh, sweetie, what happened wasn't your fault. Evil abounds in this old world, and there are dark forces at work."

Biting back tears, E. J. took a sip of the drink. "I hate him, Grams."

"I know." She leaned closer to pat E. J.'s hand. "That's your first instinct, but maybe you should pity him—"

"*Pity* him?" E. J. snorted. "I *detest* the animal." Thank God the world would be spared of Jake Kilgore. The women sat in silence, halfheartedly drinking their tea. E. J. had lost her thirst, and the sobriety of the matter had cooled Grams's interest in trivial pursuits. The kids' voices drifted from the front room, where they were building a tower with Lego blocks.

Silence ticked away.

"What are you going to do—?"

Shoving back from the table, E. J. ended the conversation. She couldn't tell Grams she was going to abort—she was carry-ing Cora's great-grandchild! Surely Cora would try to talk her out of the surgery. She couldn't change her mind now, though her fickle emotions had turned on her yesterday when she witnessed the twins' birth. So perfect, so miraculous, so . . . Godlike in perfection. One stroke of a scalpel and . . .

"Sounds like Bea's pulling Emma's hair. I have to break it up." E. J. left the kitchen and Grams sitting at the table, staring at her glass of melting ice.

E. J.'s thoughts returned to her painting. She had to stay over until she could reschedule her appointment, or leave as scheduled this afternoon. She batted around what she would tell Grams if she were to stay. *Hey, Grams, guess what. I've decided to take another week from my heavy schedule to hang around a few more days. I don't want to talk about the pregnancy or the rape, but I don't want to leave.* Or, *You know the rape resulted in pregnancy, so I've decided to have an abortion—care if I hang out here a few more days?*

Isabel and Brian would have a conniption because she'd never taken two weeks off in a row, ever. They would freak out.

A peck at the back door interrupted her thoughts. "I'll get it," she called upstairs to Grams.

Gabe stood at the door, dressed for church in a robin's-egg blue shirt and crisp khakis. Albert wound around one pant leg, leaving orange and white hairs on the freshly ironed trousers.

E. J. pointed at his legs. "He's leaving hairs."

"Don't suppose God gets upset over a little kitty fur." He bent down and scooped Albert up, cradling the cat in his arms. E. J. wiped a hand on her pants and motioned him in.

Peach Street was quiet on Sunday mornings. Everyone went to church, Bibles tucked under their arms. Sundays had an easy feel in the Corner. A day of rest and puttering about the house.

"Grams is finishing up." E. J. returned to her paintbrush. Gabe dropped the cat and followed, watching as she hoisted herself back up on the counter.

He cleared his throat. "God doesn't mind a little kitty fur, but Mrs. Lowry will faint if you get paint on the pews."

"What pews?" E. J. dabbed a spot of paint on the top of the door. "I'm not going to church with you." She blew a painted strand of hair out of her eyes.

"Why not?"

"I'm on duty for neighborhood watch today. Sorry." She painted another strip, wincing as paint sprayed her face.

Gabe frowned. "Fred Hicks paints to supplement his retirement. Want me to send him by?"

"No, I'll be done within the hour."

Well, people, she might be done, but Gabe could see right off that the kitchen was going to suffer.

But E. J. had to keep her mind busy—you know the feeling—pass as much time as quickly as possible. Anything you can think of to do to keep from thinking. Missing that appointment had E. J. running in circles, and that wasn't like either the high-powered executive who spent her days behind a desk making multimillion-dollar decisions or the young woman who used to place her trust in a caring God.

"I have a plane back to LA this afternoon."

"So soon? You just got here." He jumped back to avoid being hit by paint missiles.

"Well, maybe . . . I don't know. Maybe I'll stick around another few days. Work's a little slow right now."

Now, folks, hold on; she wasn't lying. Kilgore's Kosmetics had work, but they needed more than work right now. They needed a new product.

"Cora would like that. I'm driving her by the hospital after services. She wants to take a few things to Maggie. I thought you might want to ride along."

"Sorry. No can do."

"No can do what?" Grams appeared, fastening her hat to her head with bobby pins. One stuck out of her mouth.

"No can go to church this morning," Gabe tattled.

"Eva Jean, I'm ashamed of you. You used to be the first one up on Sunday mornings, bursting at the seams to get to church."

"Yeah, I used to be a lot of things, Grams." E. J. touched the brush to a corner of the cabinet, squinting. "I can hardly finish the painting and catch a five o'clock plane if I'm sitting in church, can I?"

Admittedly, it was a tough call for E. J. If she went back to LA she could have the procedure there with no problem. But it felt good to be home, safe. E. J. would need safety even more if she had the abortion. A part of her sensed that, wavered.

Nobody could expect her to have the baby of a rapist, she argued silently, someone who had tricked her and then taken advantage of her. She'd had no choice in that matter. She did in this one. It's just that she would rather have been here after the procedure, not in impersonal LA . . .

If she returned to LA, however, she could call Grams and tell her the matter was settled. She could say she miscarried.

"These cabinets have been here for fifty years. I don't know why you think you have to paint them today," Grams scolded.

E. J. sighed and dismounted with a soft thud.

"Besides, you shouldn't be up and down like that in your condition." E. J. drew a quick breath and shot her a stringent look.

Gabe looked blank. "What condition?"

Grams turned and quickly covered her tracks. "She has a bad back. Has had since the day she fell out the back of Morris Ledmer's old pickup."

Gabe took the brush out of E. J.'s hand and stepped to the sink to rinse it. "I warned Morris he was going to kill someone if he didn't get that tailgate fixed."

"Morris still drives that truck?" E. J. asked.

"The odometer turned over two hundred and twenty thousand last week, and the thing is still running. They don't make trucks like that anymore."

Folks ought to be thrilled at that! With LA's emission standards the piece of junk would be outlawed, but it would do in the Corner. So would imperfect lives, if only E. J. knew it.

Grams finished with the hat. "Leave the painting to me. I'll finish up later. You go and change your clothes, E. J. This is the Lord's Day, and you need to go and thank him for your blessings."

Well, at that point, E. J. didn't think she had many of those, but she wasn't thinking too straight, either. Heaving a sigh, she frowned, but Grams only smiled and patted her shoulder, pointing her toward the stairs.

"Go upstairs and change and come with us so I can keep an eye on you. We're going to be late."

E. J. marched into the bathroom, reached for her loofah, and started to scrub paint off her arms and legs, wondering why

Grams still treated her like a child. But then she guessed maybe she was acting like a child these days—confused, hurt.

A picture of the congregation rose up to taunt her. Church wasn't exactly top priority on her list these days, and facing all those women with discerning eyes was even lower on the rung. She wasn't the only girl in town to get pregnant out of wedlock.

Oh, boy. Why is it that whenever we're insecure, we tend to assume the worst in other people? Why not just tell the truth? E. J. Roberts was raped. A travesty, to be sure, but not E. J.'s fault. It was hard for her to believe other people would not think badly of her. E. J. was insecure, and the last thing she needed was criticism, so she ran from any potential blame. What she needed was plain old love.

She emerged from the bedroom, complaining that she felt like a circus juggler. She'd showered, blow-dried her hair with one hand, and applied lipstick with the other in less than fifteen minutes. She pointed out that she was unprepared for church services, that she'd brought nothing suitable to wear. She picked paint streaks from her hair, complaining.

"Well, you look good to me," Gabe said from the bottom of the stairs. He offered his arm, and E. J., still grumbling, took it. Grams, purse in hand, waited at the front door, beaming like a fairy godmother. Apparently, it didn't take much to make some people happy.

The First Full Baptist Evangelical Church of Christ sat on the corner of Maple and Elm, a scant three blocks from Peach Street. A tall buff-colored brick structure, it was among the oldest standing buildings in town. A plaque commemorated the historical site where Union soldiers had been hospitalized during the Civil War. That fact had fascinated E. J. as a child. She would spend services lost in thoughts of dying soldiers and of how, if she had been alive at the time, she would have nursed them and written letters home to their loved ones. Of course, all the soldiers in her head suffered from wounds below the covers where they could not be identified.

Friendly faces greeted the threesome as they entered the foyer. The news of E. J.'s return had spread, and everyone seemed anxious to welcome her back.

Pastor Matthewson approached, clasping both E. J.'s hands in a warm embrace before giving her a hug. "Eva Jean, how good to see you! What's it been? Fifteen years?"

E. J. smiled. "Eighteen. You're looking good, Pastor."

He patted his ample belly. Now the honest truth was, Pastor Matthewson ate like a horse, and his ferocious appetite got worse as he got older. If the Ladies' Auxiliary didn't stop feeding him, he was going to have to weigh in at the stockyards.

"I'm in no danger of starving," he said, eyes sparkling mischievously. "You haven't changed a bit. Let me have a look at you."

E. J. shrunk in horror at the thought. But two of Grams's best friends, Edna Davenport and Hattie Myers, distracted him, approaching with arms outstretched in anticipation of a bear hug. *Babies must feel this way: pinched and smothered*, E. J. thought.

The three elderly ladies had attended grade school, junior high, and high school together, all marrying men who served in World War II. E. J.'s grandfather came back. Hattie's and Edna's husbands didn't. The women, who were also sisters, moved in together and opened a boardinghouse, never to marry a second time. "Too much heartache," they declared. They'd just serve the Lord and others.

The women engaged in pleasantries while Gabe wandered off to a pew. E. J. grimaced when she saw him getting closer and closer to the front of the church.

"You have to come for tea this afternoon, E. J. Hattie's made one of her marvelous angel food cakes, and there are only two boarders now to help eat it."

"Yes, yes, yes," Hattie seconded. "You really must."

"Sounds great, Mrs. Myers, but I'm thinking about leaving later this afternoon."

The sisters' faces fell.

"Oh, well, I'm sorry—perhaps next time," Edna said.

"Yes, next time will do quite well," Hattie told her.

E. J. excused herself and joined Gabe. "Did you have to sit so close?" she whispered, edging into the second pew from the altar. They were close enough to see the hair in Pastor Matthewson's ears.

"Cora says the closer you are to the front, the closer you are to God."

E. J. remembered the saying from her youth. Everyone in the church was familiar with Grams's little witticisms. More often than not they were jumbled versions of other sayings mixed with something she'd made up for effect.

"A bird in the bush is worth one somewhere else."

"A pound of prevention is worth more than an ounce of gold."

"Never do twice what you can do once and get it over with."

E. J.'s eyes roamed the familiar old church as the choir filed in. Carved beams of polished oak broke the pristine white ceiling. Padded seats matched the faded red carpet running down the aisle. Hardwood lovingly hand polished by the Ladies' Auxiliary took a lot of hard work and dedication to keep it shining.

Stained-glass windows each depicted a different biblical scene: Jesus holding a child on his lap, a white dove, a wooden cross. To the left, Jesus' birth; on the right, the hill of Golgotha with three crosses.

Behind the choir loft hung a large wooden cross with a simple crown of thorns looped over the top beam.

The choir, wearing maroon robes with white silk collars, opened their hymnals. One of the members, an older, attractive lady with salt-and-pepper hair and arresting blue eyes, pinpointed E. J. and smiled. E. J. politely smiled back. She had never seen this woman before this morning.

The woman waved. E. J. lifted a hand and from the corner of her eye saw Gabe return the greeting. She dropped her hand to her side. The woman blushed along with E. J. at her mistake.

Cora settled into the pew, reaching for her hymnal. "That Edna and Hattie talk, talk, talk. I told them services were starting."

E. J. leaned closer. "Who's the woman waving at Gabe?"

Cora frowned. "Helen Withers."

"Who's Helen Withers?"

"Moved to town a few years back. Owns Withers' Realty. Nice lady—why?"

"No reason."

Let me stop you here and explain about Helen. Cora should have known that E. J. rarely asked questions without a reason. The lovely older woman waving at Gabe must have raised her curiosity, since new faces in Cullen's Corner were rare. But Helen was part of the town now in Cora's eyes.

"Helen and Gabe are sort of an item lately," Grams whispered.

"Really. How long has Nell been dead?"

"Almost three years." Cora leaned closer. "He wouldn't date for the longest time, and he'd say he wasn't dating Helen now if you asked, but the two have been seen together in the last few months. It's been long enough," she added as if to legitimate the relationship.

The choir finished the opening hymn, and Pastor Matthewson rose and approached the pulpit.

E. J. stared at her empty hands. She should have brought a Bible. The one she'd carried as a child sat on the nightstand in the spare bedroom.

Closing her eyes, E. J. listened to the pastor's voice, the voice that had soothed her so many Sundays.

"'I know all the things you do, and I have opened a door for you that no one can shut. You have little strength, yet you obeyed my word and did not deny me.'"

E. J. glanced sideways at Grams's large-print reference Bible. Cora was following the lines with the tip of her finger, keeping her place as the pastor read.

"'Because you have obeyed my command to persevere, I will protect you from the great time of testing that will come upon the whole world to test those who belong to this world.'"

Tests and trials, E. J. thought later as she filed past to shake the pastor's hand. Was that what the pregnancy was? A test? If so,

God had picked the wrong person to test. She figured from his perspective, she'd already failed her share of tests. Pastor Matthewson could preach about forgiveness all he wanted, but how could she forgive Jake Kilgore for what he had done? She couldn't—not now, not ever.

E. J. waited for Grams and Gabe on the sidewalk. Cora stood visiting with the same group of women she'd chatted with before services. Gabe emerged a few minutes later with Helen in tow.

"E. J." Gabe called her over. "I don't believe you've met Helen Withers. Helen's an old friend."

"Not too old," Helen corrected with a friendly laugh.

"No, I meant . . ." Gabe grinned boyishly. "Now, Helen, you know what I meant."

"E. J." The well-dressed woman extended her hand. "I've heard so much about you. Welcome back to Cullen's Corner."

The two women clasped hands. E. J. suspected that Helen had heard an earful recently.

"Helen wants you to join us for lunch. She has a roasted chicken about to come out of the oven."

"Thanks, but there's a paintbrush with my name on it calling me." E. J. realized whatever she said would be taken as a lame excuse. "I have to catch a plane late this afternoon."

"Well, next visit," Helen conceded. "By the way, I love your hair."

"Thank you," E. J. said, slipping away to wait for Grams in the car.

Sunday afternoons were for napping. Ever notice that? A man or woman can do about anything as long as he or she has that early Sunday afternoon snooze. Television going, air cooler blowing fresh air throughout the house. E. J. felt that need for a quick nap. Feeling full and sleepy, she'd closed her eyes for a second . . . just one blissful second before she packed. . . .

When she opened her eyes and stretched, her sleepy gaze meandered to the clock. Five-fifty already! In ten minutes, the final boarding call for flight 454 Raleigh to Denver would blare over the PA system.

In one quick leap, she sprinted off the couch. "Grams! Why didn't you wake me?"

Grams appeared in the doorway, wiping her hands on her apron. "Oh, honey, I know I should have, but—"

"But what?"

"You were sleeping so soundly. I didn't have the heart to wake you."

E. J. sank back down to the couch. She'd missed the flight. She couldn't believe Grams would let her sleep the afternoon away. "I told you not to let me sleep over forty-five minutes."

She'd been asleep for four hours!

"You can get another plane ticket tomorrow if you're so set on going back." Cora turned and disappeared back into the kitchen. "Stop your caterwauling. You might as well help me with dinner. You won't be leaving Cullen's Corner tonight."

Later, E. J. sat on the porch, fuming. She would have been back in LA by midnight. The whole visit had been a comedy of errors. Sure, she'd thought about staying over, but . . . that was irrelevant now. Grams was inside cleaning the kitchen. She had insisted on doing it herself, even though E. J. offered to help. Grams kicked her out of the kitchen and told her to cool off on the porch.

"Get some fresh air. Maybe take a little walk. It would do you good to get out of the house."

Taking a walk would only bring her into contact with other people, and there would be questions. "Why, Eva Jean, I thought you were leaving tonight. Overslept? You've got to be kidding!"

Gabe appeared at his back gate and let himself out, a bundle of fresh-cut flowers in one hand. He turned and walked east.

E. J. watched until he was nearly out of sight before she got out of the swing and descended the steps. It was hot, with a thunderstorm brewing in the west.

Gabe rounded a corner, and E. J. did a small sprint to catch up to him. She stayed back far enough to keep him in sight, but not close enough to risk an encounter. E. J. had been a fanciful child, often playing Nancy Drew, uncovering mysteries that would have stumped even the most observant sleuth. Ironically, Nancy also didn't have a mother. E. J. didn't have a father, either; Nancy did.

Biologically, of course, E. J. did have a father. It just seemed that no one knew who he was. There were rumors and speculation, but Marlene had never mentioned him, and the one time E. J. had tried to ask her, Marlene teared up and wouldn't answer. The identity of E. J.'s father was a stubborn case that not even Nancy Drew could crack.

Maple Cemetery was coming up. Gabe was picking his way through the tombstones, pausing before a small marble marker under a spreading oak.

Creeping past the gate, E. J. maintained a safe distance between them. He knelt at a grave site and spoke softly as he arranged daisies in a vase, removing a couple and laying them on two small graves beside Nell's.

E. J. recognized the private moment and turned away, walking toward the back of the cemetery where her grandfather was buried.

❧

The stone bothered E. J. the first time she'd seen it. Grams's name was on it too, with a blank for the date of death.

"It's cheaper," Cora had explained to a sobbing Eva Jean. "I'm not going to die anytime soon, sweetie. My name's on there because someday the Lord will bring me home to live with Grandpa."

E. J.'s throat knotted at the memory. She was surprised she'd remembered the grave's location. Grams kept the site preserved, and a fresh spray of peonies was in the vase at the side. E. J. bent to smell the flowers. "Wish you were here to tell me what to do, Gramps," she whispered.

A leaf blew across the grave as the wind pushed a cloud

across the setting sun. Storm clouds threatened, and E. J. turned to leave. As the sun broke through again, it illuminated a grave behind her grandfather's.

Marlene Clova Roberts. Born, June 2, 1950. United with the Lord, January 9, 1973.

Stepping closer, E. J. swallowed against the tightening lump in her throat and read the name and dates over and over. Twenty-two years old. Marlene had died so young.

Suddenly, as if the wind were encouraging her, she moved toward the grave. The headstone was not as elaborate as others around it—a plain gray marker set at a slight angle as if the ground had sunk under the right side.

Mesmerized by the sight of her mother's grave, E. J. knelt down. Angrily, she ripped a clod from the earth and hurled it at the tombstone.

"Why?" she asked. "Why? Why? Why?"

A clump of grass hit the headstone with each demand. The dry dirt fell limply to the grave and lay there as if to mock her. There were no answers here.

Softening, E. J. curled up on the grave like a wounded animal. She'd cried for her mother many nights, waiting, looking out the window. When told of her death, the crying had ceased and a bitter pain replaced it.

The service for Marlene Roberts had been held on a weekend, but E. J. hadn't gone. She hid in the toolshed and refused to come out until dark. Grams had been worried sick, but there'd been no spankings, no admonishments that day.

Grams had rocked her to sleep that night, grandmother's and child's tears soaking a pink handkerchief.

When the pain subsided, E. J. slowly pushed herself upright and began replacing the earth. She had told herself she didn't need anyone then.

But she needed someone now. Needed someone desperately to tell her what to do.

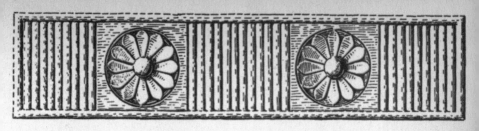

CHAPTER SIX

Oh, the problems we create for ourselves. Ever notice how one lie leads to another, then another?

Sleep didn't come easily for E. J. that night. She had too many thoughts running around in her mind. Go back to LA and have the abortion, or stay here and have it in Raleigh? Raise the child, or give it to someone who would love and care for it in a way E. J. couldn't? How could she love a child of violence? Would God expect her to love that child—well, maybe she was beginning to feel something. Nothing maternal, but . . . knowing life grew within her was humbling.

For the first time she considered the option that had skittered around the edges of her mind since Maggie's twins were born: not having the abortion. Immediately, her mind rejected it. But it was as if she'd poked her finger in a beehive and a thousand questions flew out to sting her. How could she endure the physical and emotional discomfort of having the baby, of answering other people's questions? What would she do with a baby? What about Kilgore's Kosmetics?

No, it was unthinkable. She had no option. And yet . . . unbidden, the sweet faces of those babies lined up in the hospital nursery rose to haunt her. She hadn't allowed herself to think of what was inside her as a real baby. To her, it had always been the personification of Jake's evil. But Dr. Strobel had reminded her that two lives would be affected by her decision.

Two lives . . . there was now someone else to think about. Like it or not, her decision would affect more than E. J. Grams was involved. E. J. had seen the concern in her eyes. Grams would try to have the child and go on, but E. J. wasn't Grams, and Grams respected that E. J. was a grown woman, needing to make her own decisions.

A pain in her left temple throbbed. Having the procedure might solve one problem, but it was no longer clear to her that her life could go back to the way it was. Ever.

The close air in her bedroom meant a storm was brewing. Clouds had hung over the Corner all afternoon and evening.

A lightning bug worked its way through the hole in the screen. E. J. watched the intermittent flash, wondering, like all of us do from time to time, if she wasn't losing her mind. Missing Friday's appointment had given her too much time to think. Too much time to consider what she was about to do.

Up until now, E. J. had considered abortion to be the only option because she had made it her only option. Loving the child in her womb, or even considering it a child, had been beyond her immediate capacity. But witnessing the birth of Maggie's twins and watching how she cared for her children made E. J. think that maybe she was selling herself short. So what if her mother hadn't been June Cleaver; did that mean E. J. couldn't do better?

She flipped to her back, focusing on the bug. Isabel and Brian would be upset if she took more time away from work, but she couldn't go back to LA pregnant.

Eighteen years ago she would have prayed, but now she didn't see the point. She might ask of God all she wanted, but she doubted he'd be listening.

Grams would say he's always listening. But E. J. didn't necessarily buy it. Oh, she felt in her bones there was a God, somewhere. Did he love her? Care about her, E. J. Roberts, personally? If so, where had he been two months ago?

Something leapt onto E. J.'s bed. She started, then went limp with fright. A moment later a soft purr calmed her thumping heart. Reaching for the light beside her bed, she flicked it on. Albert's orange eyes narrowed to slivers and blinked.

"Albert!" she hissed. "How did you get in here?" The cat blinked and meowed as if to say, "So? Who wants to know?"

E. J. stared at the cat as he calmly went about the business of preparing the bed for a restful sleep—his. He kneaded the bedspread in circles, turning around and around until he wound himself into a ball and tucked his nose under his tail.

Waiting until her racing heart slowed, E. J. eventually heard the cat's purrs turn to snores. She slid out from under the sheets and into her slippers, tiptoeing around the squeaks in the floors, careful not to wake the sleeping pest. Halfway to the door she realized what she was doing and stopped. Now she was tiptoeing not to wake a cat? She massaged her temples, wondering if hormones were messing with her head.

Downstairs she paused on the lowest stair when she realized that the front door was standing wide open, the screen lightly flapping in the rising wind. Her pulse took a proportional leap, landing somewhere in the vicinity of her left shoulder bone. Had someone broken in? Adrenaline surged. As E. J. fumbled for the wooden cane Grams kept by the bottom of the stairs, her heart sank when she discovered it wasn't there. Her hand groped along the wall in the dark, searching for the weapon until she gave up, realizing that the cane had been there when she was a child twenty-five years ago. Grandpa Neil's heavy, crudely fashioned walking stick could be anywhere by now. Anywhere but in its normal place.

Holding her breath, she listened for intruders, but her pounding heart drowned out every other sound. Upstairs, Grams slept like a log, so it was doubtful she'd come down in search of a midnight snack.

Folks, have you noticed that when you're scared, the slightest whisper is like a lion's roar? Especially in the middle of the night when you've been awakened from a fitful sleep. Your mind plays tricks, and they aren't nice ones.

Hugging the wall, E. J. crept around the corner and into the kitchen, where the thief or murderer could be hiding anywhere—crouched behind the counter, in the pantry—anywhere. Swallowing, she fumbled for the light switch and light flooded the room. Her eyes scanned the area. Nothing.

"Silly," she murmured. No intruder could have sneaked up the stairway; she would have heard, since the warped wood squeaked.

Convinced her imagination was working overtime, she took a deep breath and opened the refrigerator. Undoubtedly she'd forgotten to latch the front door when she'd gone to bed earlier, and the wind had blown it open. She chuckled. A murderer in Cullen's Corner—a hick town in the middle of nowhere? Murderers wouldn't be able to find the place if they were looking for it.

Well, common sense is slow to materialize at the midnight hour, E. J. told herself as she studied the refrigerator's contents.

Helen's leftover chicken looked pretty good. Gabe had dropped it by after lunch, saying that Helen had insisted E. J. have it. E. J. had stuck the meat away and refused to eat it out of principle . . . though she wasn't exactly clear what principle forbade her to eat fried chicken when she was hungry. Sighing, she pulled the foil-wrapped paper plate from the shelf and sat down at the table. Even cold, the chicken had the supermarket stuff beat hands down. She got up for the bread and finished off a drumstick and a breast, washing the midnight snack down with a tall glass of milk. Real milk, not skim. At this point fat grams lost significance in her life.

Halfway through the second drumstick, she took the glass and went to the front porch. The clock in the living room chimed midnight. It seemed like predawn.

A quarter moon darted in and out of building storm clouds. The porch swing she'd spent youthful nights on with boys or girlfriends still hung before the front window, swaying lightly.

She sat down and finished the drumstick, licking grease from her fingers. Helen knew how to fry a chicken. By noon that day she had started feeling better, nausea absent for a time, thanks to the medication, she guessed. Now, absently setting the swing into motion, she stared at Gabe's front porch. All was quiet at the Faulkner residence.

What would it be like to have a marriage like the one Gabe and Nelly had enjoyed? Few couples found the dedication they had shared. Divorce was too easy in E. J.'s world. Five of Kilgore's women employees had filed for divorce this year alone, and the year wasn't half over.

Grams was right: The whole world was going to Hades in a handbasket.

The moon slid behind a cloud, and E. J. rested her head on the back of the swing as a sudden cool gust rattled the swing. Thunder rolled in the far distance. Summer rainstorms sprang up out of nowhere this time of year. E. J. hoped it would rain and drop the temperature a few degrees. The old window air conditioner ran wide open, barely cooling the downstairs, much less the upstairs bedrooms where Grams and Albert lay sleeping.

The wind picked up, sending neighbors' hanging plants gyrating sideways. The front moved in with surprising force.

Trees suddenly bent toward the ground. A dead limb in Gabe's yard crashed to the ground with an earsplitting crack. E. J. hurriedly picked up the empty glass that had rolled to the other side of the porch and ducked inside.

No sooner had the door shut behind her than rain started, splattering big drops against the front window. Moving through the house, she closed an open window. The kitchen light flickered twice and then went off as a crack of thunder shook the floor beneath her.

Albert shot out of the darkness, nearly tripping her in his haste to get under the couch.

E. J. stood in the middle of the kitchen floor, wondering whether to wake Grams and go to the cellar. The thunderstorm rocked Peach Street with full force. Lightning flashes lit

formerly moonlit pavement. The fast-moving front was poten-
tially destructive.

Somewhere across town, a siren went off and E. J. flew into
action. Tornado!

Loose shutters banged against the side of the house as
she sprinted up the stairs two at a time, shouting for Grams.
Memories sprang up—hours spent huddled in the musty-
smelling cellar amid all of Cora's jars of canned fruit and vegetables. The dank hole had all sorts of creeping things lurking
in the dark corners, and she wasn't anxious to go there again.
Lightning flashed and thunder cracked.

A wide-eyed Grams, hair standing on end from a roused
sleep, appeared at the top of the stairs, cupping a candle in her
right hand. "Get to the cellar!" she yelled.

E. J. waited for her to descend the stairway. Latching onto
one another, the two women made their way toward the cellar
staircase as wind buffeted the house.

Blaring sirens warned of the approaching storm.

"Hurry, E. J., it's coming."

"I'm hurrying, Grams."

As they scurried past the kitchen they heard someone
pounding on the back door.

"That's Gabe," Cora shouted above the moaning wind.

"Go on—get to the cellar. I'll let him in!" E. J. said, motioning
her to the stairway.

Well, now naturally, Cora protested. Her first concern was
for E. J. and the baby, but E. J. gently urged her grandmother
toward the cellar door. Holding the candle aloft, Cora started
down the steep steps, peering over her shoulder as E. J. undid
the latch and let Gabe in.

"It's a bad one—got to get to shelter," he ordered, taking E. J.
by the arm and sprinting her across the room. She could see
the sky swirling green with intermittent lightning through the
open doorway.

"Where's Cora?"

"Already in the cellar!"

He shone the beam, and E. J. started down the stairway

as the kitchen window blew out and glass sprayed the room.

When they reached the bottom of the stairs, Gabe muttered softly under his breath when he saw Cora sitting on the dirt floor, holding her hip. Pain contorted her features, and she moaned and then cried out, "Albert! He's still upstairs."

Gabe shifted the flashlight to his left hand and bent to check her injury. "What happened, Cora? Did you fall?"

"Never mind me, go get Albert! He'll be scared to death!"

Gabe moved E. J. next to Cora, then took the stairs two at a time.

"Oh, Grams—I'm sorry. Are you hurt?" E. J. whispered. She slapped at something that brushed by her leg.

"Lands, I don't know—think I might have broken my hip." She grimaced, sucking in a breath, biting on her lower lip.

Gently making her more comfortable, E. J. bit back hysteria. A break at Cora's age was serious. E. J. blamed herself for letting her come down the darkened stairway alone. But Gabe was at the door and Grams had ordered her to let him in.

Now folks, at this point, E. J. did the very thing you're not supposed to do to an injured person: she tried to lift her.

"Let's sit you up—"

"Be careful, E. J." Cora shrugged off her advance. "I'm more worried about Gabe and Albert than I am about a broken bone. It could have been my neck."

Her neck? Cora's absence of self-pity was almost laughable if the situation wasn't so deadly serious. But, that's Cora Roberts for you: always looking on the bright side. You had to hand E. J.'s grandma that.

Unfortunately for Cora and E. J., things were going to get worse before they got better.

Gabe returned, carrying an Albert who had blown up to twice his normal size with fear. Spotting Cora, the cat leapt from Gabe's arms and flew into a corner, hissing.

"It's okay, ole boy," Cora soothed as the fury of the storm penetrated the old cellar. "We'll be safe here."

The excitement was too much for E. J. She covered her ears with her hands, trying to blot out the sounds. A tornado had ripped through the elementary school during her sixth-grade year. Tornadoes weren't all that common in North Carolina, but when one hit, it was bad.

"Dear Lord," she heard herself shouting, "stop this! Please don't let the house blow away!"

Overhead, wind slowly abated. Gabe stared at the ceiling as if he could see through the floor above him. By the look on his face, he didn't trust the sudden stillness.

And then there was silence, the eerie kind that makes the old-timer's skin crawl.

"It's not through with us yet," Grams whispered, hugging Albert tight to her chest. The storm switched directions and, howling like a banshee, ripped through the old house. E. J. clung to Cora, silently praying to be heard. They clung together, calling out to the Lord for help.

Then, it was over as quickly as it had started.

"Now, Cora, you lie still and wait for help," Gabe said.

"I'm fine," she protested, but E. J. could see that she was in terrible pain.

Gabe held the light as he and E. J. cautiously climbed the stairs. The sound of dripping water met them as they entered the kitchen. Gabe pointed the flashlight beam into the living room.

"The roof's still on," he said, panning the ray of light around the room. The large window to the west was shattered, and the branch that had done the damage still hung halfway out of the window.

Knickknacks were scattered about, most of them in pieces. Water puddled and dripped from tabletops. The room glistened with raindrops.

"Well, you won't be doing much in here for a while." He reached out and retrieved a sofa cushion. Water pooled on the rug. "We'll get Cora some help; then I'll find something to cover that window."

E. J. went to the kitchen for towels as Gabe went in search

of a phone; Grams's didn't work. E. J. had offered her cell phone, but Gabe said phone lines were probably down everywhere.

In a few minutes, he returned.

"How bad is it out there?"

"Trees are down, branches everywhere. Phone lines are out, but I stopped a policeman and he radioed for Dr. Strobel."

Sirens began to wail. Police. Fire. One by one they cranked up and pierced the night.

Gabe returned to the basement and Cora. "Are you all right?"

She waved his concern away, clutching Albert to herself protectively. "I'm a tough old bird."

"I think she's broken a hip . . . and maybe sprained her ankle," E. J. said.

"I'll wait for the doctor. You run and check on Mrs. Leary and the other neighbors."

Grams winced in pain. "Is Doc Strobel on his way?"

E. J. patted her head. "He's on his way, sweetie."

The Grams E. J. found in the nursing home bed an hour later looked pale and weak. Her hair was mussed, and the white gown the attendants had made her change into swallowed her small frame. There were tubes running into her arms, their needles buried in the skin.

"Oh, Grams. Are you in much pain?"

"A little." Cora managed a weak grin, waggling a tube at E. J. "But they can't keep a good woman down."

"What did Dr. Strobel say?"

"Oh, he's hem-hawing around, trying to spare my feelings. But I know it's bad." She sighed and fidgeted with a corner of the sheet. "It's my hip. Broken in two places. They want to send me to the hospital in Raleigh for surgery tomorrow morning."

E. J. sank into a nearby chair. Grams never complained. If she got sick, she usually discarded prescriptions and doctored herself with herbs from the Faulkners' garden. But herbs weren't going to help this time.

"When will they be taking you?"

"Said they'd be transporting me within the hour." Grams turned to look out the window. "I don't want to go to the hospital in Raleigh. I was just there with Maggie. I don't like hospitals. They make me nervous."

"But you have to go, Grams. I'll be there with you."

"Oh, really?" The old Cora surfaced. "I can't make this all go away?"

E. J. smiled, biting her lip. Cora Roberts was about to make a point, one E. J. wasn't sure she wanted to hear. Until now, Cora had been awfully quiet about the baby. Since Saturday over glasses of iced tea, Cora hadn't mentioned the rape or pregnancy again. That wasn't her nature.

"Meaning?"

Adjusting her gown, Cora started. "Eva Jean, sometimes things go wrong; I don't know why, but they do. I didn't try to be a gymnast last night. It just happened."

E. J. glanced away.

"Whatever this man did to you, you can't punish your baby for it."

"I'm not punishing the baby, Grams. I'm—"

"What is it you're doing, then? You're considering aborting it, aren't you?"

E. J.'s mouth firmed. "Who told you that?"

"No one told me. I can read you like a book, Eva Jean. Always have. You've had something on your mind from the moment you showed up back in Cullen's Corner, and it isn't going away." Her eyes narrowed. "You haven't done anything foolish, have you?"

"Grams . . ."

"Eva Jean." Cora's eyes snapped. "You haven't done something foolish?"

E. J. supposed Grams's idea of foolishness differed somewhat from hers. "No," she conceded. "I haven't, Grams. I'm still carrying the baby."

Relief filled Cora's face. "Good . . . that's good. Your mother considered abortion, do you know that?"

At the mention of her mother, E. J. stiffened. No, she didn't know that, but it didn't surprise her. Her mother had never wanted her.

"I told Marlene the same thing I'm about to tell you, dumplin'. Life is good and bad. We want good, but it doesn't always happen. It's our decisions that make the difference."

E. J. covered her face with her hands, trembling. Grams didn't know . . . she couldn't know what E. J. was going through.

Cora motioned her to the bed. By now, E. J. was sobbing.

"I don't want to be a . . . mother," she choked out.

"And I don't want to be old and suffering from a broken hip," Cora whispered, gently soothing E. J.'s hair back from her face. "But you are a mother, E. J., and I am old and I did break my hip. Old age and accidents creep up on us. And rape, well, rape is pure black sin, honey, sin we can't do a thing about. Sometimes we don't like what life gives us, but denying our state won't help. And that poor baby doesn't have a say in the matter one way or the other."

E. J. allowed Cora to comfort her. It'd been a long time since anyone cared about her the way that Grams cared.

"I'm so sorry, Grams. I should have come home more often. I've been so busy in LA, and I didn't come home for Christmas."

"I know, hon. I know." She patted E. J. lovingly. "I missed you, dumplin'."

"We've lost all that time. . . ." E. J. broke down again.

"There'll be plenty of time to catch up. My goodness, Eva Jean, I'm not dead. Just out of commission for a spell." Cora smiled and then winced as she shifted to a more comfortable position.

"I guess maybe I'd better go on to Raleigh and have that surgery. Maybe Maggie can keep me company until she goes home."

"I'll be with you every second," E. J. promised. She couldn't think of going back to LA now. Grams needed her, and she needed Grams.

"I know, dear. Now, dry your eyes and fix your face. I want you to take care of Albert and see if you can't do something about getting the house back in order. Lands, what a mess! They won't be operating until tomorrow. You could drive up then."

"I want to ride with you in the ambulance."

"You see to things here and drive up first thing in the morning. They'll put me through tests and X rays, and then I'll rest a bit. You find Gabe and thank him and tell him I won't be able to bake him that pie for a couple of days."

E. J. grinned, patting Cora's face affectionately. "I love you, Grams."

"I know, sweetie. I know." Grams closed her eyes. "I love you, too, puddin'. We'll talk more when I'm feeling better—meanwhile, don't do anything foolish, E. J. Promise me?"

E. J. couldn't make that promise. What might be foolish to Grams might be imperative to E. J. Patting the old woman's hand, E. J. bent down and kissed her. "You get some rest. I'll go see about putting the house back in order."

❧

E. J. pulled up in front of the house in the early morning hours to see a crew of men dragging a fallen tree away from the house. One greeted her with a tip of the cap as she approached the house.

"Howdy there, Eva Jean. It's been a long time. How's Cora?"

E. J. met his bright blue eyes quizzically, searching her memory for a name. The face, older now, looked familiar but she couldn't place him.

"She's fine . . . going to Raleigh later this morning . . . Sam Clark! Is that you?"

"Sure is!" He flashed an ornery grin. "Guess I haven't seen you since you were in my junior high math class."

"My gosh! How are you?" She smiled. From behind them, someone pulled a cord on the chainsaw.

"Just cleaning up a little before I replace that window for Cora."

"That's so nice of you." E. J. glanced at the shattered window, wondering how much the repairs would be.

"Leave a bill and I—"

"Not a dime. My pleasure. Hate to see Cora down like this. She's such a spark plug."

Everyone loved Grams, especially those who'd been blessed with one of her strawberry rhubarb pies or chicken dinners. But making the repairs for nothing? Did people really do that anymore?

Well, maybe not everywhere, but in Cullen's Corner they did. They still took "Love thy neighbor as thyself" seriously.

"Well, thank you, Sam. Grams doesn't expect . . ."

He waved her protest aside. "Glad to do it. I was lucky I didn't have much damage at my place, thank the good Lord."

E. J. said good-bye and went inside, still puzzled by the act of kindness. Apparently there were still people willing to help others at a cost to themselves. Adding to her surprise, she saw that the floor had been mopped and the glass swept up. Voices drifted from the kitchen.

"I swear, Gabe," a laughing female said, "you can make cleaning up fun."

Helen and Gabe appeared in the doorway with a mop and bucket. Helen's grin widened when she spotted E. J.

"Oh, honey, you're back. How's your grandma?"

"They're taking her to Raleigh for surgery."

Gabe frowned. "I bet Cora doesn't like that one bit."

E. J. focused on the mop. "You guys didn't have to do this."

"No trouble at all. Just a few more things and we'll be finished." Helen wiped her hands on her apron. "Leave the windows open for a few days so the furniture can air out."

"Right now that won't be a problem," E. J. said, turning to the broken window. The three laughed.

Helen sobered. "You look tired . . . go upstairs and rest. We'll finish up here and let ourselves out."

E. J. was tired. Bone tired and mentally weary. You know, the kind of weary we've all experienced when the rush of adrenaline is over and the body all but shuts itself down? E. J. was so tired she couldn't wait to fall into bed and pull the covers over her head.

Exhaustion overcame her with every leaden step up the stairs. Technically, she'd been up all night. She looked like it, too.

The bathroom mirror confirmed her belief. Her hair hung limp at the sides of her face. She pushed it around, pulled it back, swept it forward. Nothing helped.

Isabel was always after E. J. to be a model, but E. J. watched models walk in and out of the company building every day. They came in all sizes, tall, leggy, blonde, and brunette, often on the arms of good-looking men carrying designer bags. E. J. bought all the right clothes and makeup, drove a BMW, and ate at Spago's, but she didn't consider herself model material.

The brush caught on a particularly large snarl, and E. J. pulled until tears formed in her eyes. Throwing the brush in the sink, she went to the bedroom and buried her face in a pillow.

A soft rap came at the door a moment later.

"Come in," she called.

Helen eased the door open a crack. "Cora called. The ambulance is leaving for Raleigh."

"I should be with her."

E. J. sat up. Grams had told her to stay here, but her responsibility was to Cora. Lord knew she'd dismissed it too easily in the past. She bolted into the bathroom, hitting a toe on the door frame. Sinking to the floor, she moaned.

Helen came to help her up. "Eva Jean, the ambulance is already gone. Come back over here and rest."

E. J. limped over to the bed to inspect her bruised toe.

"Honey, are you okay?"

"Nothing in my life is okay right now, Helen."

Helen folded her hands on her lap. "We don't know each other that well, but I'm a good listener if you need to talk. I know that sometimes it helps to get it out."

E. J. mustered up a tired smile. It was kind of Helen, but she couldn't discuss the situation with her.

"Thank you. I'm tired and my hair . . ." She lifted a hand and felt a snarl that had worked itself into a rat's nest. She ran her hand through her hair, or tried to. The snarled mess tangled around her fingers.

"Say, I've got an idea." Helen stood up, draping an arm around E. J. "Why don't we see if Gabe can give you a trim? Cora will need you more later and if you're exhausted, you're not going to be much help. Get your hair fixed. Get some sleep. You can drive to Raleigh this afternoon. Nothing helps a gal's mood more than a shampoo and trim."

E. J. tried to protest, but she had to admit that the idea sounded appealing. Before she knew it, she was at the barbershop in Gabe's chair with clean hair and a plastic cape around her neck.

He carefully worked a snarl free. "You've certainly done this up right."

E. J. grinned. "I guess I've neglected my hair lately."

"And you're in the cosmetics business," he teased. He reached into a clear plastic jar for a glob of gel and eased it into the snarl. The hair released instantly.

E. J. glanced around the empty shop. "Storm scare your customers away?"

"Monday's my day off." He picked up his scissors. "Makes up for a full day on Saturday."

"Oh." E. J. turned. "I didn't mean to bother you on your day off. Helen said . . ."

He turned her back to face the mirror. "No bother at all. Not often that I get to work on a celebrity."

Color dotted E. J.'s cheeks. "I'm far from being a celebrity."

"Well, that's your opinion, not mine."

Gabe went to work, trimming the ends and adding new layers around the face. E. J. relaxed as he cut, enjoying the pampering. The sound of the blow-dryer and his gentle scalp massage lulled her, and by the time he handed her the mirror, she could care less what her hair looked like. She wanted a nap.

The cut was superb. Her hair fell softly around her face and on her shoulders, shiny and bouncy, unbelievably soft.

"What did you use to get this shine?" She turned the mirror first one way and then the other.

"It's a little something Nell whipped up a few years back. I call it Nelly's Jelly."

"I can't believe it!" Helen had been right . . . a good haircut could cure a number of ills. She felt better already.

E. J. thanked him until he finally insisted that she leave, sending his best to Cora.

On the walk home, E. J. felt her hair, attracting more than a few curious stares.

Wonderfully manageable.

Amazing.

What was this Nelly Jelly stuff?

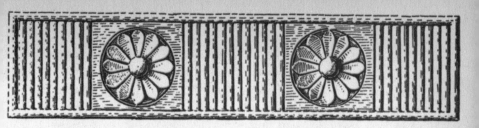

CHAPTER SEVEN

I sabel Kilgore got up from the desk and moved to the window. Sunshine shone through the tinted glass window overlooking downtown LA. Her eyes focused on the Domed Village in the far distance. Like all grieving mothers, Isabel couldn't concentrate. Friends assured her that time would ease the pain, but then friends hadn't lost their only son to a senseless, tragic automobile accident. Had it been two months? Impossible. The ache was as fresh as if it had happened only yesterday.

The police report cited careless and imprudent driving, aggravated by traces of drugs and alcohol in the blood. Lies, all of it lies. The hotshot investigating officer wanted to make a name for himself so he didn't bother to identify the source of the "drugs." Jake took prescription medication for depression. Did the police bother to check his medical records?

Alcohol? What red-blooded young Marine on leave didn't drink when a celebration was in order? E. J. had been with Jake earlier. She hadn't mentioned a word about alcohol, and E. J. didn't drink. She claimed liquor gave her a headache, but Isabel suspected her childhood played a part in the decision.

Cora Roberts had raised the young woman with strong moral convictions and the lessons stuck. Very few women had E. J.'s integrity. Isabel had recognized that the day personnel had sent her to interview for a job in the mailroom. Like all eighteen-year-olds, she had been young and idealistic, a baby, actually. Isabel had hired her on the spot and never once regretted it. E. J. had worked her way up through the company, and last year Isabel had brought her in as part owner of Kilgore's Kosmetics. Company profits were down, but E. J. was working hard to bring them up.

Turning away from the window, Isabel punched the intercom button. "Alice, connect me with Brian."

In a few minutes the head of marketing, Brian Powers, came on the line. "Something you needed, Isabel?"

"Have you talked to E. J. today?"

"Haven't heard a word. Why?"

"Where is she? It's so unlike her not to check in every day. What's she been gone? A week, week and a half?"

"Isabel, she hasn't taken a vacation in years."

"I know." Isabel's teeth worried her lower lip. E. J. usually had to be run out of the office, but this time she hadn't said where she was going or when she would be back. A brief conversation with her the other day had revealed nothing.

"Is she tracking down a lead on a new product?" Kilgore's needed one, needed one badly. That must be it; she was sniffing out a potential lead that would put the company back into the black.

"I don't know, Isabel. She called, but the caller ID said the area was unavailable."

"It doesn't make sense, Brian."

"She'll be back in a few days. Is there something I can handle for you?"

"No. I suppose I'm more curious than worried."

"Frank doing okay?"

"As well as any stroke victim." First Frank, then a few weeks later, Jake's accident. Isabel's whole world had been turned upside down in a matter of months.

Pressing the intercom off, she sat down, staring at the framed picture of her son. Smiling, wearing his blue-and-white Marine uniform, not a care in the world.

Bitterness stuck in her throat, and she wanted to scream at the injustice of it all. *Why, God? Why Jake? He was a good boy, had his whole life ahead of him. Why did you take this precious child?* What had she done to deserve this?

Shifting her gaze back to the window, she realized she couldn't think about it anymore or she would lose her mind. The loss was too great, the grief and pain too much for her to bear.

E. J. Where was E. J. and why hadn't she called her? The girl was as close to a daughter as Isabel would ever have. With Jake's death, there was no longer hope for a daughter-in-law or a precious grandchild.

Burying her face in her hands, she allowed the pain to seep out. She would never hold her grandchild, never hear him or her laugh, never buy a toy train or Barbie doll or count fingers and toes.

Never.

Why, God? Why?

Cora's surgery went well; she was resting comfortably when E. J. left the hospital around two-thirty Tuesday afternoon.

Her mind raced on the drive home. For the first time since arriving in Cullen's Corner she felt human. Even more notable, she forgot to take her medication and still she hadn't made a mad dash for the bathroom this morning. Maybe the worst was behind her.

And her hair looked terrific. What was in that gel?

Stopping briefly at the florist, she ordered a bouquet of snapdragons to be sent to Grams and then drove though a golden arch for a chocolate ice-cream cone. On the way home she phoned Brian and told him not to expect her for a while. Grams's accident had bought her enough time to reconsider her options. Brian wasn't happy about the extended leave, but he promised to calm Isabel. A second phone call to the car rental to extend the lease, and she was set until the end of the month.

Forty minutes later she parked in front of the barbershop and glanced at her watch: a little before four. Through the window she could see an old-timer sitting in Gabe's chair, passing the time of day.

Remaining behind the wheel, she periodically checked the time, frowning. To think men accused women of talking too much!

No longer able to contain her excitement, she got out of the car and entered the shop. Gabe glanced up and smiled but continued hashing over the upcoming county seat election with Fred Harris, a self-professed, bona fide, dyed-in-the-wool, Southern conservative Democrat.

"You're nuts, Fred. If Monroe gets in office, the county's done for."

"Aw, Gabe, you're way off base! Your candidate ain't got a prayer; face it."

Gabe trimmed sideburns, winking at E. J.

Now you have to admit, folks, politics is a hot topic in a barbershop. Most men can never rationally handle the subject—it only gets their dander up—but they keep at it as if they can solve all the country's problems in the time it takes to get a shave and a trim. Even more unsettling, they manage to agree every now and then.

Taking a seat, E. J. half listened to the conversation, her eyes focused on the clear jar sitting on the shelf behind the chair, trying to spot a label.

Democrat number one left the chair and Democrat number two sat down. Fifteen minutes later the conversation had somehow gone from politics to Newt Graham's new Holstein calf to the engagement of Molly Holman's youngest daughter.

When the old gentleman finally climbed out of the chair, Gabe dusted his neck with scented talc.

"I'll put it on your tab, George. Not that you'll be able to pay once we're in a recession."

George shook his head at the good-natured ribbing.

Now, people, don't be fooled. Folks in Cullen's Corner knew Gabe Faulkner liked to tease and operated on the "if you can't take the heat don't go near the kitchen" theory. Politics included. So nobody got bent out of shape unnecessarily. Not at the barbershop.

"Did you hear little Margie Holman's finally gonna marry that man from Portland? Don't know what these women see in them foreigners," the old man commented.

"Is that right? Well, she always was a rebellious child," Gabe said, dusting off the chair.

"The worst." The two men chuckled, and George tipped his hat to E. J. on his way out the door. "Eva Jean. You're looking mighty pretty."

E. J. was surprised he'd remember her. "Thank you, George. And you're looking handsome yourself."

He puffed up like a bandy rooster and sauntered out onto the street, throwing a feisty wink at old Mrs. Allen coming out of the pharmacy.

E. J. got up to stretch when the door closed, pretending an indifference she didn't feel as she watched Gabe reach for a broom to clean up.

"You shouldn't tease George. He's getting old and can't take all the excitement."

Gabe laughed. "There's nothing old about George, and besides, my teasing keeps him humble." The barber stepped over and flipped the Closed sign into place, then reached for a dustpan. "He's in here every few days for a trim. I think his mind's going. Every week we have the same conversation about Molly Holman's daughter; she's been married for two years." He dumped hair in the trash can, then folded a plastic cape and stored it under the cabinet.

Hands behind her, E. J. casually inspected the row of bottles behind the barber chair. "So you cut George's hair every week and listen to him talk to make him happy?"

"That's about the size of it. I'm not so busy that I can't spare a few minutes for a lonely man, and a trim makes George happy."

"You never charge."

"George?" He chuckled. "He barely gets by on Social Security. He lost Gladys last year—you knew that, didn't you?"

"Grams wrote me when it happened." Cora seemed to think that her friends were E. J.'s friends and was always a little hurt when E. J. had to ask twice whom she was talking about.

About to broach the topic of the gel, E. J. fell silent when a late customer wandered into the shop. She watched as Gabe welcomed him into the chair. Apparently the Closed sign on the door was used for ceremonial purposes only.

Scissors flashed as the two men struck up a conversation. Reaching for a magazine, E. J. sat down again. When the floor was covered with a fine coat of hair, Gabe opened the unmarked jar and rubbed a pea-sized dollop between his palms then into the man's hair.

Two more customers came in, with the same results. One man E. J. didn't recognize, but the young lady looked vaguely familiar. As the girl left, E. J. realized that she was a former classmate, Patty Smith, a small, shy girl who'd kept to herself.

By six o'clock, Gabe gave up on going home and poured a cup of coffee. Remembering his manners, he brought E. J. a bottle of cold water from the small refrigerator he kept in the back room. "Glad to hear Cora's resting nicely." He took a sip of coffee. "I told you everything would be all right."

"You didn't know that."

"At my age," he winked, "I know everything. Now, why are you hanging around here? Thought you might be tired after all the excitement and your trips to Raleigh."

"I thought I'd watch you work. Do you mind?"

"No, help yourself." He took another sip of coffee. "Learning anything?"

"Some. Business hours mean nothing to you. You're a workaholic. You know with enviable certainty who'll win the county seat election next month, Molly Holman's daughter married a louse, and honestly? Your suggestions for improving the Onion Days Festival were great. The name you suggested to Old Man Lukas for town council sounded interesting, and the way you single-handedly persuaded one of the sitting members of the council to check into paving Cherry Street, which I understand is currently no more than an alley—" She flashed him a thumbs-up. "Brilliant."

Gabe took the bantering in stride, unperturbed. "Maybe I should think about raising prices."

"You might. A good therapist rakes in the money these days."

Gabe didn't ruffle easily. "Cullen's Corner is a good place to live. I want to keep it that way, peaceful."

"And how long have you lived in Cullen's Corner?"

Right now he didn't act much older than she, but he had to be on the downside of fifty. He had been old in her mind twenty years ago.

Gabe chuckled as if he'd read her thoughts. Now, Eva Jean was bad at hiding her thoughts, or at least she was as a child, and everyone in Cullen's Corner knew that. Even E. J. knew her transparency, so it seldom surprised her when folks knew what she was thinking before she did.

"Long enough to know better than to answer a loaded question like that."

E. J. feigned innocence. "I wasn't asking your age. I simply wonder how long you've been a major political force in Cullen's Corner?"

"Long before you were born, little girl."

Well, of course, he was pulling E. J.'s leg now, and she knew it. He was older, but he wasn't ancient. As Gabe might say if he weren't on the defensive, "still man enough to put in a full day's work and stay around to visit with inquisitive women. Still man enough to appreciate a pretty woman in his shop on a Tuesday afternoon."

He set the mug aside and reached for the broom. "Let's say I'm looking straight down the barrel at fifty, and you're a young whippersnapper with time on her hands. Now what do I have in my shop that interests you enough to keep you around an hour and fifteen minutes after closing?"

She opened her mouth to speak and was interrupted again

when the door opened. She released an exasperated sigh. Gabe grinned.

"Evening, Max. How's that daughter of yours doing at Julliard?"

Max shut the door, taking off his straw hat. "Real good. She's studying violin and cello. Everyone says she's headed for Carnegie, or maybe a spot with the National Symphony."

"You gotta be proud of her. What can I do for you today?"

"I know it's late, but could you work in a cut for me? Just got out of a business meeting and on my way home."

"No problem."

While Gabe cut Max's hair, E. J. wandered around the shop, looking at pictures on the walls. She straightened magazines and carried empty coffee cups to the back room, waiting for Gabe to finish.

Max left, and while Gabe cleaned up, E. J. wandered over to the shelf, picking up the jar of gel.

"What's in this stuff?"

He glanced up from the register. "Stuff. Why?"

"It's a marvelous product. It worked great on my hair."

Gabe counted bills and stuffed them into a bank bag. "Nelly concocted it a few years ago. Customers seemed to like it."

"Nell made it?"

He shook out a cape and draped it across the back of the chair. "She raised her own herbs, knew medicinal uses for almost any plant in the yard. Always experimenting in the kitchen."

"Did she ever think about marketing it?"

"The pomade? No. She made it for the shop and personal use. Mrs. Lavender gave her a bad perm one time, singed her hair to the root. She didn't cry about it, simply traipsed out to the garden and gathered some herbs and boiled them." He picked up the jar, his eyes softening with affection. "It wasn't long before I was using it in the shop." He set the gel back on the shelf. "Now I make a batch a couple of times a month."

"You have a recipe?"

He tapped his head. "Right in here."

"You haven't written it down?"

"Why? I'm old, not addled, Eva Jean."

"E. J.," she corrected shortly. "And you're not so old."

Inclining his head politely, he amended his slip. "My memory is as sound as a dollar, E. J. I won't forget the recipe."

"You wouldn't sell me a jar, would you?"

"Sorry. Nell made me promise never to sell it—not that I would. It's herbs, nothing special."

E. J. sighed. Maybe to him it wasn't special, but she was dying to know what herb could produce such an effect when a whole research lab in LA couldn't.

She was about to ask him to let Kilgore's distribute the gel when he reached behind her for an empty jar. "Can't sell it to you, but there's nothing to prevent me from giving you some for your personal use."

E. J. stared at the dusty jar he'd pulled off a top shelf. He blew the dust away, wiped the jar off with a rag, and scooped up some of the pomade with his first two fingers. Before she knew it, the miracle product was in her hand.

"This should last you a while, if you don't go overboard. Isn't like those fancy products that you have to use a whole handful of." His eyes met hers over the rim of the jar good-naturedly. "These big fancy companies have to do that to sell their products."

She refused to cave to his banter. "Who's 'they'?" As if she didn't know what he was implying.

"Now you're smart enough to figure that out, Eva Jean." Her eyes steeled. "E. J."

E. J. wanted to take offense, but she couldn't. He was so accommodating, and giving her a generous sample of pomade put E. J. in his debt. She grinned. "Any way to make a buck."

He gave her a sour look. "Rub a little of the gel into your hair before you dry it. It'll take care of your dry ends."

"Thanks."

"Hey—Eva . . . E. J. Are you by any chance hungry?"

Actually, her appetite was better than it had been in weeks. "A little, why?"

He glanced at his watch. "According to my stomach, it's suppertime. How about I buy you a hamburger and a milk shake at the café?"

She'd had worse offers. Glancing at her watch, she entertained the thought. She was dying to get home and see if she could identify the herbs in the pomade, but she supposed she could take time to eat. Since she hadn't done much of that lately, a hamburger sounded good. She could send the gel to Brian and have him run it through the lab. Within a day, she'd have an answer. Since it was Nelly's formula, though, the analysis would be useless without Gabe's permission to market it.

A few minutes later Gabe locked the door to the barbershop, and they crossed the street to the café.

The hall clock struck 9:00 as E. J. let herself into the house. Throwing her handbag on the sofa, she carried the jar into the kitchen.

Sitting down at the table, she unscrewed the lid and took a dab of the gel out, gently rubbing it between her fingers. She sniffed it.

Eucalyptus.

Maybe some ginger?

Other scents mingled in her senses, ones she couldn't identify. Closing the jar, she set it back on the table, quickly jotting a note to Brian on a paper napkin before going in search of another little jar and a mailing box to send part of her sample.

Of course she wouldn't do anything with the analysis; Gabe would be appalled if he even suspected her intent. She was merely curious about the gel's ingredients. You could attribute that to years in the hair-care industry. A product with the gel's potential would raise anyone's curiosity—and that's all hers was—simply curiosity.

It was Nelly's Jelly, not E. J.'s.

Then again, it was a product Kilgore's Kosmetics desperately needed.

She mailed the package early the next morning. Returning from the post office, she picked up the phone for the call she'd been dreading.

"Kilgore's Kosmetics."

"Louise, it's E. J."

"E. J.! Where on earth are you? We've been worried sick! Why haven't you called?"

"It's a long story. Is Isabel in?"

"Yes, I'll connect you." She paused. "Is anything wrong?"

"No, I'm fine, Louise. I'm working on a new product."

Oh, folks, now that was an outright lie, and E. J.'s behavior can't be excused at this point. She was thinking straighter than she'd thought in weeks, and deception never had been her style, yet here she was, still spinning tales.

Cora Roberts contended that lying was for the weak, and E. J. was anything but weak. But in this case, E. J. thought lying was still the best course. And of course, there was a tiny bit of truth in it. The gel had potential. E. J. wasn't about to steal a product, but with a little persuasion, in time, Gabe might be agreeable to let Kilgore's market the product for him.

Isabel came on the line. "E. J.? Where are you?"

"Isabel, I'm sending you a product to be analyzed. I just mailed it. See that it gets down to the lab."

"What's going on? Are you on some kind of marketing trip? E. J., we need you back here."

"I know, I know. Don't panic. I'm . . . onto something that could be what we're looking for, but I need time to get the permission to market it."

E. J.'s hand slipped to cover her stomach. "It may take me a few weeks . . . could even be months."

"You can't be serious. Months? Can't we send someone else to get permission? You're needed here."

"No. This is tricky, Isabel. We need the patent on this prod-uct, and the owner isn't interested in selling at this point. Besides, Grams fell and broke her hip, and I need to stay here for a while. I'll handle what I can over the phone, and someone else will have to pick up the office slack until I get back."

"But . . ."

E. J. tapped the phone on the counter.

"What's that?" Isabel asked.

"Phone problems." She whacked the receiver harder. "Sorry, Isabel . . . have to go. I'll call you later."

E. J. hung up, sagging against the counter. She hadn't asked about Frank.

Or how Isabel was coping with losing Jake. Jake she didn't give a rat's nest about, but Frank had always been good to her. She should have asked about him.

⚜

Picking up the phone, she dialed again.

"Winston Health Center. Can I help you?" a Mickey Mouse–sounding voice greeted.

"Yes, I had an appointment last Friday, but I missed it."

"Which clinic?"

"I'm not sure which clinic. I made the appointment under the name Laura Smith. I think it's family planning."

"I'll transfer you."

"Muskrat Love" came on again. Did the clinic have only one recording, or were they fond of animal life? E. J. clung to the phone as if she were drowning. This was it. Nothing was going to get in the way this time.

A knock at the front door competed with a voice on the other end of the line—

"Hello! Anyone there?" Maggie's cheery voice called.

E. J. kept the phone to her ear.

"Family planning. Can I help you?"

The knocking grew more persistent.

"Yes, I need to . . ."

"Helloooooo? E. J.? Are you there?"

E. J. hung up the phone and knocked her head against the wall.

"Hi. Bad time?" Maggie appeared in the doorway, her friendly eyes taking in E. J.'s disarray. These days E. J. knew she routinely looked like an unmade bed.

"Never seems like there's a good time."

Maggie stepped back. "I'm sorry. I could come back later."

E. J. sighed. "Don't go. I didn't mean to be rude. Come in, I'll fix us a glass of tea."

Stepping back, she watched Maggie herd the oldest kids inside and settle them with books she pulled from a string bag. She had a Tupperware carryall bag that contained something that smelled delicious. Maggie looked exceptionally good for having given birth less than a week before . . . better than E. J., even with her new haircut.

"How're the babies?"

"They're beautiful. And so good. They hardly ever cry, and they wake up around the same time to eat at night, around every three and a half hours."

"Three and a half hours, huh?"

Yikes, folks! Three and a half hours for most folks, E. J. concluded, would be about four hours short. For those with newborns, three and a half hours is edging toward a full night's sleep.

"The other kids had me up every two hours to nurse. It's really something that both babies would sleep for so long, and mostly wake up together. Could be a lot worse."

And it could be a lot better, E. J. thought. *Three and a half hours?*

"Enough about my flock. It's my day to take Jill a meal, and I thought I'd stop by and see how Cora is doing."

"Doing well," E. J. said. Maggie looked as if she wanted to sit down but didn't have the time, which was all right, too. Company for E. J. at this point was not only inconvenient, it was downright frustrating. She had to get that appointment rescheduled.

"She's a tough old bird. How old is she now? Seventy-five? Eighty?"

"Grams won't say for certain."

Maggie lifted a brow curiously, and E. J. looked away.

"Are you all right? You look kinda—" Maggie paused, her eyes skimming the robe, then E. J.'s face. Her eyes moved back to E. J.'s stomach and lingered.

"Fine—tea, anyone?" E. J. said, giving up. She'd have to reschedule the appointment when Maggie left.

"Yeah!" Pete yelled. "Kool-Aid!"

Maggie ignored the child's request and trailed E. J. to the kitchen, Emma on her hip. She suddenly stopped in the middle of the doorway, her mouth ajar. "E. J. Roberts! You're not!" She gasped.

E. J. pulled glasses from the drainer. "Not what?"

"You are! You're—" she dropped her voice "—you're pregnant."

Blast that womanly radar! E. J. reached for the sugar. "Don't be absurd."

Maggie shook her head. "No, you are. I've had five kids. I should know. Trust me." She squeezed Emma tighter. "Well, why didn't you say so? That explains the weird attitude."

E. J. tensed. This was overstepping friendship and bordered on downright rudeness. Banging an ice tray on the counter, she clammed up.

"So. When are you due? What is it? Have you had the ultrasound? What are you? About two months?" Pouring tea into a glass, E. J. handed Maggie her drink.

"I have no idea what you're talking about."

"Oh, come on." Maggie shifted Emma to her opposite hip. Her tone sobered. "You look like you could use a friend."

E. J. pulled out the nearest chair and eased into it, shaking her head. How had she gotten into such a mess?

"Maggie, please don't tell anyone. I don't think . . . I've been thinking about . . ."

Maggie leaned over and hugged her with one arm.

"I'll never breathe a word. A baby." Maggie shook her head. "Miracles, miracles."

"Yeah." E. J. managed a weak smile. "Miracles."

"Who's the father?"

"It doesn't matter. He's not in the picture."

"Oh . . . sorry."

E. J. got up and poured her tea and the last of the lemonade for Pete. Fighting back tears, she changed the subject. "What are you taking Jill? It smells great."

"Oh, it's nothing, really. Tater Tots casserole. Easy as pie."

E. J. knew Maggie was still hoping for some elaboration of her strange and mysterious news, but E. J. didn't intend to give it. "It smells great."

"Hey." Maggie plopped a squirming Emma down on the floor to run off to the other room. "Why don't you take this over to Jill? It would sure help me out. I still have to pick up the twins at Jerry's mother's."

E. J. balked. "Oh, no. I wouldn't know what to say." She hadn't seen Jill since high school. Besides, she wouldn't know what to talk about. "Sorry you're ill" . . . that was so trite.

"Just catch up! There must be something to say if you guys haven't seen each other since high school."

"I've got to clean the house. And then call the hospital to check on Grams . . ."

"Nonsense, this house is spotless. And you'll only have to stay long enough to chat and have lunch with Jill and then you can do whatever else you need to do. She'd be happy to see you."

Before E. J. could say Jack Sprat, she was standing on Jill's porch, carrying the Tupperware bag and ringing the doorbell. What had happened to the competent, self-assured leader who ran Kilgore's Kosmetics? Since the rape she'd become a leaf in the wind, whipping here and there, following orders instead of giving them. She was strongly thinking of leaving the casserole on the doorstep when the door opened.

Jill Bentley, looking pathetically frail, mustered a brave smile. Cancer had taken its toll on the once beautiful young woman.

"E. J. Roberts. As I live and breathe! I heard you were visiting."

"In person." E. J. smiled, tying not to stare at Jill's skeletal frame.

Jill's eyes lit up. "Oh, my gosh! I can't believe it's you!" She opened the door wider. "And you made my lunch?"

"Actually, it's Maggie's casserole. I can't take the credit."

"Come in, come in! Let me look at you! Oh, excuse the way I look." She touched the scarf covering her chemo-thinned hair.

Still, even cancer couldn't extinguish the joy of seeing an old friend. A long tube leading to an IV bag was attached to Jill's right arm. E. J. shifted from one foot to the other and tried not to look at her. Looking death in the eye is never easy—coming face-to-face with the reality of one's own mortality.

E. J. cleared her throat. "I won't stay long. Maggie thought I should just deliver the casserole and say hello."

"Well, I'm glad you did. Come in for a few minutes, please. I hope you'll forgive me for not being more gracious. I can't do much with George following me around."

E. J. peeked into the living room. A pet?

"George?"

Jill tried to laugh, but the attempt ended in a fit of coughing. "My tall, thin friend here." She tapped the IV holder.

E. J. managed a weak laugh. At least Jill still had her sense of humor.

"I'll get your lunch," E. J. said, carrying the casserole into a spotless kitchen. Jill returned to her recliner in the living room and put Alex Trebek on mute.

"So, E. J., tell me about yourself. It's been so long." E. J. opened the bag and began scooping food onto a plate. Hunger gnawed at her. There really wasn't any reason why she couldn't stay a few minutes. It wasn't as if she had any real place to go, and Jill seemed eager for company. She got out a second dinner plate.

"Not much to tell, Jill. I'm co-owner of a small cosmetics company in LA, Kilgore's Kosmetics. Maybe you've heard of them?"

"No, I don't get out much," Jill managed before a coughing spasm overcame her. E. J. winced and set Jill's plate on a nearby tray.

Once they were settled in the living room to eat, E. J. started talking, keeping her eyes off Jill. She looked up finally to see Jill, eyes closed, head down. E. J. froze. Jill had answered a minute before. Now her head hung to her chest as if she were sleeping.

Quietly setting her plate aside, E. J. got up to check on her, but Jill's head snapped up.

"Yes?"

"I thought . . . you might need something."

"I'm sorry. I thought we would say grace."

"Oh. Did you want me to?"

"Please."

Bowing her head, E. J. blessed the food.

When she finished, Jill took her hand and squeezed it. "Thank you."

"Are you all right? For a minute I thought . . ."

"I was dead? Oh, no. Not yet. The Lord doesn't seem to want me home with Jack yet." She pushed meat and potatoes around the plate, taking an obligatory taste.

E. J. found her own appetite cooling.

"Anyway, more about you. What have you done with your life?"

E. J. didn't know where to start. As much as she hated to admit it, the Lord had blessed her greatly. Should she tell about buying her first new car? Graduating evening college with honors? That until the date rape and her unwanted pregnancy, she was healthy, happy, and had been given more than she'd ever dreamed of? And even her problems paled in comparison with what Jill was dealing with. E. J.'s problems weren't life and death . . . at least not for her. Now, where had that thought come from?

"I haven't done anything important." Clicking forks filled the silent void. Finally, she couldn't keep from addressing the obvious. "It isn't fair, Jill." E. J. could barely swallow around the growing lump in her throat. Jill was dying and E. J. was inwardly complaining that life had given her a bad break.

"Oh, don't be upset. And please don't feel sorry for me. Life's a journey, E. J. Brief and complicated sometimes, but necessary. I'll have eternal life before long, be reunited with Jack. I'll get to see my mother again." She leaned over and handed E. J. a tissue. "I'm not saying I'm jumping up and down, eager to go, but I'm okay with it."

"But why you? You're so young."

"Why anyone?" Jill pushed her plate aside. "I'm lucky to have the time I've been given. Jack's death, then months of chemo and radiation, and . . . well, God's been good to allow me to remain here this long."

"My gosh, Jill," E. J. patted a Kleenex to her nose. "How do you do it?"

"You just do. I don't know how. It would be worse if I didn't have friends to support me. I guess it would be worse if we would have had children—having to leave them behind, not getting to raise them."

"And now?"

"Now I wait."

E. J. was speechless.

Jill leaned over to hug her. "The Lord knows what he's doing. And look at the upside." She motioned around her. "I don't have to lift a finger, my house is spotless, and people bring me casseroles just like that," she snapped her finger, trying to laugh through tears. "I live like a queen."

"You make me feel very inadequate," E. J. said, dabbing her eyes.

Sobering, Jill stared at her nearly untouched plate.

"I know you're probably busy and don't want to spend your vacation sitting with a sick friend, but Helen Withers is coming over tonight to play Scrabble. You want to join us?"

"I'd love to," E. J. said. When she realized she meant it, she felt even better.

Folks, here's a lesson we all should learn: when we give of ourselves, how great is the blessing. That evening, E. J. laughed more than she had in months. All of them were horrible Scrabble players, and Jill spent ten minutes arguing for the word *wagon*.

"But you can spell it with two *g*s," she argued. "I saw it on Martha Stewart."

Jill tired after the third game and E. J. excused herself around nine. Back at Grams's house she found a message from the clinic waiting on the answering machine: "Miss Smith, this is Winston Health Center. I'd like to talk to you about rescheduling your appointment."

E. J.'s earlier elation waned as she reached for a pen and paper to take the number down and then paused. Sinking heavily into a kitchen chair, she stared at the blinking light on the machine. For ten minutes she sat in silence. The ticking clock and Albert moving to the chair next to her, begging for a bedtime snack, went unnoticed. E. J. finally looked up and sighed.

Getting out of the chair, she hit the Delete button on the machine.

"Albert," she said, flipping off the kitchen light, "what am I doing here?"

In the darkness, Albert stared at her as if humans never failed to confuse him.

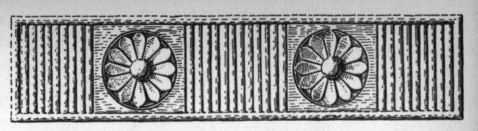

CHAPTER EIGHT

When E. J. deleted that message on the answering machine, she realized she'd crossed a line. Suddenly she knew with certainty: She didn't want an abortion. She'd never really wanted it. Why else had she come back to Cullen's Corner than to get back to her true values, values that would not allow her to take another life? Why else had she let things like oversleeping or interruptions deter her from her goal? Seeing one of Maggie's twin babies being born, her encounter with Dr. Strobel, visiting with Jill—all were potent reminders that there was another life involved besides her own, and that life is precious. Abortion was not the answer to her problem. However this child was conceived, it deserved to be born.

But giving birth didn't create a mother. Days, weeks, months, and years make a mother, and E. J. wasn't kidding herself. She didn't have what it took to raise a child. Like mother, like daughter? Maybe. Marlene had deserted her child five years after the birth. It made more sense to E. J. to give the child away before bonds were ever formed.

So, she'd stay in Cullen's Corner and have the baby. She had no idea how she'd stall Brian and Isabel, but she'd faced worse problems. Grams and Maggie already knew about the baby, and others would find out soon enough. If she returned to LA, there would be more questions than she had answers. Isabel would want to know who the father was, and what would E. J. say—"your son? He put something in my Coke and when I was unconscious, he raped me, Isabel. He was your baby, the light of your life, but he was my worst nightmare." Had he not been killed that night, he would be sitting in a jail cell, facing criminal prosecution, because as God was her witness, she would have prosecuted him so that he could never do the same to another woman.

Why, God? she thought. *Why did you mercifully keep Jake's secret from harming Isabel and leave me to face the consequences?*

In her confusion, E. J. was blaming God—but folks, at least she was talking to him. That was progress for someone who hadn't given God much thought over the years. But you see, she was beginning to realize her problem was bigger than she could handle. She thought that God's love is easily deterred—that her ignoring him for all those years would surely mean he had written her off and she was on her own. She was wrong, of course. For he has said, "I have called you by name. You are mine."

But E. J. hadn't opened her Bible in a long, long time. She believed God had spared Isabel the agony of knowing the truth about her son and was allowing her to bear the brunt of that man's sin. Hatred for Jake seared a blistering hole in E. J.'s heart, and she had no idea what to do with that hatred. The only thing she did know now was that she was not going to let another innocent person pay for his sin.

"Where did you get this stuff? Some witch doctor out there in the boonies?" Brian Powers guffawed on the other end of the line.

E. J. had read the lab analysis the moment FedEx delivered it. Herbal. Harmless yet effective. There was a note for her to call Brian as soon as the report reached her.

"I've been trying to get you for days. Where have you been?"

"Grams's phone is acting up—we've had a storm."

More half-truths. The storm had taken down telephone lines, but Grams's had been fixed the first day. E. J. bit her lip. She was getting good at avoiding calls from Brian and Isabel.

"I tried Sunday morning. Was the phone out then?"

"No, I was in . . ." She paused. "I was out. Sorry."

"So I discovered." Papers rustled in the background. "You never answered my question. Where did you get this stuff?"

"A friend gave it to me. I've never used anything like it."

"Neither have I. It's great stuff. We packaged some sample product and messaged it to a couple of area salons for feedback."

E. J. closed her eyes. "Oh no, Brian, I just wanted to know what was in it. We don't have permission to market yet." She backtracked. "You'll have to run it through the FDA, won't you?"

"No. It's herbs. The ingredients have already been approved, and when that's the case, they don't have to be retested. E. J., you know that. Has this little vacation fried your brain?"

"I'm working and looking after Grams, Brian. It's not a vacation."

"Whatever. How is it going down there in Cullen's Corner? Learning how to play banjo? Run into Sheriff Taylor and Barney at the local café?" He chuckled.

Jerk, she thought. She'd never liked him, merely tolerated him because of Isabel.

"How's the third-quarter report coming?" E. J. asked.

"Dismal. We need something to give the Christmas season a kick in the potster. Like this stuff here, what did you call it? Belly Jelly?"

"Nelly's Jelly. And Kilgore's won't be putting the gel on the market. We don't have a patent."

Of course there was no patent. The gel was made of herbs, and herbs couldn't be patented. Could they?

"Come on, E. J. If the market proofs come back okay, we could be sitting on a gold mine. L'Oréal will eat our dust."

"Brian, I am still the boss, in case you've forgotten. And I say no. Has Isabel seen anything on the gel?"

"No. I've kept it quiet like you asked, though I don't know why. Isabel's been very distracted lately, and not very interested in the company. Today she's taking Frank in to the hospital for more tests. He's been getting gradually worse since Jake's funeral."

E. J. butted her head against the wall. She should be in LA taking care of business, not in Cullen's Corner sentenced to have Jake Kilgore's baby. Maggie's recent delivery popped into her head. Two living, breathing, innocent little souls. This pregnancy may have felt like a sentence, but at least she knew she was doing the right thing.

"Don't sit on this too long," Brian said. "Kilgore's needs this gel, E. J."

"It's not ours yet, Brian. Keep that in mind."

"Your call, but I wouldn't hedge on this one. The company needs this shot in the arm."

No one knew that better than E. J. Another quarter like the last two, and Kilgore's would be drowning in red ink.

"Keep me informed. And don't market the gel until you get an okay from me, you understand?"

"Duh. I'm trying," Brian mocked.

Hanging up, E. J. poured a cup of coffee. Locating the bread, she pushed a piece into the old toaster. Every appliance in the house needed to be replaced. What did Grams do with her money? Grandpa Neil's postal pension should have allowed her a good income, but the house was run-down and needed repairs, and that old Monte Carlo was a disgrace.

Drumming her fingers on the worn kitchen counter, she waited for the toast. This time it wasn't going to give her a heart attack when it catapulted to the ceiling. This time she was ready for it.

The phone rang, momentarily diverting her attention. The toaster popped. She jumped, knocking the cup of coffee over. The phone shrilled again.

"Just a minute," she yelled, as if yelling would make it stop.

The cooling toast waited for her. Should she answer the phone, or butter the toast? It could be an important call, but spreading cold butter on cold toast . . . The phone won out.

"Hello?"

"There you are! I was about to hang up. Beautiful day to be alive, or so I've heard."

E. J. sighed and stared at the burnt toast. "Good morning, Grams."

"Now, I know you can't be bothered, and I don't want to be a burden, but you're going to have to make another trip up here. It's an emergency."

"What's wrong?" She straightened, sopping up the dripping coffee with a tea towel. Emergencies were never good things. "Is it about your hip? Are you in pain?" E. J. felt her heart struggling to come out her throat.

"I've forgotten my peppermints."

E. J. took a deep breath, trying to steady her pounding heart. "*Peppermints?* That's the emergency? Doesn't anyone there have a few they'd share?"

"My roommate, Fern Parsons." It sounded like Grams covered the receiver with her hand. "But she won't share. Tight as a cheap suit."

"Grams!"

"Well, she is."

The toast hardened.

"Okay. I'll call the store and see if Martin will drop some peppermints by on his way home."

"No. That Peabody doesn't know a peppermint from a pickle. Thirty-three and thinks he knows everything. You'll have to bring them, hon. It won't take but a minute—you're feeling okay, aren't you? The morning sickness still bothering you?"

"It's getting better. Are you okay?"

"Got a case of indigestion that could fell a mule."

"Then you need an antacid—"

"I need peppermints; antacids don't do a thing for me."

"I'll see that you have a new stash of peppermints by the end of today. Right now I have to go. My breakfast is getting cold."

"Thank you, dear, and since you're coming to the hospital, bring Albert with you. He must be wondering what's happened to me."

Cats weren't allowed in the hospital. E. J. rolled her eyes at Albert, who had come into the kitchen, apparently to see if any of the food being prepared was for him.

"We'll see . . . I have to hang up now, Grams. I'll be there later." Dropping the phone in the cradle, she flew to the stove to pull the coffeepot off and switch off the burner. The burner knob came off in her hand. She tried to stick it back on, but couldn't get it to line up evenly. After a few minutes it clicked into place, and she poured a fresh cup of coffee, holding her toast over the steam to add moisture to the dry bread.

Chewing, she studied the old kitchen. It was a mess. Frayed curtains . . . knobs that came off in her hand. Some walls were covered with cabbage roses, and yellowing paint covered others. The old E. J.—the more cash-endowed E. J.—would have already made arrangements to have it renovated. The appliances were at least fifty years old; pipes needed replacing. The roof leaked, and every window in the house needed new sills. But Cora was independent and refused to ask for help.

Money wasn't the issue; between her and Grams surely they could scrape up enough to put the old house back in order. Oomph was the problem. Lately, she hardly had enough energy to walk to the store, much less drive to Raleigh to deliver peppermints in this heat.

The cat clock above the stove caught her attention, eyes and tail twitching back and forth. Back and forth.

Back and forth.

Ten o'clock in Cullen's Corner. She dryly wondered where the morning had flown.

For that matter, what day was it?

July rode in on a blur of heat and humidity. The Fourth of July found E. J. consuming ice-cold watermelon slices in Maggie's backyard while dodging sizzling sparklers and getting a nose full of pungent-smelling gunpowder.

Grams remained in a Raleigh nursing home, her hip slow to heal. E. J. visited her whenever possible.

E. J. made trips to the grocery store and pushed the cart around with the little energy she could muster. She studied the frozen foods, as if by miraculous intervention she might discover a new vegetable—maybe a corn-pea or a lima-asparagus.

One day at the store a voice startled her. "Going to Onion Days tonight?"

E. J. whirled to see Maggie wheeling a full cart of babies and groceries. The two older children played tag down the center aisle. Bea tagged Pete with a slug, and tears welled in the little boy's eyes. Maggie shot both children a warning glance, and they darted behind the cart.

"Onion Days?" E. J. said, pretending she'd never heard of the occasion. The whole town celebrated onions. "What's that?"

Maggie laughed. "Don't tell me you haven't heard about it! Why, everyone in town knows about Onion Days."

What Maggie said was absolutely true. And E. J. did know about the Onion Days Festival . . . banners and flyers were everywhere. There wasn't a shop in town that hadn't made sure everyone would not only be there but would sign up to participate in some way.

"How exactly do you celebrate an onion?" E. J. asked. "Cry?"

Maggie giggled, reaching out to prevent a child from falling.

"Honestly, E. J., you're a hoot! No, with a carnival, jail cell, that kind of thing."

"Jail cell?"

"Fund-raiser. The mayor, sheriff, local dignitaries get arrested by deputized charity officials and thrown in jail—in a cattle pen set up on the square. They have to try to get passersby to donate money to bail them out. A riot. Last year, old Doc Strobel and the vet, Del Thompson, got thrown in and had to spend three hours trying to raise twenty dollars. Seems Doc's wife is ornery and spent her time paying people *not* to donate."

E. J. shook her head when Maggie doubled over at the

thought. "She raised more money than her husband," Maggie hooted.

Very funny, E. J. thought. She would have killed the woman.

It wasn't that E. J. was averse to having fun or even hated onions. These days she ate onions on everything. But the thought of making a public appearance in her obviously growing condition was unbearable. By now word was certainly out that Cullen's Corner's second most prodigal—taking a backseat only to her brother, Chris—was home, pregnant, and not married.

"Listen, you've got to come."

E. J. turned back to the shelf. "We'll see."

"Pooh. That means no," Maggie complained. "You've got to come. Gabe raised the most money last year. Of course, that happens when you're thrown in jail four times." Maggie detached Pete's hands from the hem of her skirt and warned him with a stern look to stand still.

"I can't imagine Gabe doing anything as frivolous as allowing himself to be the butt of an Onion Days joke," E. J. said.

"Are you kidding? It's the most fun he has all year. He really believes in what the money goes for. The town needs a clinic so we can bring in more doctors so we don't have to go to Raleigh for medical services. See—" Maggie leaned closer—"if there'd been a clinic here, Nell Faulkner might be alive today."

E. J. paused, balancing a jar of olives. The sobering thought took her mind off her swelling feet. "I'm sorry. I didn't know. . . ."

"They were only moments too late getting her to Raleigh, even with air evac. It was her heart, you know."

The women stood in silence for a few moments. Even the children called a temporary truce and gaped up at the women curiously.

Maggie finally broke the silence. "Anyway, I've gotta feed the bitty ones. Think about coming, okay?"

"No promises, Maggie." E. J. playfully squeezed Pete's arm as he passed by. The boy grinned.

Walking home with her groceries, E. J. felt a flutter. Tiny, almost imperceptible, but definitely a flutter. Or maybe gas? She stopped in the middle of the sidewalk, nearly dropping her shopping bag. There was a life growing inside her. She thought about the babies she'd seen and wondered what hers looked like. Not now—she knew it barely had a face at this stage—but it would. And ears and a nose . . . and feet.

She rushed to the barbershop, giddy with the news. Almost to the door, she realized that Gabe didn't know about the child. She tucked the excitement away and straightened her hair.

He waved her into the barbershop. "Come in and keep me company. I'm lonesome."

As much as she'd have liked to get home, her swelling ankles warned her she should sit for a minute. Gabe took the bag of groceries, setting it on one of the wooden chairs that lined the shop's west wall.

"Perishables? I could run them next door. Edna lets me store perishables in the pharmacy refrigerator."

"Fruit and bottled water." E. J. sat down and succumbed to the urge to slip off her shoes and rest her feet on the cool tile floor. Her eyes traveled the small shop, empty this morning. "I hear you're going to be jailed tonight."

Gabe took a seat in his barber chair, grinning boyishly. "Not guilty, to all charges. Where'd you hear that?"

"I bumped into Maggie and her brood at Peabody's. She said you were the top moneymaker at Onion Days last year."

"Well," he grinned modestly, "that's not overly hard when you have your hands in almost everyone's hair."

E. J. tsked at him. "Gabe Faulkner! You wouldn't blackmail people with bad haircuts to take their money, would you?"

"It could happen."

E. J. smiled, her hand absently moving to rest on her stomach. "At least it's blackmail for a good cause."

"Yes, it is. And Onion Days wouldn't be nearly as successful if Maggie didn't help coordinate the events. She can rearrange an entire seed catalog alphabetically while feeding the kids, mowing the lawn, and putting a second coat of paint on the house—and still have time for charity events." He picked up a swatter and nailed a fly. "She's quite a woman."

"So was Nelly." Her eyes moved to the shelf behind the barber chair.

Gabe's expression sobered and E. J. bit her tongue.

"That she was."

The two sat in silence, listening to everyday sounds going on outside the open door.

"You coming tonight?" Gabe slid out of the chair, stretching. For a man "staring down the barrel at fifty," he was remarkably fit and athletic.

"I rather doubt it."

"Why not? You'd have a good time."

"I'm not feeling my oats, as Grams would say." She lifted her feet, surveying the ankles. "Is Helen going?"

Now, folks. Gabe's not an idiot. He'd put two and two together and come up with an unmarried young woman in trouble, but he didn't think E. J.'s situation was any of his business. If she wanted advice she knew she could come to him and he'd give it. Apparently she wasn't looking for counsel at this point.

But she was one of Cullen's Corner's own, and if one of its own was in trouble, the town would be there to help out.

"Helen Withers miss Onion Days?" He rolled his eyes, restraightening his work area.

E. J. grinned. "Is Helen a touchy subject?"

For Gabe, Helen was. He still felt a tad guilty that he was seeing her, though not a soul in Cullen's Corner resented his and Helen's growing relationship. Everyone remembered those first dark days after Nell's death. Gabe had been beside himself with grief.

"She seems very nice."

"Yes, I suppose so." He picked up a brush.

"Pretty."

"I guess."

"Very active in the church."

"She does her part," he conceded, picking hair out of a brush until it was spotless.

"Most definitely interested in you."

He picked up the sack of groceries. "Little nosy, aren't you?"

E. J. grinned.

"Think about coming tonight," he told her as she slipped her shoes on to leave. "And bring your wallet."

She took the sack of groceries from Gabe. "If I don't, have a nice time . . . and by all means, eat lots of onions."

"You can count on it."

She squeezed out the door with the sack on her hip.

"And Gabe," she said, turning back to face him.

He lifted a brow. "Yes?"

"Don't volunteer for the kissing booth. I hear Helen's got money to burn."

Gabe refused to acknowledge her feistiness, and she laughed all the way home until she remembered she'd promised Grams she'd give Albert a bath tonight.

Toward dusk, with Albert cleaner than he wanted to be, E. J. meandered outside to sit on the front step and listen to the festival taking place. The smell of fried onions reached her.

Going back inside, she flipped twice through the three-channel selection, and decided to go to bed. The cat clock said nine-thirty.

Closing the kitchen window, she flipped the watercooler on high and wondered if Gabe had been bailed out of jail yet.

Albert joined her in bed and set about his nightly cleaning. The bed shook with his efforts. E. J. turned over and tried to ignore the music coming through the open window. The fiddles and guitars found their way into the line of sheep she was counting. Bluegrass. Not exactly LA kind of music.

She wadded a pillow over her head and squeezed her eyes shut. Within minutes, she was covered in sweat. Gasping, she took the pillow away and breathed more easily. The hands on the bedside clock pointed to ten.

"How long can people eat onions?"

In the darkness she could see Albert extend a leg back over his head. Shake, shake, shake went the bed.

On, on, on played the music.

E. J. wiggled a foot under Albert and eased him to the floor.

Ten minutes later she threw the sheet aside and marched into the bathroom, tying her hair up with a ribbon. Her face was puffy in places she didn't know existed. Pulling from the closet a large skirt and blouse she had recently bought to accommodate her growing middle, she prepared to meet the town and eat an onion.

The festival was in full swing as she approached. This would be the first celebration in years that Grams couldn't attend. That afternoon when E. J. had visited her, Grams had made sure E. J. knew she wasn't happy about it.

"The doctor's full of it. I could make it. All they have to do is get me one of those little wheelie chairs."

"The doctor said you have to stay off that hip for another few weeks," E. J. scolded.

Grams made a face. "What does he know, anyway?"

E. J. would be the only representative from the Roberts household to attend Onion Days this year. If the farmers had a good crop this year, it could go on all night.

Carnival rides and concession booths filled the streets. The smell of Kettle Korn saturated the air. She threaded her way around the outside of a large group of senior citizens, spotting Maggie and Jerry surrounded by sleeping children sprawled on benches.

"Oh! E. J.! Yoo-hoo! Over here. You made it," Maggie said, shifting a sleeping twin to her other shoulder.

"Better late than never," Jerry teased, balancing the other twin on his shoulder. "Join the party."

E. J. sat down on the bench beside him, smiling at little Sid sleeping in his father's arms. Jerry caught her looking.

"Wanna hold him?" he said, offering the baby to her.

E. J. gingerly took the infant and settled it on her shoulder. The baby shifted in his sleep.

"Oh! He's moving!" She tried to hand him back.

"It's okay. He's getting comfortable." Jerry touched the baby's cheek. "My beautiful little boy."

Out of nowhere, a huge fried onion appeared in front of her. The bloom smelled wonderfully greasy. She turned to see Gabe and Helen smiling at her and quickly passed the baby back to Jerry.

"Figured since you came, you'd need to eat an onion like the rest of us. Thought you'd be dying to try one." Gabe winked at Maggie.

E. J. managed a feeble smile. "Thanks . . . but I can't possibly eat all that . . . thing."

The thing stared back at her.

The onion covered nearly all of a paper plate. Steam wafted lightly from its breaded center. Grease spread outward underneath it, and the very smell made E. J.'s mouth water. Onions. Yummy.

"Try a tiny piece, honey," Helen urged. "It's really very good. What you can't eat I'm sure the men will clean up."

Helen and Gabe sat down on opposite benches, and everyone began talking at once. Before E. J. could say "bluegrass" she had polished off the onion and was looking around for more. Somewhere in the distance a band shifted into the "Missouri Waltz," and couples drifted toward the center of the street.

Gabe got to his feet and held out his hand to E. J. "How about an ice-cream cone and a ride on that Ferris wheel?"

"Oh no, I haven't ridden a Ferris wheel in years. I really couldn't." She glanced helplessly at Maggie, who only grinned.

"Come on, Eva Jean. You need to loosen up a little. Don't take life so seriously." Jerry punched her playfully on the arm.

The rest of the small party stared at her expectantly. She looked over at Helen, who nodded encouragement.

"Go on," she said gently. "It'll do you good."

E. J. could feel her defenses lowering. "Do they have Rocky Road?"

Gabe grinned. "I expect they do."

"Double dip?"

"Triple if you can eat it. I'm buying."

"Well . . ." E. J. turned to study the humongous wheel. "I do love Rocky Road, and the Ferris wheel does look pretty with all its lights. . . ." She sighed. "Oh, why not? What's another pound or two?" She reached for Gabe's hand and they moved first to the ice-cream stand, then on to the colorful wheel going round and round.

Once aboard, E. J. almost lost her stomach as the ride whisked her to dizzying heights. The lights of Cullen's Corner stretched out below as the wheel paused at the top to allow loading below. Taking a deep breath, E. J. inhaled the sights and sounds of life and then tried to keep up with her melting ice cream. It had been so long since she'd taken in such simple pleasures. Reaching over, she laid her hand on Gabe's. "Thank you."

He smiled as if he knew her thoughts. "You're welcome, pretty lady."

E. J. felt more alive than she had in months. Life could be good; she'd almost forgotten.

Another onion and three glasses of lemonade later, E. J. walked home, reliving the evening in her mind. She'd had fun. And having friends wasn't all bad . . . in fact, it was quite good. Maybe she needed more times like tonight in her life.

That night she dreamed of multicolored Ferris wheels, ice-cream cones, carousel music, and the sweet smell of innocent babies.

And onions.

Those marvelous, greasy, gastric delights that'd given her one dilly of a case of heartburn.

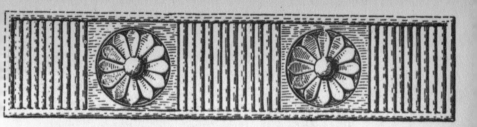

CHAPTER NINE

August arrived and with it, sweltering dog days. Talk at the barbershop centered on the upcoming November presidential race; the Republican presidential nominee, George W. Bush, and Richard "Dick" Cheney would take on Democrats Al Gore and Senator Joseph "Joe" Lieberman in the political arena.

One particularly blistering afternoon, E. J. stood in front of the mirror in Grams's room at the nursing home. Grams was allowed to sit up in a wheelchair for a few hours a day, and she beamed during E. J.'s daily visits.

"My goodness." E. J. patted her rounding belly. "I'm less than five months and look at me. How much bigger am I going to get?"

"Depends on whether you're carrying a football player or a ballerina," Grams replied, tatting a baby bonnet for one of the twins. She patted the chair next to her. "Pumpkin, you've been avoiding the subject for weeks. I think it's about time you and I had a long talk."

Tears ballooned in E. J.'s eyes as the implication of Cora's words sank in. "Yeah, Grams, I guess it is." For months E. J. had been trying on her own to deal with the rape; maybe it was time to accept help.

Sighing, E. J. sat down. "I don't know where to start."

"At the beginning, E. J. How are you dealing with this?"

"Not well. At first I was angry, then bitter, and now I just want to get through the pregnancy and have it over."

Cora bit off a thread. "You think having the baby will put a stop to the nightmare?"

"It will help."

"Oh, honey, you still have so much to learn about life and its ups and downs. The pain of what's happened will never go away. It will lessen, be more bearable, but every time you see a young man with the father's characteristics it will all come rushing back—black and ugly and despairing. What happened, happened. You can't erase it or hide it or pretend that it never took place. It's a terrible thing for a woman to go through—"

"It's so unfair, Grams!" E. J.'s voice caught with emotion. "Jake didn't have to pay for what he did—he was killed in an automobile accident on his way home that night. He never—" she broke down, sobbing—"he never had to face what he did."

Cora shook her head, her features solemn now. "You've never told me what happened that night."

"I've wanted to spare you, Grams." Life hadn't exactly treated Cora Roberts fairly. Marlene had borne two children out of wedlock—and E. J. had never once heard Cora speak bitterly of her daughter. It couldn't have been easy for Grams to face the critical looks and whispered innuendos, but Cora was made of sturdy stock—sturdier than E. J., it seemed. And now E. J. was back, a victim of rape, carrying a rapist's child.

"I'm Grams, honey. Remember? Whatever touches you touches me. What happened that night, E. J.?"

Haltingly, the story came out, uncut, uncensored. "I was doing Isabel a favor—"

"Isabel Kilgore? The other half of Kilgore's Kosmetics?"

E. J. nodded. "Her son, Jake, was home on leave from the Marines to help Isabel take care of Frank after he had a stroke. Jake had been underfoot for a few days and restless, so Isabel asked if I would take him out to dinner, maybe a movie to relieve the monotony. I'd met Jake a few times and never cared for him. He was too brash, overconfident, not my type." Reaching for a tissue, E. J. blew her nose. "That night I took him to Spago's. He was his usual self—arrogant, annoying. I ended the evening as quickly as possible, but he insisted on coming into my house for a cup of coffee. Since he'd been drinking pretty heavily at the restaurant, I figured maybe that wasn't a bad idea. The last thing Isabel needed was to have Jake involved in a car accident." A bitter laugh escaped E. J.

"But that's what happened?" Grams asked.

E. J. nodded, tears swimming in her eyes. "He asked for a Coke, and I got him one. He insisted he didn't 'drink' alone, so to humor him I fixed a second soda for me. I was anxious to get rid of him, so I pretended the meal hadn't set well with me and excused myself, saying I was going to take an antacid. When I returned, Jake was sitting on the sofa, all smiles, holding my glass of Coke.

"Drink it," he said. "The carbonation will make you feel better."

"By then I just wanted him out of there, so I downed the soda and asked him to leave. He lingered, in no hurry to go. A few minutes later I began to feel woozy and disoriented—" Drawing a ragged breath, E. J. looked away. "When I woke up I was on the floor with my clothes half off. . . . I heard his car drive off, tires screeching onto the highway. . . ."

Grams reached over to take her hand. "Go on, honey, you need to get this out."

E. J. buried her face in her hands, her voice muffled as she went on. "The next morning the phone rang at 5:30. Isabel was hysterical, babbling something about Jake and a car accident. By the time I got to her, the doctor had given her a sedative. Jake was killed instantly . . . drove straight into the path of a semi and the trucker couldn't stop." E. J.'s voice broke on a strangled sob. "Oh, Grams, I had to make the funeral arrangements; I had to bury that filthy animal. It made me sick to look at him, sick to think he had slipped something into my Coke and then date-raped me."

"So Isabel doesn't know about the rape?"

Shaking her head, E. J.'s shoulders shook with grief. "She and Frank were inconsolable. Jake was their only child, and they doted on him from the day he was conceived. I couldn't tell Isabel—what good would it have served? The damage was done; her son was dead. I would only be adding to her grief. I couldn't bring myself to do that, though I hated Jake Kilgore with every ounce of my strength. When I discovered I was carrying his child, I hated him even more."

"Oh, darlin', what you must have gone through. Why didn't you come home immediately? You knew I would help you through this, E. J. No one here in Cullen's Corner is going to judge you."

"I had my job, Grams. And I haven't exactly been thinking straight these days. Honestly? I didn't know I was coming home the night I showed up here. I flew into Raleigh on business, rented a car, and . . . and suddenly I was home." Closing her eyes, she wondered if she shouldn't have gotten on the plane that same night for the return flight to LA. A million questions, and as many missing pieces.

"Home is exactly where you ought to be," Cora said. "Have you sought counseling on this, E. J.?"

"I spoke to a psychologist briefly when I discovered the rape had resulted in pregnancy. He was no help. Dr. McPherson insinuated it would take months, maybe years to work through; I couldn't bear the thought of reliving it week after week."

"You always were a headstrong child, E. J. Stubborn as the day is long, always thinking you can do things alone. Maybe you didn't give the doctor a chance—"

"It's my problem, Grams, and I don't want everyone in the world to know about it." Springing out of the chair, E. J. moved to stare out the window. Outside, the world looked so normal: sprinklers shot sprays of water across flower beds filled with colorful impatiens and deep violet-colored petunias.

So beautifully normal, yet nothing in E. J.'s life resembled normalcy.

"You were immediately examined by a doctor?"

"No. I was too embarrassed and terrified that someone would find out what he'd done. I know I wasn't thinking clearly. In retrospect I know I should have gone to the emergency room. They could have given me a shot to prevent pregnancy and venereal disease, if needed. Thank God Jake didn't have—" E. J. bit her lip. "I mistakenly thought everything would be all right and it wasn't."

"Oh, my." Cora shook her head.

E. J. hated to upset Grams when she was beginning to feel better after her fall. A humorless laugh seeped out. "Marlene all over again, huh?"

"Now just a minute, young lady." Grams's lips firmed. "Are you suggesting that the circumstances of your and Chris's birth had in any way affected my love for you children?"

"No, but I know my mother must have hurt and humiliated you by her actions."

"The point is, she hurt and humiliated herself, and that hurt me. I wish I could tell you who your father is—I wish I could tell Chris. Don't think I haven't lain awake nights wondering where Neil and I went wrong. We raised Marlene the best we knew how; we taught her right from wrong, but ultimately she was left to make her own decisions, and they weren't always wise. But I loved that child dearly, and her death nearly destroyed your grandfather and me."

E. J. turned to look at her. That was the most she'd ever heard Grams say about her wild, rebellious daughter.

Cora reached for a tissue. "What are you going to do? We can raise this child, you know. I'll help you."

"No." The word ricocheted through the room. Taking a deep breath, E. J. tempered her reaction. "I don't know what I'm going to do—" She still wasn't certain adoption was the answer.

A thought suddenly occurred to E. J., one she'd toyed with for days. "Why don't you come home, Grams?" She suddenly realized she wanted Grams's company and wisdom more than anything she could think of at that moment.

"I don't want to be a burden, honey. I'll be in a wheelchair for a few more months, and you're not up to seeing after me. There's lifting involved and—"

"You wouldn't be a bother. I'm feeling much better now, and we can hire home nursing. I want you to come home, Grams." E. J. paused, eyes focused on the flower bed outside the window. "I need you."

Silence hung between them. Outside the door the hallway bustled with noon activity, trays being pulled from carts, glasses filled with ice. Lunch would be served momentarily.

"You'll get through this, E. J." Cora's voice was soft and persuasive. "You've been through a terrible ordeal, but you're strong, and you can't allow this to ruin your life. The hurt and pain and degradation will pass, sweetie. It won't be easy, but you'll be able to put this behind you, and I'm going to be right here to help you every step of the way."

Turning around, E. J. stepped back to the wheelchair and into Grams's Cashmere Bouquet–scented arms.

"I hope so, Grams," E. J. whispered, hearing her voice reduced to a frightened whimper. "I'm so afraid."

"Don't be afraid. God's with you, and so am I. You couldn't have a better team in your corner."

September gradually settled over Cullen's Corner, and E. J. continued to put on weight. Cora came home, and E. J. arranged for a nurse to care for Grams's immediate needs. Hattie Nelson, a pleasant woman, kept to herself and visited her own family on weekends.

Fall cleaning began in earnest: shutters were taken down and repainted, gutters cleaned and repaired.

By mid-October, maples burst forth in glorious colors, and crisp, cool air mingled with wood smoke and apple cider.

Of course, the never-ending fall craft festivals offered thick, rich molasses and every craft imaginable to mankind. You know, people, it's amazing how a simple thirty-two-ounce plastic soda bottle can be made into so many colorful whirligigs and Demofloggies. And those aluminum pie plates? Painted the right way they can scare the rabbits out of anything. E. J. visited the festivals, studying the interesting crafts, and even bought some sort of yard ornament from one of the booths.

Brian kept after her for the go-ahead on the gel. She delayed, telling him she was working on it. She hadn't broached the subject with Gabe again because he was dead set against marketing it.

"It's big," Brian claimed.

"I know, Brian, I know. It's also someone else's formula."

Halloween exploded with spooks and goblins. Before E. J. knew it, the holidays were looming around the corner. Her brother, Chris, had called needing money, so she sent him a couple hundred dollars.

"I'll pay you back," he'd said.

"Right," she replied. His chances of paying her back were about as good as her chances of fitting into a size six again any time soon.

"Grams doing okay?"

"Getting better every day."

It was about this time that Helen began her campaign for E. J. to join the church choir. She'd heard that E. J. had a good alto voice and since Florence Watts had gone to live with her sister in Portland, the choir's alto section had been reduced to one: Lets Marley, who everyone knew couldn't carry a tune in a bucket. A lot of caterwauling, Grams recalled. Not a musical bone in that woman's body.

E. J. was cleaning the garage Friday afternoon when Helen stopped by Gabe's briefly for a cup of coffee. She was in the neighborhood showing property, she explained, as she stepped over the hedge to visit. Her eyes took in the stack of boxes, lawn mowers, and paint cans lining the drive.

"Looks like you've got your work cut out." She set her keys and purse on the hood of the Monte Carlo.

E. J. paused, shoving a ball cap further back on her head. "I don't think Grams has cleaned the garage since Grandpa died."

Helen grinned, her eyes fixed on the mess. E. J. could see why Gabe liked her. She was a nice-looking woman for her age. She dressed right, wore her makeup flawlessly, and kept her hair tinted the shade of red E. J. envied. Helen was the kind of woman who got out of bed looking good and only got better as the day wore on.

"So how about it? Care to join the choir? We could sure use you."

E. J. threw a pair of worn men's boots in the trash. "Helen, have you heard me sing? I'm more of a shower singer than a songbird."

"Don't give me that—I heard you were the choir's lead alto during your youth."

"Ha." E. J. pitched a dented minnow bucket. "I can't read music."

"Neither can I."

E. J. glanced up, frowning. "You can't?"

Helen smiled, and when she smiled, Helen was beautiful. "Not a note. We don't care if you can read music or not; we need voices. Alto voices," she added.

Church choir. Now wouldn't that be dandy. She was getting as big as the Goodyear blimp, and they wanted her to stand up in front of the congregation and open herself for further speculation? "Helen . . ."

"Come on, a lot of the members don't read music. It's as simple as memorizing the part."

"You make it sound easy."

Helen brightened when she heard signs of surrender. The alto section was desperate, especially with "A Cullen's Corner Christmas" about to begin casting. The choir needed E. J.

"We practice Wednesday evenings at seven. In the choir loft. I'll pick you up if you like."

E. J. paused, leaning against the trash can. Clearing her

throat, she sighed. "Look at me, Helen. Do I look like choir material?" She patted her rounding belly.

Helen viewed her condition calmly.

"Tell me honestly, what do you see?" E. J. demanded.

"I see a lovely young woman with the glow of impending childbirth."

"Well, put on your glasses, Helen. You're too nice. I'm E. J. Roberts, Cora's unmarried granddaughter, carrying a rapist's child."

To her credit, Helen recovered quickly. Compassion flickered briefly in her eyes, but other than that small concession she seemed genuinely neutral about the announcement.

"I'm sorry. This must be very hard on you."

E. J. lifted a brow. "You mean the gossip mill hasn't reached you?"

"Of course there's always gossip, but I haven't heard anything malicious, and I didn't know what your circumstances were. Figured you'd tell me if you wanted me to know."

Ha, E. J. thought. *Ha*. "Well, you know now." She picked up an old shovel and pitched it.

"So? Shall I pick you up Wednesday night?"

"You're nuts, Helen. I hardly think the church is so desperate for an alto they'd accept someone in my condition."

"E. J." Helen picked up her purse and keys. "What happened to you shouldn't happen to anyone, but it did, and there's no reason for it to ruin your life. There isn't a one in church who will think less of you for your circumstances; it could have happened to any one of us. Now I have to run, but the choir needs you. The Thanksgiving program and Christmas cantata are coming up and we have one alto. One alto, E. J.—Lets Marley. Need I say more?" She winked. "Be a good sport and help us out—I'll be happy to drive."

E. J. watched the big Lincoln with the Withers' Realty sign on it back out of the driveway. Giving a friendly wave, Helen drove off. Glancing resentfully at Gabe's house, E. J. adjusted her ball cap.

It would be so much easier to dislike that woman if she

wasn't so nice. E. J. turned back to the pile of junk stacked at the back of the garage. It was evident why Grams didn't park the car in there—you couldn't squeeze a bicycle between the boxes.

"Need some help?"

E. J. jumped, dropping a box of photos, which scattered across the floor. "Oh!" She put her hand to her chest. "You scared me half to death."

"Sorry. Didn't realize you were so engrossed in your work." Gabe bent to pick up the scattered pictures. E. J. tried to help, but couldn't quite reach her toes. She straightened.

"It's like carrying a basketball on your lap. You can't move." She eased into a folding chair and fanned herself with an old flyer. Gabe stood by, watching her, amusement evident on his face.

"Are you hot?"

"Hot, cold, I'm always something. It doesn't matter what it's like outside, my body's thermostat is broken."

She watched as he looked at a few pictures. She'd finally gotten up the nerve to ask him about marketing the jelly the week before. He'd flatly refused. Nelly's Jelly would not be sold in any form by anyone. Subject closed.

The production date neared, and ads were already reaching the test market. Brian was just waiting for the go-ahead.

"E. J.," Brian had said on the phone earlier. "I don't understand what the holdup is."

"Gabe doesn't want to market the gel, Brian. I realize it's not patented, but it is . . . sort of." It was as good as patented. It was Nelly's "secret" formula.

"It doesn't have a patent, E. J. It doesn't matter."

"It does to me," E. J. snapped.

Truth was, E. J. had been snapping a lot lately. The whole matter set her on edge. If Gabe didn't want the gel marketed, she couldn't force him to change his mind.

With Kilgore's Kosmetics knee-deep in red ink and more on her mind than she could deal with, Eva Jean Roberts the country girl and E. J. Roberts the corporate tycoon warred with each other.

"Who's this?" Gabe held up a faded snapshot of two small children and a dog. E. J. leaned over to look. He moved the picture closer.

"Chris and me. We found some stray and talked Grams into keeping it even though she had a resident cat."

For less than a second E. J. allowed herself to wonder if the baby would look like the children in the picture with their high foreheads and blond hair. Before the answer surfaced, she had squashed the thought.

"Looks like a nice dog." He held the photo up for closer inspection. "Well, I'll be—there's your mother in the background."

A chill shot up E. J.'s spine. "Really?" She wiggled out of her chair and sorted through a box of clothing. "I didn't notice."

Gabe put the last of the pictures in the box and secured the lid tightly. "Okay, what are we trying to do here?"

"I thought I'd surprise Grams and decorate the house early for Thanksgiving. I'm trying to sort through her decorations. She hasn't thrown anything away in forty years." She held up a cardboard turkey with a missing wing to emphasize the complaint.

"Good idea. I'll help." He hefted a box onto a shelf. "Hey. Haven't seen much of Chris over the years. Thought he might come around more often."

"My brother? What on earth would make you think that?" Chris was not exactly family-oriented. He was Chris-oriented.

"Cora said something about his calling the other day."

That was news to E. J. Chris calling Grams could mean only one thing. He wanted more money . . . money Grams didn't have.

"I hope for Grams's sake he doesn't decide to show up. All he ever wants is money or a place to crash until he's out of trouble."

Gabe glanced up. "You and your brother don't get along?"

"Not really." That was putting it mildly.

Gabe appeared to let the assessment ride. He scanned the messy garage. "Quite a stockpile Cora has here."

Stockpile wasn't an adequate word to describe Cora Roberts's garage. She kept everything. E. J. could hear her sputtering defense.

"If I throw it away, I'll need it later. . . . Waste not, want not. . . . I can use those old clothes for quilt filler. . . . I may need a replacement cord one of these days and I'll have one," she'd say, holding up a ratty old lamp. "There's got to be something we can do with these old tennis shoes."

E. J. smiled to herself and opened another box of old clothes. She riffled through skirts and shirts from her high school days. Grams could make twenty quilts from the filler in here.

"Look at this," Gabe said, holding up a hatbox with a broken lock. E. J. lifted the lid and peeked inside.

The hatbox was full of photos, letters, and dried pressed flowers. The scent of age pricked her nose, and a faint memory struggled to surface. Where had she seen that box before? Ah yes. The box under her mother's bed that she and Chris were never allowed to touch. E. J. picked up a letter and noticed that it was addressed to her mother. From some man. Her father? Boyfriend du jour?

"Put it up there," she said, pointing to a high shelf.

"Don't you want to go through it? Reminisce?"

"I have nothing to reminisce about. Those are Marlene's things, not mine."

Gabe moved toward the shelf and then, apparently thinking better of it, stopped to stare at E. J.'s turned back. He set the box down.

"You really have a problem with your family, don't you?"

E. J. folded and refolded a shirt. The compulsion to get it perfect overwhelmed her. "I don't know what you're talking about."

"You don't want your brother home for the holidays, and you aren't even curious about your mother's things."

"I don't think I need to go nosing through her things."

Gabe set the box aside, dusting his hands. "I saw you at the grave site that day."

E. J. spun around, forgetting the shirt. "You had no right to spy on me!"

"I didn't spy on you. I didn't say anything because I didn't figure it was any of my business. Visiting a grave is a private matter, and I don't like to interrupt."

Red crept up E. J.'s neck. He had no right to pry into her life, no right at all. "I don't want to talk about it."

"Maybe you should. Maybe getting rid of the bitterness would help."

Turning back to the box of clothing, E. J. murmured, "Like you talk about Nell? Like you have dealt with her death and moved on?"

Shock registered on his face, and he turned away from her. For a moment, the two riffled through boxes in silence.

E. J. knew she'd crossed the line. "Look, I'm sorry. I shouldn't have brought that up," she muttered, ashamed of herself.

He continued to sort through some old dishes, making more noise than he needed to. Finally he turned around. "I miss her, E. J. There isn't a day that I don't think about her." He smiled and absently touched his wedding ring. "Life hasn't been easy, but I'm trying to move on. Maybe you should, too."

E. J. turned her back, wishing that Maggie would come over or Grams would need something. Anything to prevent the conversation she could feel coming.

"Nelly's gone. I know that. And it hurts. We had good times and bad times. She wasn't perfect, and Lord knows I wasn't either. But she was the best part of life, and I'd give anything to have her back again. Every time I go into the bedroom, every time I see that row of pines lining the back lot . . ."

E. J. bit her lip. The thought of Nelly and Gabe's pines in the backyard, one for every year they were married, brought tears to her eyes, and she wished she could ease his pain. She couldn't see him, but she could feel his eyes on her back.

"Your momma wasn't a bad person, Eva Jean. She never got a chance to grow up before she had you and your brother."

"That's not my fault," E. J. reminded shortly.

"I didn't say it was, but you can't hold on to your anger forever. It's not good for you. It's not good for the baby."

E. J. whirled to face him. Anger welled from deep, deep inside her.

"You know what isn't good? Leaving your children with their grandmother, running off with a siding salesman! It isn't good never to send a Christmas present or birthday present. It isn't good never to attend PTA meetings or your kids' Christmas play—or even call on the phone. It isn't good to just up and disappear from your kids' lives! If we're talking about harm, let's talk about those things."

Gabe reached for her shoulder. By now she was trembling with fury.

"You can't change your childhood, Eva Jean. All you can do is be a better mother to the baby you're carrying."

She turned, shrugging his hand away. "A mother? I can't be a mother. I don't know how."

"You'll learn."

"I won't have the chance."

His hand rested on her shoulder again. Their eyes met, and she could see suspicion surfacing in his.

"What's that mean?"

"It means I'm giving the baby up for adoption."

"I didn't know." He dropped his hands to his sides, and they returned to sorting.

Silence hung between them, heavy and oppressive. E. J. found the Christmas decorations and brushed dust off the box. She looked inside and found old ornaments, pieces of her childhood.

"I suppose you think I'm an awful person," she said, breaking the strained tension.

"No. I think you're a little confused and too stubborn for your own good."

Disapproval. Disappointment. Both were evident in his voice.

E. J. sighed. "It isn't like you think. I was date-raped."

Surprise flashed across his face, then compassion. Then anger. "Who?"

"It doesn't matter. I'm trying to move on." E. J. thought about Grams's nightly lectures about getting past the unpleasant. "I'm planning to give the baby up for adoption."

Gabe pushed himself off the cooler and walked over to her. Reaching out, he offered his arms, and she went into them.

"Eva Jean. Honey. Are you sure? You can't blame yourself or the baby for what happened."

"I don't," E. J. sobbed.

"I think you do," he softly corrected, holding her at arm's length to search her eyes.

She didn't look up, but focused on his brown leather work boots. "It's not the baby's fault."

"Then why won't you keep it?"

"I can't, Gabe. I can't be reminded of what happened every day of my life." She and Cora had this conversation every day. Cora wanted her to keep the child and promised to help raise it, but E. J. couldn't. "I close my eyes and see his face. I see the birthmark on his neck, I see his nose, his eyes. I can't stand the thought of raising his child. What would I tell the baby about his father?"

"It's your child, too. Your flesh and blood, a part of you. There are two victims here, E. J. Have you forgotten that?"

"How could I keep it? I go back to LA with a baby. There would be questions . . . Isabel would want to know . . ."

"Have you thought through all the options? There must—"

"There's no other choice . . . except abortion, and I decided not to do that."

"Not to do that? You were considering abortion?"

E. J. flared. "I know you and Nell lost two babies, babies you wanted very badly. But tell me what you'd do in my situation, Gabe. Tell me abortion wouldn't be your first thought if Nell had been raped."

Gabe ran a hand through his hair. In all his years, he'd never had to face anything like E. J.'s dilemma—had never had to think of something like this. Of course there were tough decisions to make when a pregnancy resulted from rape. But aborting a baby?

"You live under different rules, E. J.?"

"Rules?"

"Commandments. My Bible says, 'Thou shalt not kill.'"

Tension built between them. *Rules, rules*, E. J. thought. *That's all Gabe's generation knew.* What would he know about rape and rage? He'd had a good marriage and lived in Cullen's Corner all his life. The world was different on the outside; he didn't know a Jake Kilgore. For him, life was tied in a neat box with a colored ribbon.

Frustrated, Gabe broke off the discussion. Reaching for the box of decorations, he let himself through the back door, calling hello to Cora as he passed the kitchen.

"I guess I could make you lunch," E. J. offered, trailing him to the living room, where he set the box down. The conversation had ended abruptly, leaving E. J. wondering if he was angry with her. She was still a little angry herself. If he couldn't see her dilemma, then where was his so-called brotherly love?

"Helen brought me lunch, but thank you." He turned to go, then paused at the front door.

"Eva Jean, I'm not here to judge you. No one is. We want to support you no matter what you decide to do. Your choice is difficult, but I will say this: The Lord doesn't say you can't be angry. He doesn't say that you can't cry and beat your chest and rail against injustice. He doesn't expect us to like being a victim. But he wants you to lean on him through this. Lift your eyes, E. J. There you will find help."

E. J. stifled a bubble of laughter. "I haven't consulted God in years, Gabe. I wouldn't know where to start." She perched on the edge of the sofa. "I don't know where God is anymore."

Gabe turned the knob and opened the front door. "Right where he's always been," he offered. "Where did you leave him, E. J.? Where did you walk away?"

An hour later, E. J. began pulling out decorations and dusting them off. It had taken her that long to cool her engines. Baling-twine scarecrows clung together, and a cornucopia with plastic vegetables caught on the bottom of the box. Frustrated by Gabe's admonishment, she got up and went to the kitchen for a glass of water. Grams was napping and the house was quiet.

The problem wasn't going back to where she'd left God; the problem was finding him in all the clutter.

Frustrated with herself and the situation, she did something she had been putting off for weeks. She went to the phone and dialed.

"Barrett Agency. How may I help you?"

"Yes, I'm wanting information on . . . adoption."

"You'd like to adopt a child?"

"No. I'm thinking of giving up my baby." Hand resting on her stomach, she made herself continue. "I'd like to make an appointment, please."

Look, Gabe. God seems so absent at this moment.

Late October, Helen and Maggie hovered over E. J., laughing with delight when the ultrasound produced a shadowy image. Grams moved her wheelchair closer. "My, oh, my—my great-grandchild! She's a beauty!"

"We don't know that it's a she, Grams," E. J. reminded shortly.

Grams grinned at the nurse. "Maybe you don't."

"Look, E. J.! It's your baby!" Maggie exclaimed.

E. J. refused to look; instead, she kept her eyes on the ceiling, enduring the procedure only because Dr. Strobel had insisted, claiming her age put her into the high-risk category.

"Oh, E. J., it's so precious," Grams scolded. "Don't you want to look?"

"No." E. J. averted her eyes.

Maggie and Helen sighed, squeezing her right hand.

Cora moved the wheelchair until she was holding E. J.'s left hand. "It's too soon, girls. Give her time—she'll come around. I know my Eva Jean."

❧

No one was more surprised than E. J. when she found herself in the church parking lot three weeks before Thanksgiving. She hesitated at the door, feeling like a blooming spectacle in a tent dress big enough to fit a cow. Grams lovingly teased that she needed a Wide Load sign.

Helen was talking with a couple of women in the foyer, but she spied E. J. immediately.

"E. J.," she called out, hurrying over to her. "I'm so glad you came. I'll introduce you to Michael Gray, the music director, and get you a folder."

"Helen, I'm not sure about this," E. J. hedged.

What made her come? Boredom? Grams, insisting that a social life would do her good? Or did the thought of singing again actually appeal to her? Lifting her voice in praise could calm a number of fears, and E. J. in a small way hoped that it would lessen hers.

Actually, it was a combination of Grams and the Lets Marley thing that had won her over. Lets had sung in the choir for forty years and refused to step down to newer blood. She couldn't hit a note with a machine gun, but her dedication was admirable. And the holidays were a special time of year. . . .

E. J. had spent the afternoon vacillating about whether or not to come. Even now that she was here, she wasn't so sure she was doing the right thing. She didn't want to be a source of pity, and she certainly didn't want to be the center of attention.

"Michael, E. J. Roberts, alto." Helen flashed a pleased grin.

The studious young man in horn-rimmed glasses extended a hand. "Welcome to the choir, E. J. We need all the voices we can get this time of year."

"I'm not sure I'll be much help. I don't read music."

"I'll introduce you to a couple of ladies who, frankly, don't read music either and they do fine. Judy, come meet E. J. Roberts."

Ten minutes later practice began, and thirty minutes later E. J. was surprised to find she was enjoying herself. By the time the hour ended, she was able to laugh at herself for singing two whole lines in melody rather than harmony.

"Well, what do you think?" Helen asked as the two women pulled on their coats in the foyer.

"I had a good time," E. J. admitted. "Thanks for asking me, Helen."

Helen linked arms with her as they walked outside into the crisp night air. "Up for a cup of coffee?"

"No, I need to get back and check on Grams." Other than local craft shows and an occasional Scrabble game with Grams, Jill, and Maggie, she'd kept to herself. She'd never been a person to make close friends, but friendship seemed to be the status quo for Cullen's Corner. First Maggie, then Jill, now Helen. She didn't know what to do with all these new relationships.

Problem was, she was beginning to like the feeling, and that frightened her. "Maybe next week?" she found herself agreeing.

Helen squeezed her arm. "I'll hold you to that. The choir meets fifteen minutes before service begins. See you Sunday?"

Sunday? Rats. Of course if E. J. sang in the choir she'd be expected to show up for Sunday services.

On a regular basis.

Every Sunday.

E. J. wondered what she'd committed to. "Okay. See you Sunday."

"Are you feeling all right?"

"I'm fine," E. J. reassured her.

"Good. Don't forget, Jill wants to play Thursday evening if she's up to it." Buttoning her coat, Helen waved and set off for the car. "Take care."

E. J. inserted the key into her car door. *Take care.* If only she'd known a Helen seven months earlier.

On Sunday, she arrived in the choir room a few minutes early and claimed her music.

"E. J. Roberts, I'm thrilled you've come to help me out," Lets giggled, adjusting her glasses on the end of her nose.

The choir seconded the sentiment loudly.

Lets shot them a sour look. "Let's not get carried away."

E. J. latched onto Judy as the choir lined up to file into the choir loft.

The congregation looked very different from E. J.'s vantage point. Instead of the backs of heads, she saw faces. Gabe's face. He grinned at her like a proud papa, and she couldn't help but return the smile. Big as an elephant, here she was in all her glory.

Suddenly she was standing and carefully watching the director as the intro began. She was so nervous she hardly knew when the piece was over. But when the choir exited the loft, she found herself heading toward Gabe and Grams, right along with Helen.

"Congratulations." He took her hand, ushering her into the pew. Leaning closer, he whispered, "The alto section sounded better this morning than it's ever sounded."

"Thanks," she said proudly.

Rev. Matthewson delivered his sermon in his easy way. Still, it seemed he was talking directly to her.

Didn't he know someone else with flaws? Didn't he preach about anyone other than people who made poor choices? What about those who had no choice, whose future was forced upon them? Did he still have the same pat answers— ask God for wisdom and guidance? turn your life over to the Almighty who knows all and sees all? practice faith until you feel it?

The next week it was the same message. God was the answer. Seek and you will find, knock and the door will be opened.

E. J. was short-tempered these days. She came home from choir practice one night to find Grams busily knitting a pink baby bunting. "Look at this," she preened. "Isn't it darling?"

Throwing her coat on the sofa, E. J. stalked past the sofa on her way into the kitchen.

"Aren't you even going to look at it? It's so cute—"

"Forget it, Grams! I'm giving the baby up for adoption."

"Maybe not." Cora's muffled voice sounded on the other side of the door.

Pushing the door open a crack, E. J. fixed her with a cold stare. "Did you say something?"

Cora flashed a grin. "Said I was hot. See what the furnace's set on, will you, hon?"

E. J. adjusted the thermostat, then returned to the kitchen and a sack of microwave popcorn.

"Bet you will," Cora's voice came back.

The week before Thanksgiving, Cora talked E. J. into helping with the canned-food harvest. She always helped, Grams contended, and urged E. J. to go in her place this year. The baskets would be delivered to the needy the afternoon before Thanksgiving Day.

While it was something E. J. had never done, she found herself enjoying the work. Maggie was there, so she didn't feel quite so out of place. The satisfaction of doing something needed, something so simple as feeding the poor, filled a need she didn't know existed.

"You look tired," Helen said when they were finished. The three women sat around, drinking cups of hot chocolate.

"I am, a little." E. J. sat down, resting her back.

Maggie nodded. "You've been on your feet too long."

E. J. glanced down at her ankles. They were the size of water balloons—ugly water balloons. She thought of all the cute strappy heels in her closet in LA. Would she ever wear them again?

"These days anything longer than five minutes is too long."

"You need to take better care of yourself. Gabe mentioned that over dinner last night."

"If I took any better care of myself I'd die of boredom." E. J. grinned. "But thanks, Helen. I appreciate your concern."

"Going to the Turkey Trot Saturday night?"

"No. I'll trot my turkey at home on the sofa, thank you."

Helen grinned. "I've been thinking . . . do you have every-thing you need for the baby? Clothing, high chair, those sorts of things?"

The baby was a subject E. J. still wasn't comfortable discuss-ing with anyone, not even Helen and Maggie. Of course she had nothing because she needed nothing. Grams had a stash she kept in the cedar chest, but E. J. refused to acknowledge the clothes or encourage Cora. The baby's new parents . . . the thought jarred her. The baby's new parents would be buying the baby whatever it needed.

She reached for her purse. "Look at the time. I have to get home. Thanks, Helen, I really enjoyed helping."

She was heading for the door when Helen's hand on her arm stopped her. "Like I've said before, I'm a good listener when you need to talk. If not me, then Maggie or Jill. We love you, E. J."

"Yeah. We love you," Maggie seconded, coming over to give her a big hug. "Honest."

Leaning closer, E. J. hugged both women, trying to speak around the tight emotion crowding her throat.

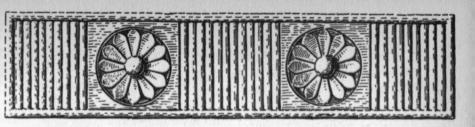

CHAPTER TEN

Thanksgiving arrived with turkey, dressing, and all the trimmings. E. J. pushed back from the table, about to explode. "Helen, you've outdone yourself."

Helen beamed, handing her a slice of pumpkin pie mounded with fresh whipped cream. E. J. groaned. She'd done nothing but eat the past few days. The baby was in her rib cage a lot, and lettuce gave her heartburn these days, but she kept eating. She reached for the whipped cream and added another dollop. "This stuff is great."

Sunday, E. J. tried her hand at cooking from scratch, something she rarely practiced. Grams said she had a hankering for meat loaf and mashed potatoes.

"Those instant mashed potatoes you've been making aren't bad, but I want the real thing."

E. J. thought instant *was* the real thing. "Grams, you know by now I can't make a decent piece of toast, let alone make a meat loaf and mashed potatoes."

"Your cooking hasn't been bad, hon. Cooking isn't a science."

E. J. took Grams's word for it and dug into the steaming boiled potatoes with a potato masher.

"No, sweetie," Cora chided, watching from her wheelchair. "Your potatoes are going to be lumpy if you don't use the electric mixer. And add more milk."

E. J. splashed more milk in the bowl and dug out the electric mixer from the bottom drawer, which was no small feat those days. She straightened with a groan to face the potatoes, mixer in hand.

The last late leaves fluttered past the kitchen window, and a cool sunshine hinted of the coming winter. Despite the light breeze coming through the kitchen window, E. J. wiped beads of sweat off her forehead and turned the mixer on high, splashing potatoes on the walls and cabinets.

"Oh, honey, you're getting it everywhere. Sit and relax for a minute. There's no hurry."

E. J. turned the mixer off and left it cockeyed in the bowl. The baby had been kicking all day, and her ankles were the size of pumpkins. Ugly pumpkins. Sitting down at the table, she focused all of her concentration on the potato bowl, as if by thought alone the potatoes would finish themselves.

It wasn't really frustration over the potatoes that was getting to her as much as uneasiness about the Thanksgiving program that night. She was nervous as a cat although she'd attended rehearsals for the past three weeks. But she was getting so large! Her pregnancy would be on display for all to see and wonder. . . .

Thinking of Maggie's surprise at the birth of a second baby, she'd asked Dr. Strobel if twins were possible. He'd laughed. "No. Not unless we have a conspiracy going and your baby is an expert at playing hide-and-seek."

"I'm a lousy cook, Grams."

Cora reached over to pat her. "Calm down and rest. Don't worry about dinner. I'm sure it'll taste fine, lumpy potatoes or not." She wheeled herself over to the cabinets and started digging.

"Oh, my, will you look at this!" She pulled an implement from the drawer, beaming.

For a moment, E. J. couldn't tell what she was looking at.

"I don't know how many times I've made butter in this. My mother gave it to me, and her mother to her." She held up an old, wooden mold with a cracked wheat design. When she pressed the two halves together, the mismatch was instantly evident.

"You remember this, don't you?" Grams lovingly ran a finger around the chipped wheat pattern.

"Yes, I remember it," E. J. said, pushing herself up and returning to the potatoes. "You used it every holiday." It was the one reminder of her youth she found pleasant.

"Every Thanksgiving and Christmas. I couldn't guess how many plates of butter I've made with this. It's very old. That's why it's so special."

Memories, events that touch our hearts—isn't that the best part of holidays? Family gatherings, hugs and laughter, and those unforgettable traditions. Cora always had fresh, sweet butter on the holiday table. The mold was part of the Roberts celebration tradition, though E. J. couldn't imagine using the old thing. A part of the wheat pattern was chipped, and the butter never came out even. Still, the keepsake brought back memories.

E. J. had been very young, barely old enough to understand the conversation. A vague memory surfaced. What had her mother been trying to say to her?

E. J. felt the blood leave her hands. She began wiping the splatters off the wall with a damp rag.

Her mother. They were standing at the kitchen counter, making butter pats for dinner. Marlene told her something. What it was remained fuzzy, but it slowly emerged from the recesses of her mind. . . .

"Eva, I need to talk to you," her mother said as she laid creamy yellow butter pats on Grams's good china.

"Yes, Momma. I know what it is." Eva Jean pushed her glasses farther up on her nose. "You're going to marry that man, aren't you?"

Marlene sighed.

Eva Jean felt that nothing about her made her momma proud enough. Not even trying to like Bruce, who smelled funny, like beer and grease, and sold some old stuff that went on houses.

"Did Grams tell you that?"

Eva shifted onto her other foot. "She doesn't like him. She doesn't think he'd make a good daddy."

"I know, honey. Your Grams isn't exactly subtle about how she feels."

Subtle, Eva thought. *S-u-t-l-e. Sutle.* Folks said she was bright for her age. Why, she could even spell dinosaur. *D-i-n-a-s-o-r-e. Dinasore.*

"Actually, we're not going to get married right away. We want to do some traveling first, find ourselves."

Eva Jean brightened. "We're going on a vacation!"

Marlene stiffened. "No, honey. You and Chris are going to be staying here with Grams. This is a grown-up vacation. You understand, don't you?"

Eva wasn't sure what she was being expected to understand, but she was sure that she wasn't going with Momma. Momma had left before, sometimes for months.

"How long will you be gone?" Tears pooled in her eyes. Somewhere outside she could hear her brother yelling at his friends.

"Just mix until they're smooth," Grams's words broke into her thoughts. "And turn the mixer on slowly."

E. J. shoved the memory aside and tried to concentrate on what she was doing. She glanced out the window as she did, half expecting to see her brother playing with his friends, waiting to be called inside to wash up for dinner. All she saw was the line of pines at the back of Gabe's lot.

How many things were imperfect in E. J.'s world? More than just a butter mold.

"You know," Grams murmured, picking up the mold to examine it again. Her eyes softened. "For years I grieved Marlene's death, desperately wanting a second chance to be a better mother. Of course, that couldn't happen. But I got the chance to raise you and Chris. Maybe, like this butter mold, the most imperfect things in life bring the greatest joy." She glanced at E. J.'s swollen middle. "Yes, I think that's a good thought for us to keep in mind this Thanksgiving weekend."

The choir began congregating half an hour before evening services. Everyone was tired from the long holiday weekend but eager to present the finale.

E. J. adjusted her dress, a loaner from Maggie's rotating maternity collection. It didn't fit right, and the huge collar made her look like a clown instead of a choir member.

"Eva Jean!" Judy called. "Hurry up and get into your robe."

E. J. ran to the robe cabinet and pulled out the last one. She slipped it on. It fell just above her knees. She got in line with Judy.

"This isn't my robe," she whispered. The choir leader shot a warning glance.

Judy looked down.

"You're right. Clara Zigby must have forgotten which robe is hers again."

Sure enough, the elderly lady in the front row had on a robe two sizes too big. The garment hung off her shoulders laughably.

Judy lowered her voice. "You'll have to catch her before we go in."

The warm-up started. E. J. felt the baby sitting low on her bladder and excused herself to the bathroom.

While she was gone, Judy talked Clara out of her robe.

"But I'm sure this one is mine," the tiny woman insisted. Everyone knew Clara was as blind as a fool's heart.

"Now, Mrs. Zigby, just look. It's two sizes too big for you," Judy said.

The older lady pursed her lips. "Well, if you say so, but I still think this one is mine." She slipped the robe off, and Judy carried it to E. J. and returned the proper robe to Clara.

E. J. quickly changed. From the choir room she could

hear the voices of the congregation as the choir members began warming up. Michael hit a high C on the piano. "La, la, la, la."

She was most definitely not ready for this. She couldn't remember a word to any of the songs.

In the sanctuary, the choir started filing into the loft when E. J. grabbed her folder and hurried to catch up. Falling into step, she flipped through the music one last time and put a hand to her belly. *Well, kid,* she thought, *it's show time.*

E. J. took her place on the second row. Pastor Matthewson began the opening prayer. With her head down, E. J. sneaked a peek at the congregation. The church was overflowing. Everyone was in his or her regular church pew. Faces bowed in grateful reverence. Gabe sat near the inner aisle of their pew with Grams wheeled in beside him.

"In Jesus' name we pray! And the people said . . . ?"

"Amen!"

E. J. flipped open the folder and tried to summon up some moisture to clear her dry mouth. Nothing came. She could hear a quiet murmur from the congregation and then the first song began. Voices swelled.

"We gather together to share the Lord's blessings . . ."

E. J. waited for the altos to enter on the second page. Around her, the voices of the choir brought the words back to memory. She would live through this after all.

The congregation was riveted to something behind her, and she wondered what it was on the podium that interested them. She half turned to look. Seeing nothing, her eyes returned to the music. Before long, a blush crept up her cheek. A little boy pointed and whispered something to a brother, and they both giggled.

The room suddenly began to swim. Everyone was looking directly at her, and suddenly she realized what was going on. They were making fun of her. Between the robe and her stomach, she looked as big as a braggart's mouth!

Anger and pain wrestled inside her. How dare they make fun of her? How dare the parents let their children mock her? She could make out grins throughout the congregation, and their rudeness cut to the bone.

E. J. glanced to Gabe, who smiled at her and made some sort of motion with his hands. Her color deepened. Was he mocking her too? She quickly turned the page, struggling to keep up.

She missed her entrance on the next measure and tried to find her place. She heard a snicker, then a child's laugh. Dear Lord, this was awful. She had to leave. She had to get out of there.

Mortification paralyzed her. Gabe . . . of all people, Gabe was laughing at her. His earlier words echoed in her mind. *"God doesn't say we can't be angry. He doesn't say we can't cry."*

Eva Jean was raped. Eva Jean is carrying a rapist's child, her mind taunted.

Whispering something inaudible to Lets Marley, she quickly moved around the woman and out of the loft.

Bolting through the side door, she unzipped the robe. The zipper jammed, and for a moment she thought she would break down in a crying fit in the middle of the choir room. Yanking the robe off over her head, she threw it on a folding chair. She could hear the choir begin the third song, "Bringing in the Sheaves," as she slipped out of the door and into the back hall.

Gabe caught up with her as she tried to escape out the back door. "Whoa."

Shrugging out of his hold, she squared off angrily. "They're making fun of me!"

"Eva Jean." Gently, he adjusted the collar on her dress. "No one's making fun of you. Your collar was sticking straight up."

"My collar?"

"Your collar."

Dissolving into tears, she went into his arms, and he held her. The smell of his aftershave oddly comforted her. He felt warm and kind. Exactly what she needed right now.

"You know what? I think I know where there's a piece of pumpkin pie with your name on it."

"With whipped cream?" she asked, her voice muffled against his shoulder.

"With whipped cream."

"I thought they were laughing at me."

"I know, I know." He held her until the moment passed. "Sometimes what we think and reality are two different things. Don't make things hard on yourself by imagining everyone is out to get you. Relax and let us take care of you."

Folks, pregnancy is a complicated mix of emotion and chemicals. A woman barely recognizes her own body, but she has to live with it. As E. J. stood there with Gabe, her thoughts and emotions were jumbled. She didn't know if it was the pregnancy making her act crazy, or the guilt that gnawed at her insides. For as the baby grew, so did her awareness of life. Everywhere she went she saw mothers with babies. Even puppies made her conscious of the baby growing inside her—and of her decision not to keep it.

Life was precious, the pastor had preached.

Life is sacred, Gabe had said.

Was she being abnormal for not keeping her baby? Was she bucking some immutable law, like jumping off a three-story building and expecting not to get hurt?

Thanksgiving had just passed, and E. J. had tried to focus on all her blessings. Maggie had called children miracles, blessings. That's not how E. J. had thought of this child . . . but now she wasn't sure how she felt.

Soon it would be Christmas, the time the world celebrated another child's birth. One who entered this world, I guess you could say, through a young woman who also found herself in a situation not of her own making. Could something good really come from E. J.'s imperfect situation, as Grams had suggested?

Perception and reality. They're not always the same, Gabe said. She'd thought people had been laughing at her. Her imagination had run away with her and she hadn't realized it. Could she even trust her own sensitivity?

Her thoughts still whirling, E. J. picked up the remnants of her pride and followed Gabe to Cora's home for that piece of pie and whipped cream. Nothing imaginary about that; it was time to get back to the comfort of what was available—fellowship and good food.

Back at Cora's place, Gabe cut a gigantic piece of pie and put it on a plate. E. J. waved it away with one hand. Suddenly she realized she needed the company more than she needed the pie. She poured a cup of coffee, and for a moment the two sat in silence while Gabe slathered on whipped cream and dug in.

"So, what's been on your mind?" He wiped his mouth with a napkin.

E. J. sipped her coffee, finally catching on to his tactics. He was humoring her. Why hadn't she seen that earlier?

"Do you want to talk about it?"

"I can't do it, Gabe. I can't stay here anymore."

"Why not? I thought you were adjusting to small-town life again."

She gave him a wry look. "I can't stay, knowing that everyone knows what happened."

Gabe chewed thoughtfully. "Did you ever stop to think that maybe they don't? And if they do, they consider it to be your problem and not theirs?"

"How could they not? Don't tell me people don't talk. . . ."

"Sure they talk," he finished off the pie, avoiding her eyes. "But could be they're talking about something other than you."

E. J. paused. She felt color rising up her neck. She was in no mood for another Gabe Faulkner lecture on God or the meaning of life.

"I'm going back to Los Angeles," E. J. said, surprising herself with the announcement. She'd go back, have the baby—she would ignore the stares and whispers. At least most LA people were strangers. No one had to know the circumstances of her pregnancy.

"If that's what you want."

She shot him a peeved look. Obviously, he had no compassion, no idea of what she was going through. She was coming too close to a change of heart, and that scared her. Did she want her child—putting the child's heritage aside—to be raised fatherless as Marlene had allowed her to be? Never having a daddy to show off, take to school, play ball with her on sunny afternoons. Well, if and when she had children, she wanted more than a bare existence for her son or daughter. She wanted a June Cleaver influence—Carol Brady—Clair Huxtable!

He calmly put his fork on his pie plate and pushed back from the table. "I'll get your suitcases."

Now, everyone knew that Gabe Faulkner wasn't insensitive, but if E. J. had her mind set on leaving, she was going to leave, come flood or famine. And Gabe was about fed up at this point. The girl had to grow up, and in his opinion, there wasn't a better time than right now.

She met his gaze evenly. "I'll get my own suitcase, thank you. You can go home."

"No, I wouldn't sleep, thinking of you in your condition alone on the highway at this time of night."

"It is always about my 'condition,' isn't it?"

Gabe sighed. "You know what I mean, Eva Jean. Could you change a flat by yourself?"

"I certainly could—and have. Many times."

Folks, you know by now that Gabe doesn't have a heart of stone. Of course he softened a bit. E. J., unwilling to cave in on principle alone, stared stonily at him, but Gabe knew that the way to the heart was not through criticism. Whether or not E. J. remained in Cullen's Corner was not something he or anyone else could determine. It was up to her to decide what she'd do with the rest of her life—and more importantly at this point, her baby's life.

"You have to do what you have to do. I'll make you a cup of coffee to keep you awake. Wouldn't want you driving off the road."

Her bottom lip curled.

Sighing, he took her elbow and led her out of the kitchen. "You're leaving in the nick of time. Weatherman's predicted a bad winter. LA will be warmer."

Shrugging free of his grip, she returned to the kitchen table.

The man had the heart of a warthog. "Suitcases in the attic?"

"Only one. Under the bed."

"Well, that's handy."

She shot him a resentful look. Patronizing her only made it worse. She wasn't a child; she knew her own mind. She was determined to return to LA, have this child, and piece her life back together.

E. J. went upstairs. Without a word, she dragged the suitcase from beneath the bed, hoisting it onto the old mattress. She turned and realized that Gabe hadn't followed her. Her anger blossomed.

Ever notice how there are certain times in life when we're bound to do something, yet we're dying to be talked out of it? Like when you run away from home as a child. You're waiting for someone to talk you out of it, hoping and praying someone will. This was one of those times for E. J. Roberts.

Scooping underwear out of dresser drawers, she flung it into the suitcase willy-nilly.

Gabe came in and glanced at the drawers hanging agape. He shook his head. "Is there a fire?"

"I'm in a hurry."

He nodded. "No use wasting time once you've made your decision." He glanced at his watch. "Shouldn't have much traffic at this hour." Smiling, he handed her an unmentionable she missed. "Coffee'll be ready in a few minutes. Cream and sugar?"

Straightening, she glared at him. "Three of each."

"Got it." He left and came back a few minutes later with a cup more full of cream and sugar than coffee.

She took a rebellious sip before setting the coffee on the corner of the dresser.

His eyes scanned the contents of her closet. "What about these dresses?"

"They're Maggie's. Could you please see that they're returned to her?"

"Why don't you return them yourself?"

E. J. refused to answer.

"You didn't bring a lot, did you? Didn't plan on staying long?"

"Four days. I was going to be here four days." She reached for the coffee, her anger draining. Gulping the hot liquid brought tears to her eyes.

Oh, brother. Now aren't we all this way once in a while? Quick to flare, slow to realize common sense. The brisk walk home, the fragrant coffee aroma, the warmth of the old house, Gabe. All worked together to finally calm the troubled woman. Sitting on the side of the bed, she shook her head, trying to speak around the lump in her throat.

"I'm sorry," she whispered. "It's these stinking hormones."

Gently removing the cup from her hands, Gabe set it on the nightstand and sat down beside her. She went into his arms unthinkingly.

He gently stroked her hair, softly comforting her. "What did you come here for, E. J.? You packed for a few days, you seemed eager to get the visit over with, and yet you stayed."

"Grams fell—"

"No," he rebuked softly. "It's time for honesty. No more stories. What did you come here to do?"

"Have an abortion," she whispered. She felt dirty, hurt, and alone. But free. Free to finally let the words come out, one after another. She told him about the emotion and decision that had gone into making the trip back to Cullen's Corner. Planning to have the abortion. Not having the abortion. Everything that had occupied her time the past few months.

Well, Gabe had been around long enough that nothing much surprised him anymore. But E. J. and abortion? The two didn't tally.

"What happened to change your mind?"

Wiping her nose, she sat up straighter. "So many absurd things stopped me, you wouldn't believe me if I told you." She blew into a tissue. *Maggie's twins. Grams's accident. Over-sleeping!*

"And now?"

She refused to meet his eyes. "Now I'm having the baby, but I'm not keeping it."

She got up and moved downstairs to the living room. Gabe

followed. She explained how she couldn't conceive of ever loving the child, not under the circumstances.

"The only option is to have the baby and give it up for adoption. Somewhere out there a couple is desperately seeking a child . . . a couple who'll have no emotional ties other than love for this child. I want that couple to have my baby." Her hand slipped to her stomach protectively.

E. J. realized that her anger toward the child, if there had ever been any, was gone. The baby was an innocent victim, as she had been. The only compassionate thing for her to do was allow Jake's child to be loved. For the first time, Isabel's role in the matter briefly flashed through her mind. Isabel was suffering unspeakable grief over losing her only son. This was her grandchild, flesh of her flesh. Why hadn't E. J. considered Isabel's feelings?

Bile rose to the back of her throat, and the realization stunned her. This baby was the only grandchild Frank and Isabel would ever have.

Gabe's eyes softened. "I'm sorry for what he put you through."

"Thank you," she whispered, wiping her nose again. People could be sorry all they wanted, but it didn't change anything.

"Well—" he leaned over to close the case— "if you've got your mind made up, all I can offer to do is drive you to the airport."

"Thank you . . ."

"No problem."

Well, now they were behaving like strangers. And, actually, they weren't much more than that. He'd talked about Nell; she'd talked about a number of things the past few months, even about the baby. But yet they really didn't know each other.

"What about your bathroom articles?"

"I have to pack them."

She got up and carried the overnight bag into the bathroom and carefully put the shampoo, hair dryer, makeup, and the sample of Nelly's Jelly into the bag.

"Ready?"

She slammed the medicine cabinet door. "Almost finished in here."

He closed the one suitcase, mashing down hard to secure the latch. She'd bought a few more articles during her stay.

"Good. Let's get a coffee for the road. If memory serves me, there's a red-eye out of Raleigh that we can make in plenty of time."

Midnight? E. J.'s heart sank. She was exhausted, her feet were killing her, and it was only nine o'clock. No one in LA would know she was coming back. She'd have to rent a car . . . wrestle her luggage . . .

Picking up her cup, she followed him to the kitchen. The pleasant aroma of pumpkin spices scented the room. They drank coffee in the warmth of Grams's old kitchen. Outside, a cold wind whistled around the eaves. Conversation was sparse, confined to neutral topics. The impending winter. The stores that had already decorated for the Christmas season. Topics that didn't mean a hill of beans but helped to fill the awful silence.

Finally, Gabe got up and set his empty cup in the sink. "Better be heading that way. I'll come back and clean up later. Or Hattie will do it."

"Sure. Oh my goodness . . . Grams . . ." Grams was still at the church, wondering what had happened to her!

"Helen will bring her home after the service. You can call Cora from the airport and tell her you're leaving."

E. J. studied him. Was he serious? Was he really condoning her stupidity, encouraging her to leave? Wasn't he supposed to be trying to talk her out of her anger?

Gabe carried the case and bag to the car. E. J. followed more slowly, trembling as she locked the front door. She was closing another door on her life, and it was scary.

He settled into the driver's seat, buckling his seat belt and adjusting the mirrors. E. J. stared out the window as he backed out of the drive.

Gabe turned right, toward town, but instead of taking the highway, he turned toward the outskirts of town.

"This isn't the way. . . ."

"Yes, it is."

"Gabe."

"Relax. Enjoy the scenery. The plane doesn't leave until midnight."

"But you said—"

"I *know* what I said. I've been hoping you'd change your mind, but I see all that coffee has affected your thought processes. Okay, this is the way it is, E. J. I'm going to do my best to talk you out of leaving. If you get on that plane tonight you'll have to shoot me first."

She sat back, wondering where he was taking her, and even more puzzling, why she was so relieved he *was* going to talk her out of it—because now that her anger had cooled, she knew she wasn't going anywhere. And she didn't own a gun. She couldn't possibly leave Grams alone; she knew it and Gabe knew it even better. Hattie was a wonderful nurse but she wasn't family.

"Where are we going?"

"Oh, I thought we might take a drive. The silhouettes of the trees are nice in moonlight. Haven't you driven out this direction?"

"I haven't been out here in years."

"I come out every once in a while. Trees are peaceful. They listen, without comment, without judgment."

"That would be nice. No judgment."

"You feel people have been judgmental against you?"

"What else can I feel? They must be wondering."

"Wondering never hurt anyone."

"Isn't Helen upset about your spending so much time with me?" After all, he'd left Helen behind at church so that she could take Grams home.

"Helen doesn't worry about you, not in that sense."

She didn't know whether to feel relieved or offended. "So I'm being oversensitive."

Gabe didn't answer, but turned the car into the parking lot of a small grocery.

She looked at the sleepy little store with a night-light burning in the window.

Braking, Gabe slipped the transmission into park. "I'll be right back."

She waited as he strode across the lot to the store porch and took the steps two at a time. She envied his ease. He was a man comfortable with himself, with who he was. He was never uncertain about life, though it had dealt him his fair share of disappointments.

When he returned he carried a paper grocery bag that he put on the floor of the backseat. "Thought we'd picnic when we got hungry."

"I've eaten enough the past few days I don't want to think about food."

"Charlie was nice enough to open up for me, and a person can always eat."

Gabe drove, and E. J. watched the passing scenery, barely aware of much more than the trees growing thicker and the road growing narrower. He turned on an oldies radio station, and the Platters softly crooned "Harbor Lights." She found herself relaxing and enjoying the drive.

Gabe located a small turnabout with a wooden picnic table. He parked, and they got out. She was cognizant of the quiet. The area was peaceful and lit only by a full moon. Only the rustle of leaves teased by a light wind high among the branches interrupted the silence. Even the air smelled different up there. Cold, fragrant with the scent of pine.

Gabe set out two decaffeinated soft drinks, a sack of rye bread, a white wrapped package of meat, one of cheese, a small jar of pickles, a squeeze bottle of mustard, a jar of black olives, one of banana peppers, a purple onion, and a bag of potato chips. E. J. slid onto the wooden bench.

She stared at the mini deli. "Exactly what kind of snack were you thinking of?"

"A dagwood. Ever hear of one?"

"Of course. Dagwood Bumstead's favorite sandwich in the Blondie comic strip."

She began making sandwiches, slicing the onion, piling on a slice of ham, one of beef, and one of chicken, opening the

bag of chips. She made her own slightly less complicated
and smaller version. When she got on the doctor's scales next
time, she wouldn't be surprised to see a ticket pop out, saying,
"One at a time, please." Gabe twisted open a bottle of soda and
set it in front of her.

"It's beautiful up here."

"I find it peaceful. I like to come up here when the world
closes in on me."

She glanced up at him. "Are you implying my world has
closed in on me?"

"Hasn't it?"

She couldn't say it hadn't.

He sat across from her and bit into his sandwich. She sipped
her drink, shivering from the cold.

"Need a heavier coat?"

"No, I'm fine."

He took a bite, staring at the stars. "May and Charlie have
owned that store for as long as I can remember. I think their
main business is from people who come up here, stay longer
than they'd planned, then decide they're hungry. Fresh air will
do that to you. A couple of times someone has been lost and
they've fed the searchers."

They ate in silence for a few minutes.

"Tell me something," he finally said, reaching for a pickle.

"What?"

"Why are you running back to Los Angeles? The real reason."

She bought time by pretending to be interested in her soda.
"I have a business to run there . . . personal matters that need
my attention."

"You think your problem will disappear once you get
there?"

She shrugged, and he changed the subject. "What's Chris
doing these days? Seen much of him?"

"He's around. Calls once in a while when he needs something."

"Your checkbook?" Gabe guessed.

She hated to admit the truth, but her brother was a user.

"Well, God has a plan for Chris."

"Sometimes God's plans seem illogical."

"He has a plan for your life, too."

"He doesn't have a plan for my life. I'm on my own."

"Oh, he has a plan. And he'll reveal it to you in a way you can most readily understand at the point of your most basic need. Remember that." He took another bite of sandwich.

E. J. didn't believe that for a minute. If God had a plan, why wasn't he letting her in on it? "God has a plan for my life?"

"Have you consulted the Lord about the problem?"

Reverend Matthewson's words popped into her mind, about people not taking problems to God. No, she hadn't done that.

"If God cares so much, he knows my problem, Gabe. And if he's so concerned about me, why didn't he prevent the rape from happening? I was doing a favor . . . was that so bad?"

"Not bad at all, only unfortunate." He smiled gently. "Bad things happen."

"I don't believe in this God you talk about."

"What kind of God do you believe in?"

"I'm not sure—certainly not a personal one." Not one who cared about her.

"Well, I think I'd have to ask myself a few things if I felt that way. Like, what keeps this world together, this universe spinning? What is it that keeps the planets in their paths, in a rhythm that hasn't deviated in thousands of years? What is it that keeps the sun from hitting the earth and turning us into a fireball? What is it that keeps us the exact distance away from the sun so that we don't freeze in the winter, or burn up in the summer?"

"Come on, Gabe."

"You know the answer, but you don't want to admit it. To admit it would mean you'd have to believe in someone other than yourself."

"I'm all I've got to believe in. God's made that very clear to me. If God's in control, then I think he messed up."

Gabe leaned back. "Nope. Jake did. You've been left to pick

up the pieces." He leaned toward her, his forearms resting on the picnic table. "But you can't. Not alone. You'll have to go to him and ask what his plan is for you, E. J. Roberts."

She stared at her drink, wishing she could feel as sure about life as he did. "You make it sound so easy."

"It's the hardest thing you'll ever do. But do it, E. J. Because you deserve to know God cares about you, even when events happen beyond your control."

He began cleaning up their picnic remains, and E. J. watched how easily he worked. Nell had been lucky to have a man like Gabe—a man who made sandwiches and took her for long, moonlit trips on cold November evenings. Had Nell known she'd been lucky? E. J. bet she had.

Suddenly it was clear that she'd never had a good friend, not one who genuinely cared about her. Getting to know Gabe was an adventure. One she cherished. There was nothing quick or superficial about it. It was a relationship that had grown slowly over the months. She would miss him.

Miss him.

She would. Badly. So why punish herself more when she could stay and enjoy the friendship?

She wadded the rest of her sandwich in her napkin. "I'm changing my mind."

"Oh?" He picked up trash and disposed of it. "About leaving?" He tossed the last used napkin into the grocery bag.

She sighed. "I'm staying." She glared at him resentfully.

Affection lit his eyes. "Pick you up for church next Sunday?"

She had to smile. How predictable he was. "Sure—and get there ten minutes earlier. We were almost late last week."

Folks, the people in Cullen's Corner might be far more interested in her than E. J. wanted them to be, but perhaps it was, as Gabe said, because they cared, because they wanted to help. That was a new concept for E. J., one she'd get used to . . . eventually.

Viewing the situation from that perspective meant that E. J. was growing. In Los Angeles, no one cared what she did or with whom she did it. But here in Cullen's Corner E. J. began to hope that maybe God noticed her. And—this was something she was going to work on—maybe she'd notice God a little more, too.

Did God work like that? Did he have an investment in her that he wanted to protect: such a deep investment of love that he protected her even when she ignored him? She didn't know, but Gabe had given her something other than her own needs to think about.

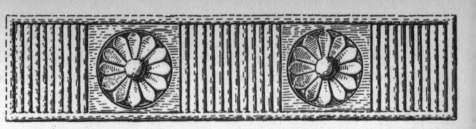

CHAPTER ELEVEN

A thick haze hung over Our Lady of Hope, a peaceful cemetery in the outer suburbs of LA. Mourners gathered in the early December chill at the grave site for the interment of Frank Kilgore.

The day of Frank's funeral was cool for LA. Low fifties, wind out of the north. Brian Powers put his arm around a frail, sobbing Isabel Kilgore, a woman broken by grief.

As the minister said a few final words, Isabel suddenly collapsed to the ground. "Frank," she wept openly.

The sting of death can be harsh, and Isabel had felt that sting not once but twice in seven months. The service paused as mourners knelt to comfort the grieving widow. So much had happened to Isabel in such a short time. Jake's death, then Frank's. She had also learned that had he lived, Jake would have been court-martialed for rape of a female officer. How much could one woman bear?

"Take me, too, Lord," she sobbed, grasping hold of Brian's hand. "I have nothing left to live for."

Gently lifting her to her feet, Brian supported her slight weight as the minister intoned, "Ashes to ashes, dust to dust."

The coffin was lowered, and one by one mourners passed by to pay their final farewells. Many of Frank's closest friends were in full Marine uniform and saluted the coffin out of respect for their fallen leader.

Each person paused to clasp Isabel's hand and offer condolences, several with brimming eyes. They promised support whenever she needed it.

She thanked each one, but in the back of her mind she must have thought of E. J., who had sent flowers but failed to attend the service.

Isabel must have thought that now she was completely alone. That even God was absent today.

The second week of December brought conclusion to the dramatic and unusual presidential election, along with Cullen's Corner's first snow. Lovely, wet, irregular flakes drifted from a pewter-colored sky. Childlike, E. J. pressed her nose to the windowpane and beheld the splendid sight. LA could offer three hundred and twenty-nine days of sun, but not this. The baby kicked and squirmed as if he, too, wanted to be out in the world to experience the first snowfall of winter.

E. J. spent the morning writing a long letter to Isabel, expressing sympathy about Frank's death. It didn't seem fair that one woman had to suffer so much in so short a time. E. J. used Grams's recovery as an excuse not to attend the funeral, but guilt gnawed at her. Isabel was a close friend, and E. J. loved Frank. She should have attended the service, but how could she? The baby's birth was only weeks away now. Even if she could have discarded her pride and fielded questions about her pregnancy, Dr. Strobel had warned that the child could come early and that travel at this time was out of the question.

Flakes mounted on lawns and bare tree branches, painting a winter wonderland. Around ten, she heard the familiar clink as Mr. Dangby dropped mail into the slot.

Shrugging out of the chair, she got clumsily to her feet and padded across the floor, wondering if she would be reduced to shopping for clothing at an awning store before the baby arrived.

Pulling a bundle of letters from the box, she felt a sudden sharp pain in her right side. "Oh, baby." She held her breath, and the pain receded, replaced by a slow ache that started somewhere in her middle and slowly spread to her back.

Grams looked up from the Grisham novel she was reading. "What's wrong?"

"I don't know—there's this pain. . . . It's nothing, really."

For a moment E. J. thought about calling Maggie, but decided she was being paranoid. The baby wasn't due for at least another month, and Maggie had her hands full with the twins.

By noon, she paced the floor, keeping an eye on the clock as the pains narrowed from being fifteen to ten minutes apart.

"Call Gabe," Cora said. "You're in labor."

Snatching up the phone, E. J. dialed the barbershop.

Gabe picked up on the second ring. "Barbershop."

"Gabe . . . I don't know—I think the baby's coming—"

The receiver banged against the wall, and she heard Gabe telling someone he had an emergency, to close up shop for him. Five minutes later he burst through the doorway, and before E. J. could protest she was bundled and in the car on her way to Dr. Strobel's office. Grams wheeled to the doorway, concern dotting her face. "Call me the minute you know anything!"

"How close are the pains?" Gabe asked, running the stop sign at the corner.

"They're erratic, but some have been as close as a few minutes apart."

Gabe stepped on the gas, and the Chevy surged ahead.

A nurse met them with a wheelchair. E. J. bit her lip, frightened now but trying to do what she was told.

"Will the baby be all right?" she asked as she was whisked through a set of double doors. "It's not due for another month—"

"Just relax, Mommy. Everything will be fine," the nurse assured, helping her undress.

Mommy. She was going to be a mommy.

"False labor," Dr. Strobel told her a few minutes later. He read her chart, frowning. "The baby's breech right now." He paused when E. J. gasped.

"That isn't unusual, E. J. The baby can turn before or during delivery, but as a precaution I want a friend, an OB-GYN in Raleigh, to take a look at you. Do you feel like making the trip today?"

"Breech?" E. J. lay back on the table. She had read about breech births; if the baby remained in breech position they would have to do a C-section. Panic seized her.

"Nothing to be concerned about. I want you to see Dr. Grayson and get a second opinion. I'll ask Gabe if he can drive you to Raleigh."

Dr. Strobel stepped out of the cubicle, and E. J. heard him talking to his nurse, asking her to call Gabe back.

Struggling off the table, she got dressed. This wasn't supposed to happen. She was supposed to have a trouble-free delivery and return to LA unscathed. Breech? C-section? That meant a longer recovery, more time away from Kilgore's Kosmetics.

E. J. had never been afraid of a challenge, but this was different. This was more than mere challenge. This was a threat to her and to the child she carried. She didn't want the baby, but she didn't want anything bad to happen to it, either.

She looked up when the curtain parted. Gabe, followed by Dr. Strobel, stepped into the cubicle.

"I'm being a problem, aren't I?" she teased the two men.

Gabe smiled. "Up and at 'em, my lady. We're going to Raleigh."

"But what about your customers?"

"They can wait. The baby can't."

"Someone needs to call Grams—"

"Already taken care of—she says to button your coat. She doesn't want you getting a cold."

E. J. rolled her eyes.

The doctor scribbled an address on a notepad. "I've had my nurse call. Dr. Grayson is expecting you."

Ten minutes later they were headed toward Raleigh. Snow had tapered to intermittent flakes. The big old Impala took the slushy roads with the grace of an army tank.

"What if this is serious?" she asked, almost to herself.

"Don't borrow trouble. Breech babies come every day. The doctor wants to make sure he isn't overlooking anything."

"But what if this time it is serious?"

"Then you'll have to spend a little of your extended vacation in the hospital."

"I can't do that."

"You know what? Maybe what-ifs aren't the best things to dwell on at this point."

That was true, but the thought of spending much time in a hospital bed terrified her. She fell quiet for the rest of the drive.

The OB-GYN office was in an older building in the middle of two blocks of wholesale and retail shops, but inside, it was as efficient as a hospital. The nurse ushered E. J. into a room and instructed her to slip out of her clothes and into a paper robe.

Dr. Grayson examined her, his face solemn. She felt uncomfortable enough without the doctor prodding around, but when he came back with the results the doctor looked relieved.

"Pregnancy normal so far?" Dr. Grayson asked.

"Perfectly normal."

"Appetite good?"

"Too good."

He patted her leg and helped raise her to a sitting position. "I don't see anything that should present a problem."

E. J. went weak with relief. "I was afraid it might be serious."

"A breech birth?" The doctor chuckled. "I see it every day. Dr. Strobel will watch the situation closely, and if you do go into early labor, be sure and tell the hospital staff the baby is breech at that point. They'll know how to handle the situation." He patted her shoulder. "I am concerned about all the water you're carrying. We don't want you developing toxemia. I want you to stay off your feet, drink plenty of liquids, and take a mild diuretic I'm going to prescribe."

When she joined Gabe in the waiting room a few minutes later, her quick smile erased the worry from his face. "I'm okay. Just a scare, though I've got a list of directions to follow."

"And you'll follow them to the letter, young lady."

She was so relieved at the doctor's report that she would have agreed to anything. "I promise," she said, saluting smartly. She grabbed her stomach and winced. "Ouch."

As they exited the doctor's building, E. J. spotted a beauty-supply house two doors down. "Do you care if we stop for a moment? I need to pick up a few things."

Gabe peered in the window. "Sure. I might find something I need."

The snow flurried around them. The few inches of glaze left a light sheen on the sidewalks. E. J. held tightly to Gabe's arm as they traversed the slippery path to the front door.

"Hello," the clerk greeted warmly when they entered the shop. "Is there something I can help you with?"

"I might be in the market for some new clippers. Got any?" Gabe asked. The clerk pointed him to the back of the shop.

As he disappeared down an aisle, E. J.'s eyes were drawn to a shelf of Kilgore's products. An end cap featured their top model, walking through a meadow, beautiful hair streaming behind her. "Kilgore's hair: for the discriminating woman," the sign proclaimed.

Moseying over, she casually picked a jar of new product from the shelf, eyes widening when she saw the pink-and-gold label. The delicate script leaped out at her.

Nelly's Jelly. A delicate, all natural herbal conditioner for shiny, healthy, long-lasting style and bounce, developed in the Kilgore's labs and brought to you by Kilgore's Hair Care.

The air suddenly left the room, and she felt faint.

"What is this?"

She froze at the sound of Gabe's harsh voice. Standing an aisle over, he held a jar up for her inspection.

"I . . ."

"E. J.?"

"Gabe, I can explain. . . ."

"I told you I didn't want Nelly's Jelly marketed. I told you . . ." He stopped, rereading the company name.

Brian had marketed the gel without consulting her. How could he? She'd clearly told him they didn't have permission to use the gel.

Gabe's rage melted into simmering anger. "You lied to me," he accused. "You somehow got the recipe . . . now you're selling the gel . . ." He set the jar on the shelf and walked out of the supply house.

E. J. forced herself to calmly follow him outside, smiling warmly at the clerk, although she wanted to bolt and run as fast and far away as her condition allowed. Gabe paced up and down the sidewalk, clearly trying to control his fury.

"How could you do this?" he demanded. "How could you take Nell's product and market it as your own? Why didn't you tell me what you planned to do? Surely you didn't think you could get away with this, E. J."

"No, Gabe! You have to believe me. This is a mistake. Brian didn't listen when I told him—"

"But you lied to me. You took something that was mine, something that was Nelly's, for your own personal gain. For profit."

"I didn't," she insisted. "Brian Powers did this. And he did it without my authorization."

When Gabe turned away she followed, trying to explain, as she should have done months ago.

"I had Brian, our production manager, analyze the formula so we could market the gel if we secured your consent, but I specifically told him it was not to be produced by the company without your permission."

His face was as tight as a mask. "I can't believe you've done this."

"But I didn't!" She grabbed his arm. "Come with me."

"E. J. . . ."

"I'm going to call Brian right now and get this stopped. Come on. There's a phone."

He reluctantly followed her to the public phone. Using her phone card, E. J. dialed the direct line into Brian's office. When he answered, she tipped the phone receiver so Gabe could hear both sides of the conversation.

"Brian, I found Nelly's Jelly at a supply store in Raleigh. What's going on?"

"I'm marketing it. It's exactly what Kilgore's needs, and you've been dragging your feet."

"I want it withdrawn immediately. I want every jar recalled. I don't care what you have to say or do. I want it pulled today. Do you understand me?"

"E. J., you can't be serious—"

"I'm as serious as gallstones, Brian. Pull it. Furthermore, you and I are due for a long talk in the near future."

"E. J. . . ."

"I told you specifically not to produce this product for mass distribution. I told you that you were not, I repeat, *not* to put it on the market without my consent. Do you remember that?"

Brian's tone changed from one of excitement, to persuasion, and finally silence. "I didn't think . . ."

"Does Isabel know about this?"

"Isabel's grief-stricken. She hasn't come back since Frank's death."

"So you assumed authority?"

"Give me a break, E. J. Kilgore's is in financial trouble. At least I'm here trying to keep the company afloat. Where are you?"

"Pull the gel. Today." E. J. hung up.

She met Gabe's solemn eyes. "Now do you believe me?"

He shook his head and started for the car.

"Gabe . . ."

"Come on. You're supposed to be resting."

Both parties were quiet on the drive home. There was nothing more E. J. could say. After Gabe parked in Cora's drive, she attempted again to explain her part in the fiasco.

"I could apologize," she began, "but it would only be for

Brian's unauthorized actions. I never intended for Nelly's Jelly
to be on the market without your consent. I hoped you would
eventually give permission and share the profits, put them
to good use, maybe update the shop."

"The shop is fine the way it is."

E. J. sighed. "I didn't purposely lie to you. I came home
because I didn't want the people I do business with to know
I was pregnant. Then I didn't go back because I didn't want
them to know I intended to give the child up for adoption,
and I didn't want to raise questions I couldn't answer about
the baby's father. I came here to escape, Gabe, not to steal
a product. I know I should have been more up-front about
wanting to buy the formula, but you were so adamant about
not selling it."

"You must think I'm pretty dense. I knew you wanted the
gel, but I never once thought you'd take it."

"I hope you don't truly believe I would do that."

"The gel's on the shelf, isn't it? With a Kilgore's label?"

She paused for a long moment, unable to leave him so angry
with her. "I didn't steal the formula for marketing purposes."
She bit her lower lip. He wasn't buying it. "I wouldn't do
anything against your wishes, Gabe. I know it's Nelly's formula
and yours to do with as you wish. I overstepped my bounds by
having the formula analyzed, and maybe in a way I let the old
E. J. override common sense. But I didn't steal your formula."

"I have to get back to the shop," he interrupted.

Hurt that he'd totally rejected her explanations, E. J. opened
the car door.

"Please think about this with an open mind. I didn't intend
to hurt you. I never authorized the marketing. You heard what
Brian said. It's a wonderful product. Nelly's Jelly is phenomenal
and it could be a tribute to Nell. This was something of hers
that you could share with the world. What's so bad about that?"

The anger in his eyes was almost tangible.

Giving up, she got out of the car and slammed the door
shut. He'd have to cool off; then they would talk.

If he cooled off.

Ferris Knob called rehearsals every night in December for "A Cullen's Corner Christmas." E. J. was asked to fill in as the Virgin Mary when Florence Hill fell on the ice and twisted her back, but she declined. Her heart wasn't in the season now that Gabe was avoiding her.

It had been a week now, and the hurt of what he perceived as betrayal was still fresh in his mind. The weather had turned almost springlike. When E. J. stepped out of the house, the eaves dripped melted snow in a steady stream. By midweek, patches of earth were showing through the rapidly melting snow, and the branches of Gabe's pines shone bare and green.

Suddenly energized by the balmy weather, E. J. decided to walk to Peabody's. Approaching Gabe's shop, E. J. slowed her stride, wishing she could go inside and talk as before. But she knew he wouldn't welcome her. She hadn't heard a word from him since the day they'd discovered Nelly's Jelly on the supply-store shelf.

"It's so unfair, Grams," E. J. told Cora over supper the night before. "He thinks I deliberately stole Nell's formula."

"He's just upset—and rightly so. How else would it look to him? But he'll come around; give him some time." Cora reached for the apricot preserves. "And let this be a lesson to you. When someone says no, that means no."

E. J. hoped Gabe would come around. She'd grown fond of him. She'd talked with Brian again, and he'd assured her the product was in the process of being withdrawn, though he couldn't be certain how long it would take to get the gel off the shelves. The only thing in Kilgore's favor was that the product was selling faster than they could package it.

"We're losing a lot of money on this, E. J.," Brian had protested.

"I don't care. We'll find a way to make it up. What about the other product, the mousse the lab was working on when I left?"

"It didn't pan out."

Deciding to chance Gabe's rejection, she suddenly swerved into the barbershop. He looked up from sweeping when the bell over the door rang.

"I know, I'm not the most popular person in here, but I hope you're in the mood to listen to me."

"I heard what you had to say."

"And you heard Brian say that he manufactured the gel against my instructions."

He leaned on the broom. "Okay. That doesn't take care of your analyzing the gel without my consent."

"That was wrong and I'm desperately sorry. Please, Gabe, I made a mistake."

He stood silently for a moment, staring into her pleading eyes. Finally, he shrugged. "Maybe I'm overreacting. I don't have a patent on the gel. What you did was wrong, but truthfully, I don't own the herbs."

"You do as far as I'm concerned. You own that blend, and it was wrong of Brian to package it. He got a little too zealous, and he might yet lose his job over it. I have to take responsibility for his decisions, whether I like it or not. It was my company that went against your wishes. I apologize for that. I want you to believe I wouldn't have broken your trust for anything. Your friendship means more than anything to me, and I wouldn't compromise that. Certainly not for personal gain." She stopped, an idea surfacing. "I can determine how much has been sold— our profit on the product—and Kilgore's will reimburse you every cent."

He immediately shook his head. "I don't want any profit from this."

"I don't either. So what do we do?"

He thought for several moments, and she held her breath.

"What's done is done. If we have to settle this, I want the money to go for a good cause. Something Nell would approve of." He thought, then said quietly, "I want to build a clinic here in Cullen's Corner, in Nell's name."

E. J. grinned. "She would love that."

"And I guess if your company wants to manufacture

Nelly's Jelly and market it, my proceeds will go toward that fund."

E. J. nodded. "And Kilgore's should donate a sizable contribution because of the mistake." E. J. had no idea where the money would come from, but it was only fair in light of the error.

Shaking his head, Gabe muttered. "And you pride yourself on being a businesswoman? You're not going to be in business long if you offer to give your profits away."

"I know—I'm just trying to butter you up." She flashed a repentant grin. "Kilgore's will donate something for the mistake and, after that, will take the larger share of the profits, but your cut will still be sizable—enough to build the clinic and help staff it, too, if this product takes off like I think it will."

Please God, she silently prayed, *let me make amends*. Here she was asking the Lord for help, and she'd given him no reason to answer.

Gabe set the broom aside, face grave. "Okay. Set up the fund in Nelly's name."

E. J. was ecstatic, but she didn't want to overwhelm him with the mountain of possibilities the agreement could present. If the gel proved to be the success she anticipated, it would put Kilgore's Kosmetics back on the map, and it would give Gabe an opportunity to do something lasting for Cullen's Corner.

"Thank you, Gabe."

He finally looked at her.

She looked away. "Something good should come of this. I think Nell would approve."

"I wouldn't be doing it if I didn't think she would."

Giving him a brief hug, she left before the fragile truce shattered. He was coming around—she didn't want to push her luck.

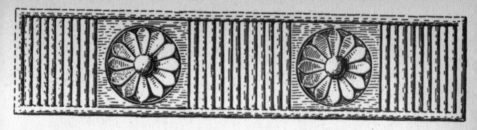

CHAPTER TWELVE

J ill Bentley died Saturday morning—quietly and with a dignity only Jill could pull off. Maggie, Helen, and E. J. held hands in the bright sunshine that Cullen's Corner wouldn't see again until spring, and they watched the casket being lowered into the ground.

Death had such finality. E. J. desperately wanted to believe Grams's quiet reassurances. She smiled as if she knew something E. J. didn't when told of Jill's death.

"She's home now," Grams said. Still, the old woman reached for a tissue. "Rejoice, E. J., don't cry."

Touching her stomach, E. J. felt only relief that her baby would be given life. Maybe not eternal life, as Grams believed Jill now enjoyed, but the opportunity to decide for himself or herself about God and eternity.

To top off a perfectly dismal week, E. J. opened the door Monday morning to find Chris on the doorstep.

"Home for the holidays!" he said with a cocky grin.

"Well, ring the bells," E. J. retorted.

He dumped his bags in the living room and disappeared into the kitchen.

"You could have called first."

"Got anything to eat? I'm starved. What's with the bottled water and pretzels?" Chris came back into the living room with a handful of pretzels.

E. J. studied his face, aware that he had changed little since childhood. Still tan year-round with streaky blond hair and a sideways grin.

"Did Grams call you?"

"Nope. I'm here because I want to be." Pretzel crumbs fell out of his mouth and down the front of his shirt. She handed him a napkin.

That night, Chris took off to the nearest bar two towns away. He dragged himself in sometime around two, smelling of alcohol and cheap cologne. He slept in until afternoon, got up, ate, and was off again. Grams never said much, but her eyes said a mouthful. She made him get his own breakfast, and instead of keeping him company, she left him sitting at the kitchen table to eat alone.

A week of Chris coming and going was alleviated Friday evening when the doorbell rang. E. J. glanced up, unable to get out of the chair. Most likely, it was just some woman hunting for Chris, anyway.

"Chris, could you come in here and get that?"

No answer.

"Chris, stop acting like you don't hear me. I know you do."

The doorbell rang again but still no response from the kitchen.

Groaning, she hoisted herself up and waddled to the door.

Gabe stood on the other side of the glass, grinning. "Hi. Are you busy?"

She brightened, affection washing over her. She'd missed that smile. "Nope, not at all."

"Then how about helping me decorate my Christmas tree?"

Christmas. Christmas tree. She'd tried to overlook Christmas traditions but could hardly do that when every light pole in Cullen's Corner held either a big red bow or a green wreath, and every store had a Christmas display in the window. The

Ferris Knob play was the talk of the town. But any chance to regain her former standing with Gabe and get a break from Chris was one she'd gladly take.

"I'll feed you Christmas cookies."

She glanced down at her tummy. "As if I needed that."

"Well, I'll eat yours."

She smiled, her eyes softening with hope. "Friends again?"

"Friends," he conceded. They shook on it.

"Hattie!" E. J. called. "I'm going next door to Gabe's!"

The nurse materialized in the kitchen doorway. "I'll see that Cora's in bed asleep before I leave."

"Thanks." E. J. put her boots on, then grabbed her coat off the hook on the back of the door and shrugged into it. Gabe helped her down the steps, which held residue of fresh snow. Cullen's Corner had already seen more snow than usual this winter, and the weatherman promised much more before the winter was over.

"You and Chris getting along?"

"Hardly."

Gabe grinned and helped her through the drifts.

In Gabe's warm living room, E. J. tossed her coat onto the couch and eyed the old box that sat in the middle of the floor. He flipped open the top, and she spotted a mass of aluminum shreds. He picked it up, and she realized it was in the shape of half a tree.

"Nell and I bought this not long after we were married."

By the inflection in his voice she could tell it was a special memory, so she refrained from commenting on its sad shape. Perched on the edge of the couch, she watched as he pulled the rest of the tree, a stand, and some sort of spotlight thing from the box. He pushed the bottom half of the tree into the stand, then the top half onto that portion and stood back to observe it.

"I usually put it in front of the window."

"Okay."

He pushed it into position at the front window, set the spotlight to one side, and attached it to a cardboard circle that had red, amber, and green cellophane circles in it. E. J. wasn't sure what that contraption was for but put off asking for the moment. The way Gabe handled the tree and spotlight was almost reverent, and she didn't want to hurt his feelings by asking what the tree setup was all about.

He opened another worn box. "These ornaments are old, but I've never seen a reason to quit using them."

They were old. So old she'd seen pictures of them in antique magazines. There was a painted Santa of thin glass about three inches high and a bird with a brush tail that apparently went with a tiny nest that had three tiny blue eggs in it. There were wreaths, and candles, and angels with delicately painted faces and feathered wings along with glass beads to drape among the aluminum branches of the tree. Somehow the delicate ornaments didn't go with the tree, but who was she to comment on that? It was Gabe's tree.

"Nell bought this bird and nest when the five-and-ten store closed on Main Street. This wreath—" he held up a piece of green braided yarn with red buds on it—"was part of a handicraft her second-grade Sunday school class made one year. And that gold cross the year after."

E. J. recalled all her childhood ornaments in Grams's boxes.

"Nelly made something every year after that, including this candy cane made with Life Savers, and this little Santa sleigh." He shrugged his broad shoulders. "Not the most beautiful things, but—"

"Full of memories," E. J. finished for him. "Just like those trees in your backyard."

"Like those pines . . . all twenty-eight of them. One for each year we were married. Full of memories." He hung the Life Savers candy cane on the tree. "I'm sure Christmas brings back a lot of memories for you, too."

She picked up a tiny wooden birdhouse. "Not any I want to remember."

He stopped rummaging in the box. "Now, why not? Cora goes all out at Christmas."

She hung the birdhouse on the tree.

"Want to talk about it?" he offered.

"I'm here to help decorate the tree."

Gabe scooted the box nearer E. J. "Then let's get it done. I made eggnog to drink afterwards."

Though she hated the ritual that Gabe obviously enjoyed, if his lingering over each ornament was any indication, he clearly cherished it. But each comment he made about the tree, an ornament, a memory of Nell and Christmases past, was like a stab to E. J.'s heart. Grams tried hard to make the holidays special, but E. J. had always found herself looking out the front window, hoping . . . well, she didn't know what she hoped for—maybe a mommy like the other girls had?

Finally every ornament was on the tree.

"Now for the *pièce de résistance*."

Gabe turned out the overhead light and plugged in the small spotlight. The color wheel began to turn slowly on its stand, red changing to green, then to amber, then clear, casting sparkles onto the limbs.

"Nell would turn the tree on as soon as it got dark. We'd sit in that chair and watch the lights play on the tree and across the ceiling." He stood back, studying the tree with his head tilted to one side, lost in memory.

"Well, let's have some of that eggnog." He glanced down at her. "Nonalcoholic, of course."

"Of course."

She followed him into the kitchen. "Do you hear something?"

Gabe paused and listened. "Sounds like someone is using a chain saw."

"At this hour?"

"Probably cutting up firewood. Started your shopping?"

"Nope. But I don't have a lot to do, so it won't take long."

She had made arrangements for gift baskets to be delivered to key people in the company and had discussed a Christmas party with Brian.

E. J. sipped the eggnog as Gabe sat next to her on the sofa with his own cup. "This is good."

"Never care much for eggnog except at Christmas. It's one

of those rituals that seems right somehow. What I've always done." He smiled. "Families need to have traditions."

"Should they?"

His gray eyes turned to her, questioning. "Didn't your family have Christmas traditions?"

"Not really. It was mostly Grams and me. She made fudge on Christmas Eve. With big hunks of black walnuts in it." That candy literally melted in E. J.'s mouth—she hadn't eaten anything that wonderful since.

"There you go. That's a tradition."

E. J. studied the cup. A heavy mug with a Norman Rockwell scene painted on the side. "I don't consider that a tradition."

"You could. Everyone should have a few good memories of childhood Christmases."

"Well, I don't. But then, it's hard to build any kind of warm fuzzy feelings since my mother was never around. She wasn't exactly the sentimental type."

"It must be nice to be perfect."

"I'm not perfect."

"Only able to see others' mistakes then. That must be comforting."

She recognized the censure in his tone and refrained from answering. Gabe and the evening had made her open a door she usually kept closed.

He swirled the eggnog around in his cup. "What about your brother?"

"Mr. Nice Guy over there? He's his mother's son. I keep thinking that I must have my father's temperament, but then, who is my father?" Her laugh sounded hollow.

"It's never too late to start your own traditions. Be good for the baby."

"You forget: I am giving this baby up for adoption."

Gabe was quiet for several minutes, and she finally glanced up at him, expecting to see . . . what? She didn't know.

"Well, there are a lot of couples out there aching for a child. I'm sure the agency will find it a good home. Have you talked to Freeda?"

E. J. nodded. She had been in contact with the lady who ran the small social services office.

She made herself drink the eggnog, holding the cup with both hands so her trembling wouldn't be so evident. "It wouldn't be fair of me to keep my baby."

"Says who? Have you stopped to consider that you know better than anyone what not to do? You know the mistakes not to make."

"Mistakes, yes, but I don't know anything about babies or what they need. I can buy things, provide toys and clothes and proper schooling. But a child needs more than clothes and toys and schooling, and I don't think I'm capable of raising a child properly." Tears stung her lids. "I don't know how to care, Gabe, how to really care about somebody. I'm like Marlene. Maybe I don't like it, but it's true."

Gabe was quiet for a long time. Finally, he said softly, "You've changed since you came here."

The observation surprised her. "Have I?"

"Of course you have. Growth is good, and you're starting to think more clearly. To see life as it is, not as you want it to be."

E. J. smiled wistfully. "You see all that in me?"

"Yep. You were fairly certain that Cullen's Corner was a town full of idiots when you first came back."

She laughed. "Now I wasn't that bad."

"Maybe not, but you didn't think we matched up to your standards. You're allowing yourself to care about people now."

E. J. stared into her empty mug, letting him continue.

"You've formed close friendships with Helen and Maggie, and even old Lets Marley has wormed her way into your heart."

Gabe reached for her hand, a gesture that surprised her. "And we both know that you can care for this baby and love it more than any other person on this earth can love it."

She wasn't so sure about that. At the moment, she didn't feel the least bit maternal . . . or did she? Didn't she wish deep down in her heart that she was among those glowing soon-to-be mommies eagerly shopping the baby section for blankets and newborn sleepers for the children they carried next to their hearts?

"I'm going back to Los Angeles as soon as the baby's born."

If you haven't guessed already, stubbornness ran in the Roberts family. Now, E. J. had learned to trust her new friends, more than trust them . . . to . . . dare I say it? . . . love them. Unfamiliar feelings of true friendship curled warmly inside her, uncomfortable yet comforting at the same time.

She was convinced that giving up the baby for adoption was the right decision. She feared she was like her mother in more ways than she cared to admit. The sobering thought hurt when she'd finally admitted it. She wasn't a drinker, nor did she go from man to man. She'd made sure she didn't fall into those traps, but a child had no place in her life. She had a career, her company. A child would mean an additional responsibility she wasn't prepared to accept.

"It's getting late," she said, setting the cup aside. "Very much of that and I'll not fit through my door."

"You look good. Pregnancy becomes you."

E. J. smiled. "You're a nice man . . . but a big fibber. Walk me home, Gabe Faulkner, before God strikes you down."

He laughed, tenderly tucking a lock of her hair behind her ear. "You're nice too, E. J. Roberts. Cut yourself some slack."

❦

Kicking off her boots outside the door, E. J. stepped inside the foyer and stopped short. The scent of fresh pine wafted through the house. A giant tree filled one corner of the front room.

"What on earth?"

Chris grinned from the kitchen doorway. "I got us a Christmas tree!"

"It's huge."

"Biggest one I could find."

E. J. tossed her coat at the hook on the back of the front door. "Good grief."

"Where are Grams's decorations?"

E. J. stopped in midanswer. "Wait a second. Why are you doing this?"

Chris pretended to be shocked. "Can't I do something nice for my grandmother and sister and her baby?"

"Not without wanting something in return."

"For heaven's sake, Evie, can't we be nice to each other for a little while? It's Christmas."

E. J. sighed. "They're in the garage."

He rubbed his hands together in delight. "Okay, let's get busy."

Her wish to forget the Christmas season ignored, E. J. was caught up in Chris's enthusiasm by what they found in Grams's old boxes.

"These are ancient," he crowed, pulling a string of lights out of a box they'd found marked Christmas.

"Make sure the cords aren't frayed."

"Grumpy," he accused, checking the strands. "They look fine."

He began looping lights around the huge pine while E. J. scavenged other boxes and found decorations at least as old as those Gabe had lovingly put on his tree. The fragile glass balls came in all colors: green, red, blue, gold, silver, and an odd color of pink. There were breakable Santas about three inches high, snowcapped cottages, a Rudolph, wreaths—enough to make a lovely tree. E. J. felt her excitement rising.

They decorated until late into the night, then turned off the lights and drank hot chocolate, admiring the results. The lights twinkled merrily, illuminating the room.

"See, it's perfect," Chris boasted. "Grams will love this. Wait until she wakes up and wheels herself into the living room in the morning."

"Yes, she'll love it," E. J. agreed.

Chris stared at the tree, lost in thought.

"Penny for your thoughts." E. J. sipped her chocolate.

"How about a thousand dollars."

"Why that much? Do you really think you're worth it?"

Chris reached over and pretended to slug her on the arm. "Watch it, Evie."

"Stop calling me Evie. It's E. J."

"Whatever, Evie."

E. J. stuck out her tongue and they both laughed. When quiet returned, E. J. turned to her brother. "Why are you here, Chris?"

"To take care of you and Grams. Grams is worried. You're helping take care of her, and you have the baby and yourself to take care of."

"We have Hattie to help take care of Grams, and people come over with food and to visit her. And I never saw you rushing back to take care of anyone any other time we needed you."

"Touché, sis." He sighed, eyeing his fingernails.

"So what gives?"

"I'm in trouble."

"What kind of trouble?"

Chris looked away. "Well, seems I'm going to be a father. My girlfriend . . . she's having a kid and she wants me to support both of them."

E. J. frowned.

"Evie, you know me. I don't want kids. They aren't for me."

"But . . ." She paused, realizing the implications of whatever came out of her mouth.

"I'm not stable like you. I don't have a fancy job and an LA loft. I can't have a family now. I don't even have a job."

"Get one."

Chris sprang up as if suddenly shot from a gun. "I tried . . . I can't do it, Evie. I've tried everything. And I have these debts . . . I've made some really bad choices."

"That's the 'thousand for your thoughts.'"

"It would sure help." He rubbed a temple, looking very boyish. "I wish sometimes I were you, Evie."

E. J. sat in silence. What could she say? She wished she were someone else. "My life . . . it's not as good as it looks."

"No, it's probably better." Chris turned and walked to the stairs. "I hate to flake out on you, sis, but I'm feeling a bit bushed. I think I'll head up to bed."

"You aren't going out?"

"Nope. Not tonight."

He began climbing the stairs. E. J. looked at the cup where he'd left it beside the couch. Still not picking up after himself. Some things never changed.

"Night, Evie."

"Hey, Chris."

He paused and stuck his head down to look at her. "Yes."

A lump caught in her throat and the Christmas tree lights blurred. "We could do better . . . maybe we should quit blaming our mother and take responsibility for our lives."

"Yeah . . . maybe." She listened to his footsteps disappear up the stairs.

❦

Saturday morning, Gabe buttered his toast, then sat at the table to eat his breakfast. Folks said he was a creature of habit. Helen accused him of it often, in a teasing way. Shaking out his morning paper, he glanced out the window at the trees he and Nell had planted over the years, as he did every morning.

He blinked and threw the paper aside. Going to the window, he stared out in disbelief. Where there had been twenty-eight pines standing in a row across the lot behind the house, now there were twenty-seven and a stump.

He recounted them aloud to make sure, then counted them again.

Twenty-seven.

Fury gripped him. Everyone in town knew what those trees meant. Nell had planted those pines to commemorate each wedding anniversary. She'd died shortly before their twenty-eighth anniversary, but he'd planted one that year anyway.

He finished breakfast, his gaze riveted on the tree stump. He'd gotten no closer to identifying a culprit when he left for the shop.

During the day, his customers commented on how quiet he was, but he didn't explain. No one would understand. No one could understand. To them it was a tree. To him it was his life.

By the time he headed home he was no longer merely angry. He was furious.

As he let himself into the house, his eyes were drawn to lights on in Cora's house. Maybe giving E. J. an early Christmas present would lift his spirits.

Trudging across the snowy yards, present in hand, Gabe knocked on Cora's back door.

The door creaked open and E. J. was framed in the doorway light. "Hey! I'm glad to see you! Come in."

Glancing past her, he saw Chris sitting at the table and surmised that some of the tension in the house had subsided.

E. J. looked good—and young—in blue tights and an over-sized blue sweater. Her hair was gathered atop her head in some kind of knot, and strands of it clung to her neck and cheek. Apparently brother and sister were playing some kind of board game. Monopoly.

"I wanted you to have this."

"Oh! A Christmas gift!"

She accepted the gaily wrapped box, grinning. She shook it impishly. "Keys to a new Mercedes-Benz?"

"You peeked." He set a second, smaller gift on the kitchen counter. "For Cora—a bottle of that perfume she favors." He glanced toward the living room. "Where is she?"

"Her hip was bothering her, so she took a pain pill and went to bed early. Thanks—she'll love the perfume, and she has something for you."

E. J. set her gift on the kitchen table. "Would you like a cup of hot chocolate? Chris and I were just having some."

"Yeah, Gabe, come on in. E. J. makes a mean cup of cocoa." Chris got up from the table and moved to the refrigerator. "Plus you can see me bankrupt my big sis."

"No, thanks. Thought I'd drop the present off early and get on home."

He didn't have to get home, but he wasn't good company. And he did have a baby cradle to finish.

"Wait a minute," E. J. said. "I've got something for you."

"Haven't seen you around much," Chris remarked, returning to his chair.

"Barbershop keeps me busy."

"E. J. said you're a workaholic. No future in that."

"Here," E. J. said, returning to the kitchen and handing Gabe a small package. "Merry Christmas."

"You didn't have to—"

"But I wanted to." Her eyes met his, affection shining in their depths. "For the first time in a very long time, I wanted to buy a gift from the heart."

"Thank you."

"Open it."

"Only if you open yours."

She laughed, ripping into the festive paper.

"A foot massager!" She flew into his arms and hugged his neck energetically. "Finally, a gift I can use! Thank you, thank you, thank you!"

Grinning, Gabe submitted to the affectionate onslaught. "I noticed you've had a lot of trouble with swelling."

"Okay, open yours."

He tore off the paper and found a Christmas card. Glancing up, he opened it.

"It's a year's subscription to a seed-and-floral-house catalog," E. J. said. "I thought—"

"It's perfect. Been thinking about ordering from this house myself and just never got around to it."

She frowned. "Seriously? You don't have one already?"

"No, I don't. I'll look forward to the first issue. Thank you."

"It's the first Christmas gift I've ever bought just because I wanted to. Merry Christmas," she whispered, giving him another hug.

His grip tightened around her waist.

Gabe spotted the blinking lights coming from the living room along with the sound of the television.

"You've put up a Christmas tree?"

"Uh-huh. Chris surprised me with it last night. Thanks to your cleanup efforts, we were able to locate the decorations in the garage. Come see it. I haven't had a tree in years."

He remembered her saying she didn't have Christmas trees, and her excitement surprised him. He followed her into the living room, where the twinkling tree dominated the room.

"It's really too big—"

Gabe choked back a stunned expletive. His pine! The tree was his missing pine! He'd recognize it anywhere.

He turned, swallowing back anger. "I've got to get back. You have a merry Christmas, E. J."

"And you, too, Gabe!"

He shut the back door soundly and hurried back across the lawn, clutching the Christmas card. First the gel, and now the tree.

Had E. J. lost her mind?

E. J. peeked out the window, watching Gabe cross the yard in a huff. "Wonder what was wrong with Gabe?"

"I don't know," Chris said, rolling the dice and moving a miniature iron around the board. "Maybe he's upset because I didn't ask him about the tree."

"Tree?" She turned from the window. "What do you mean, ask him about it?"

"I cut down one of those trees on his back lot."

"You did what!" E. J. couldn't believe her ears. Surely he wasn't that self-centered. "You cut one of Gabe's trees? I thought you bought that tree."

"Buy one? Why buy one when there are plenty next door? He's got too many. They need thinning out anyway."

"But it wasn't yours."

He shrugged. "It's just a tree, E. J. Don't make a federal case out of it."

"Just a *tree*? Gabe and Nell planted those trees together. They're not just trees; they're memories."

Chris rolled his eyes at the ceiling, an obstinate look on his face. She'd seen that look before, and it was not a charitable look.

"Besides sentiment, that tree belonged to someone else. How dare you go cut it down!"

"Well, it's done. Don't obsess over it. It's your move."

"I can't forget it. And Gabe won't, either."

She felt heartsick. Those trees were memories to Gabe, and she couldn't believe that Chris had been so insensitive as to cut one down because he was too lazy to buy one.

"So is this going to be a big deal?"

"Chris, someday you're going to have to grow up and take responsibility for your own actions." She smacked the toy iron out of his hand and shut the board.

Shoving back from the table, he shot her a dark look and went into the living room, throwing himself on the couch sullenly.

"I want you to go over there and apologize right now."

"For crying out loud, Evie, who are you? Marlene? Chill out."

"No, Marlene would have let you get away with this."

"What do you want me to do? Take the tree back and give it to him?"

"Apologize, that's all."

He got up and went upstairs.

E. J. picked up the phone and called Gabe. There was no answer. She hung up, reaching for her coat. The pine sat in the front room, gaily festooned and twinkling merrily.

How would she ever explain this?

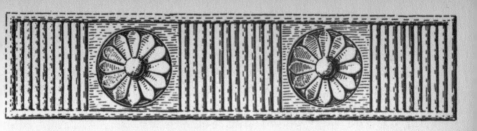

CHAPTER THIRTEEN

Explaining Chris's actions to Gabe was doomed to failure. The regrettable couldn't be explained, not logically. E. J. grieved with Gabe. But life goes on, and both E. J. and Gabe knew this. Both agreed that a tree couldn't overshadow the season. The birth of a Savior made E. J. more aware of her own child—the brand-new life growing inside her—than of Chris's mistakes. She was getting good at explaining the mistakes of others, but not so good at dealing with her own.

The week between Christmas and New Year's brought more snow, more cold. The only thing that kept E. J. from going nuts was that Chris went out every evening. She and Grams watched sappy movies and played endless dominoes. E. J. shed buckets of hormonally induced tears and prayed that she would one day find a comfortable way to sleep. She longed for the time when she could breathe and tie her shoes again.

New Year's Eve and Day passed. E. J. grew more uncomfortable every hour, both physically and mentally. The baby was real to her; each kick, each tremble within her body reminded her of the new life. Resolve started to weaken, and she found herself thinking about motherhood. Maybe she could take a lesson from Marlene and be a better mother than her mother had been. If she kept the baby she would have to get a bigger apartment—and trade the BMW off for a van. Plenty of women worked and had small children at home; if others could juggle a career and motherhood, why couldn't she?

Gabe's attic light burned long into the night. Sleepless, she'd sit at the window and wonder what he was doing. Imagining that she was with him brought a sense of comfort.

Maggie stopped by every day, which quickly became E. J.'s favorite time to look forward to.

"I remember the last month," Maggie said. "I felt like a moose."

E. J. laughed, knowing well the feeling.

"But this too will pass. Keep busy, sweetie." Maggie patted her comfortingly.

"With all this snow? Keep busy doing what? I've helped Grams cross-stitch three samplers. I've read every book I can get my hands on, and I'm sick of the limited television stations we get because Grams refuses to order cable." She sighed. "My work for Kilgore's isn't demanding right now. The gel is taking off, and Brian and Isabel are pleased. And now I'm boring you with my complaints. Tell me, what's going on in the real world?"

"Well, you know your brother is seeing Lucy Harris."

"Who?"

"Lucy Harris . . . cute little waitress at the café?"

"Really?" E. J. didn't know, but it didn't surprise her. Chris was always on the prowl, a child on the way or not. "What's she like?"

"Lucy is, well, bouncy."

"Bouncy."

"Uh-huh. Cheerful, although I don't see how she could be with her dad's recent death. But she's like that. Nothing gets her down."

"I'm so sorry."

"It was his heart. Passed on last week. It was a very good-feeling funeral . . . you know? Like Jill's. One of those services where you just know the man's in a better place and out of pain. Now Lucy can get on with her life. She can go anywhere and get a good job doing about anything . . . she's that smart.

I bet she could sell real estate. Helen wanted her to work for her but on a commission-only basis, and Lucy felt she couldn't do that. She needed a regular salary, with her father unable to work all those months. Maybe now she'll take Helen up on her offer. Helen would be real good to her."

"Helen's a very special woman," E. J. murmured. The best. She'd brought soup by twice this week, and she did E. J.'s nails. E. J. almost felt human again.

"Sure is. I wish she and Gabe would make up their minds about marriage." Maggie sipped her tea. "You know, there's been talk about you and Gabe." She met E. J.'s gaze innocently. "Any truth to that?"

E. J. patted her belly. "Of course. He's smitten with my ravishing beauty . . . can't keep his eyes off me."

Maggie rolled her eyes. "Goofball. I'm serious. You guys do spend a lot of time together. I think it's nice. Gabe's older, but experience is hard to beat. You know, the old stability effect an older man has on a younger woman. Could be a good match."

"You're the goofball, Maggie Markus. Gabe Faulkner doesn't have the slightest interest in taking a younger woman to raise."

"Hmm . . . don't be too sure about that. You could do worse."

"Gabe couldn't."

"E. J.!" Maggie scolded. "How dare you talk about my friend that way! You're a wonderful catch." She grinned.

"But I'm such a beast it's doubtful anyone, including Gabe, would put up with me."

"Well, it's my opinion that if a man had to go through pregnancy and childbirth, the population would be cut by one half."

"Don't scare me," E. J. warned.

"Piece of cake. Don't worry about a thing. Doc Strobel is a dream, and he always smells so yummy. Preferred Stock, I think. You'll sail through the birth without a problem and when it's over, you'll love this baby beyond belief."

E. J. studied her cup.

"What's the matter?"

"I don't know. Maternal feelings, I guess. Lately I've been thinking that maybe I could keep the baby. . . ."

She thought of the old butter mold. It wasn't perfect, but it was the source of so many good memories. This child was conceived in imperfect circumstances, but the joy it would bring was sweet and pure—like the butter from the mold.

"Oh, E. J. I've been hoping you'd at least consider keeping the child." Maggie leaned over to hug her. "Being a mother isn't so hard. Honest. And I'll help you in any way I can."

"I don't know, Maggie. It's only a thought. I haven't made any firm decisions. I'm still not convinced that I'm mother material."

Maggie bent forward again, laying a hand on E. J.'s, blue eyes intense. "No woman is, until she has a child. But I suspect you've got more grit than you realize."

E. J. held tightly to her hand, like a drowning woman holding onto a life preserver..

"I'm scared, Maggie. What if I'm like Marlene?"

"You're not. Forget that. Chris is like Marlene. You're the responsible one."

E. J. squeezed her hand. "Thanks. I needed the vote of confidence."

"You're welcome. You know, it's not often I get out without the kids, and with their croup and colds I've about run out of things to keep them occupied. So when I have two in school and a baby-sitter for the other three, I take advantage of it."

They spent half the afternoon talking, and when Maggie left, E. J. marveled at how much she'd enjoyed sitting with her, talking about nothing in particular. But she especially appreciated Maggie's support. Maybe E. J. wasn't Marlene after all. Maybe she was capable of raising a child.

That night before bed, E. J. located the cell phone in a dresser drawer and plugged it in to charge the battery. Snow was predicted to turn to ice, and if the power went out she wanted a phone. She hadn't used the cell phone in weeks, but Maggie reminded her to plug it in and keep it handy.

"You can never be too careful," Maggie had warned. "Especially this close to delivery."

Feeling achy and tired, she decided to go to bed early. She washed her face, then before getting into bed went to the window to look out. Gabe's house was dark. By the streetlight she could see snow coming down fast and furious. The street-light was a dim yellow glow amid the swirling flakes. Shivering, she closed the curtains and climbed into bed. The radio said it was the worst winter North Carolina had had in years. Of course, it had to be the winter she was there.

Sleep was slow in coming. She couldn't find a way to get comfortable. At least the baby wasn't beating against her ribs. She settled into an uneasy sleep and dreamed of building snowmen and tumbling in the snow with Chris as Grams peered out the front window.

Suddenly, she woke with the strangest sensation. A sudden warm gush made her sit up as a rippling pain made its way from her back across her belly.

"Rats," she whispered, sucking in her breath. "I'm not ready for this."

The slight cramping she'd had all evening was clearly the beginning of labor, and she'd ignored it. In fact, she'd ignored the actual birth part of the pregnancy the whole nine months. If this pain was an indication of the hours ahead of her, it wasn't going to be a picnic. She was counting on the epidural to get her through this.

Switching on the lamp, she groaned when she realized the power was off. The face of the digital clock was black. She care-fully got up from the bed, stripped her sodden gown off, and slipped on a housecoat. She leaned over and retrieved the flash-light from the nightstand. With the streetlight out, the bedroom was pitch dark.

Fumbling for the cell phone, she counted the pads until she reached nine, then pushed speed dial. Gabe answered on the first ring.

"My water broke and I'm in labor," she said quietly, gasping as a strong contraction gripped her. "It started about ten minutes ago."

"I'll be right there."

She'd managed to put on socks and loafers and wake Grams and get them both downstairs before Gabe knocked at the door.

"How close are the pains?" he asked, coming in with a swirl of snow.

"Ten minutes apart," Cora said. " I think we still have plenty of time."

"Maybe not. There's ice and about four inches of snow on top. E. J. where's your cell phone?"

"Upstairs on the nightstand." E. J. sat down, suddenly terrified. She'd never had to stay in the hospital—she'd never even had a broken bone. Hospitals smelled funny and the patients always looked so . . . sick.

He retrieved the phone and then dialed a number, frowning as he waited for an answer.

"Paul? Gabe here. I need your help. E. J.'s gone into labor, and without a four-wheel drive, I'm not going to be able to get her to Raleigh in this weather."

E. J. waited, closing her eyes as another contraction started. Grams patted her hand. "Hold on, honey. We still have plenty of time. First babies usually take their time coming."

Gabe hung up. "Paul will be here in a few minutes."

"I'm sorry."

"Don't worry about a thing. Paul's a customer. He's got one of the few vehicles I know of that can get around in this kind of weather. He'll get us to the hospital."

Gabe dialed a second number.

"Dan? E. J.'s in labor. I've got Paul coming with his four-wheel drive to get us to Raleigh." He listened a moment. "I don't know. Her water broke. About fifteen minutes ago. Okay."

He clicked the phone off. "The doctor will be waiting for us when we get there. Where's your bag?"

She drew a deep breath, pointing to the closet.

Gabe wasn't the typical television male buffoon. He wasn't ripping down clothes poles to take to the hospital, or forgetting the expectant mother in a mad dash to get to the car. He worked slowly and methodically, speaking in low syllables.

Cora limped toward the closet with the aid of her cane. "Let's get you into a coat and gloves, and I'll get a blanket off the bed."

E. J. got her coat and a muffler and found her gloves in her pocket.

"Boots?" Cora reminded.

"By the back door."

Gabe got them, then knelt in front of E. J. to help put them on.

He grabbed her suitcase and gave her a smile of encouragement.

"You're all so nice to me," she blubbered, suddenly overwhelmed by the situation.

Gabe winked at Grams. "Well, E. J., you're pretty easy to be nice to. Okay, let's get this baby into the world."

"I want to come," Cora declared, trying to snag her coat off the hall tree with the tip of her cane.

"Cora, all you need is to fall on this ice and break that hip again." Gabe gently moved the old woman to the sofa and draped an afghan around her knees. "You stay put. I'll phone the minute we get to the hospital and let you know what's going on. It may be hours before the baby comes."

Grams nodded, her old eyes accepting. "You're right—I can't get out in this weather. Hattie will be here in a few hours—don't worry about me. Call the minute you know anything, Gabe."

E. J. bent to give her a kiss. "Don't worry, Grams, I'll be fine . . ." She broke off in tears. "I'm not ready for this!"

Gabe calmly reached for her arm. "Come on, Momma. You'll do fine. Let's get you to Raleigh."

As E. J. discovered, that was a feat that wasn't as easy as it sounded. The porch steps were treacherous. Gabe went down first and made her sit down and slide to the bottom. He broke a path to Paul's waiting Suburban. Paul shoved the door open, releasing a blast of warm air.

"Now, E. J., don't you worry about a thing. We're going to get you to Raleigh in plenty of time."

"Thanks, Paul," she said, gritting her teeth as she managed to crawl into the vehicle.

Gabe crowded in beside her, and then put his arm across the back of the seat so she was nestled against him. She closed her eyes against another contraction.

Paul backed out of the drive, sliding sideways upon reaching the street. The ride to Raleigh was harrowing. E. J. learned that a four-wheel drive didn't necessarily mean skid-free driving. Upon reaching the hospital, she was whisked into labor and delivery and prepped. Gabe was admitted and he stayed with her, holding her hand, instructing her to breathe.

In twenty minutes, Dr. Strobel walked in, dressed in green scrubs.

"Well, well. Depend on babies to have the worst timing." He grinned. "The wait will be over soon. I'd say three or four hours. Then we'll know if we have a girl or a boy."

Girl or boy. *Maybe a girl*, E. J. thought. She'd once seen the cutest tiny pink dress with little rosebuds on the collar in a Sears catalog. . . .

When Doc had asked her if she wanted his best guess, she'd told him she didn't. She hadn't wanted to know until recently, as she hadn't wanted Lamaze classes—until right now. At the moment, she just wanted it to be over, yet her excitement grew. Her child would enter the world tonight.

Boy or girl.

Son or daughter?

The baby seemed in no hurry to cooperate, now that E. J. was settled as comfortably as possible in the hospital's birthing room. A nurse hooked E. J. up to a fetal monitor, coaching her through another hard contraction before she made a note on the chart. She efficiently took E. J.'s vital signs, comforted her through another contraction, and then went out, motioning Gabe to follow.

E. J. lay in bed, waiting for the epidural, staring at the ceiling, apprehensive and uncertain. She hadn't thought about this part of the birth and had tried her best to block out the painful images when they popped up. Most women had husbands, or at least a boyfriend or a mother to stay with them during labor. Why hadn't she asked Maggie to be her coach—or Gabe? Tears sprang to her eyes and she closed them, longing for Grams to be with her.

A warm hand picked up hers, and she opened her eyes.

Gabe stood beside the bed. "Doing okay?" he asked.

She managed a weak smile. "Think so."

"The nurse says everything is going well."

"That's good."

"Don't worry about a thing." He squeezed her hand.

A contraction started, and she squeezed back with a force that would make a linebacker wince.

"Breathe through it," he encouraged.

Throughout the long night Gabe was beside her, talking in that low, calm voice that kept her fears at bay, bathing her face and holding her hands as they watched contractions grow stronger on the monitor. Without him there, she was certain she would have succumbed to terror.

"Okay!" Dr. Strobel bustled through the doorway. "Let's get this baby born." The nurse hooked up another IV.

"I'll be outside the doorway," Gabe said, rising.

"No! I . . . I can't do this alone," E. J. cried, clinging to his hand.

Dr. Strobel motioned Gabe back to the chair. "If E. J. wants you here, it's okay. Put on a gown and mask."

From that point, everything was a blur. The only thing E. J. knew was that Gabe was beside her, holding her hand, encouraging her.

As dawn crept over a snowy landscape, E. J. heard a cry. Her baby had entered the world, screaming its lungs out.

I don't blame you, she thought, exhausted. She felt like joining in.

"It's a girl!" Gabe whispered softly, close to her ear. "Beautiful . . . just like her mother."

E. J. was worn out, but when the doctor lifted a small bundle and handed it to the nurse, she could not keep from looking at her daughter.

Her baby's blue-eyed stare caught hers. "Oh, my," E. J. whispered. "Hello, baby!"

Then she froze. On the left side of the infant's neck was a deep purple blotch—the Kilgore birthmark. Exactly like her father's. *Dear God.* Her heart sank, and she looked away.

"She looks like she's saying, 'Here I am, world. Look out for me!'" Gabe said, caressing the baby's cheek with the back of one finger. "She's a dandy."

"Take her away," E. J. murmured.

"Mommy has to rest now," the nurse said, throwing E. J. a sympathetic glance. "And we've got to weigh this little girl." She moved the baby to a scale to be weighed and measured.

"Good job, E. J.," Gabe said, brushing damp hair away from E. J.'s face. "You can rest now."

"Gabe." She grasped his hand. "The baby . . ."

How could she explain that until she'd seen the mark, she'd wanted to keep the child? Her daughter. But now . . .

"You're exhausted," he said, as if he knew. "You have all the time you need to make your decision."

"How will you get home?"

"Paul's in the waiting room. I'll ride home with him."

"Thank him again for me."

"I will." His hand brushed her hair. "Sleep."

Her eyes were heavy, and she dozed off before Gabe left the room.

When she awoke, sunshine was streaming through the hospital room windows.

A nurse glanced up, smiling. "How are you feeling?" She took E. J.'s pulse and blood pressure.

"Tired." Sick at heart. If she'd entertained the slightest notion of keeping the child, the birthmark had closed the door. She would never look at the child without being reminded of the rape, of Jake. What a cruel joke.

The nurse made notations on E. J.'s chart.

"You rest a bit more; then we'll see about getting you a breakfast tray."

"I'm not hungry."

The nurse closed the chart. "There's ice water in that pitcher by your bed. I'll bring in your baby."

"No," E. J. said shortly. "I don't want to see her."

The nurse turned, studying E. J. for a long moment. "You're sure about that?"

"Yes. Please don't make this any harder by bringing her in."

"Of course. I'm sorry." She turned to leave, then paused in the doorway. "I'm probably totally out of line, but would you like me to send the chaplain by to see you?"

E. J. turned away. "No."

"If you change your mind, press the call button."

The door closed, and an antiseptic silence closed over the room. Rolling to her side, E. J. doubled the sheet in her mouth and bawled.

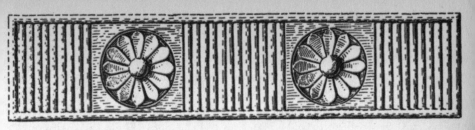

CHAPTER FOURTEEN

E. J. woke an hour later to see a huge bouquet of hyacinths and tulips sitting on the bedside stand. Gabe. She knew without looking at the card that he'd sent them. Her experience told her that tulips out of season cost a fortune.

Then she remembered the reason for the flowers. Her baby had been born this morning. Her daughter. She recalled the frantic ride to the hospital and Gabe holding her hand, talking to her, encouraging her, telling her she could do it.

The birthmark: Jake Kilgore's hereditary signature. She closed her eyes, swallowing back sobs.

She couldn't ever go back to the old E. J. What she'd felt when Dr. Strobel held up her newborn daughter had been the most amazing thing she'd ever experienced. There had been joy, expectation, and relief.

And her beautiful, innocent daughter was in itself a miracle. Nothing had prepared her for the sight of her child, not the books she'd read or even witnessing the birth of Maggie's twins.

Well, folks, we have to ask ourselves why did E. J. look at the child, if she hadn't decided for certain to keep her? Automatic reflex? Simple curiosity? The answer might have eluded E. J., but to any mother, her response was natural. There's some very basic instinct that makes every woman yearn for her child. Everything E. J. had read about surrendering a child for adoption suggested it was best not to see the baby. Seeing that tiny, marred neck, that face so new she had only just drawn breath, E. J. realized how fragile, how precious that life was.

Swiping at tears, E. J. spotted a small teddy bear lying on the foot of the bed. She reached for it and held it close, closing her eyes against a wash of tears. Gabe's goodness knew no end. She wished he'd stayed, wished she could have awakened to see him sitting beside her. But he hadn't stayed, and she felt emptier than ever.

Resting a hand on her much flatter stomach, she swallowed tears. She'd never expected to feel like this. She'd thought, or made herself believe, that once the baby was born it would all be over. But it wasn't. It felt as if it were only beginning, the pain as raw and hurtful as the day she'd discovered she was carrying a rapist's child.

Helen Withers, dressed in a smart chocolate brown pants suit with a cream-colored blouse, sat at her desk, staring at Gabe. Helen's house sat in an older neighborhood, two blocks over from Gabe's. She'd papered the living room and kitchen in the last couple of months, and the house had begun to shape up. Gabe had gone with her to choose the paint, causing renewed speculation about their relationship.

"What are you doing out so early this morning?"

"E. J. had the baby early this morning."

Surprise and elation filled Helen's face. "Wonderful!"

"A girl—seven pounds and three ounces."

"Is E. J. doing okay?"

"She was resting when I left the hospital."

"My goodness—how wonderful. Listen to me—you must need a cup of coffee about now."

"Thanks, Helen. Coffee would be nice."

Helen returned in a few minutes and handed him a cup. She'd never seen him so . . . so what? Nervous? Edgy? Uncertain?

"How did you get to the hospital in all this snow?"

"I called Paul to drive us."

"Well, the snow's stopped. I'll run up to Raleigh later today. I imagine she'll be going home tomorrow or the day after."

Gabe nodded. "She'll be going back to Los Angeles."

He sat in front of the desk as he'd done many times before, but somehow today was different. He had something on his mind, and she'd wait until he was ready to tell her. She sat across from him, holding her cup of coffee, waiting.

"Is she? I thought maybe she'd change her mind about that."

"No. I think she'll be leaving soon."

Gabe stared at his cup. Finally, he cleared his throat, and the reason for the early morning visit made itself known. "Helen, what I'm going to ask is personal. And odd, but bear with me. I know a woman has a right to expect a better marriage proposal, but neither of us is a youngster, and I'm not always so good at saying what I mean."

He paused and searched for the words somewhere outside the window. Helen smiled encouragingly at him. She had known Gabe for years. The man's quiet, soft compassion was what endeared him to her.

"I don't think a child should be raised by strangers, and I don't think that a man alone can give a child what it needs. Especially a daughter. I want to make a home for E. J.'s baby. I think together we can do it, if you're willing. Each of us has talked about how we've regretted never having children of our own. E. J.'s baby might be God's way of giving us a second chance."

Though stunned by his proposal, Helen went along. "Like Sarah and Abraham?"

He smiled. "Something like that."

She set her cup slowly back on the table. For a moment they looked at one another. She'd hoped for a long time that their relationship would lead to more, but she was also well aware that Nelly's memory still overshadowed Gabe's life.

Until lately. Until E. J. came home.

"What are you saying, Gabe? That you and I raise the child? At our age? We're not quite as old as Sarah and Abraham, but like you say, we're not getting any younger. We're getting to the age where you never know about health. What if . . ."

"I know, I know. Don't think I haven't considered all possibilities." He got up and paced to the window, staring out at the snowy landscape. "It's sudden, and I shouldn't ask you in this way. I still believe that E. J. will eventually decide to keep the baby. I want to give her every opportunity to change her mind, but if she doesn't . . ." He paused. "I want the child to remain in Cullen's Corner."

Helen focused on the stack of contracts needing her attention on the desk. Contracts from young couples starting out with their first home. Contracts full of hopes and dreams and youth. She remembered when she and Ed bought their first house shortly after they were married. They dreamed of children, but they put it off. Years flew by, Ed fell ill, then years and years of battling the sickness. Then it was too late.

"So what exactly are you proposing that we do?"

"I thought that we'd . . ." He turned back to her, eyes softening.

At that moment, Gabe was caught by Helen's simple elegance. Poised on the edge of her chair, hands clasped before her . . . he was suddenly rendered speechless. He was trying to do a good thing and be fair to Helen in the process. But oh, how he wanted that child, that small piece of E. J.

"We'd . . ."

She motioned him to go on.

"I thought we'd get married, adopt the baby, and raise her. I know this isn't the most romantic proposal you've ever had—and I do have feelings for you, Helen, it's just—"

"You don't need to explain," she said. "And if E. J. doesn't change her mind?"

"Then praise God that she doesn't. I continue to believe in E. J. Once she's had time to sort through her feelings, she's going to realize she can give that baby everything she will ever need, including—especially including—love. She needs time alone, Helen. She'll be back; and if she isn't, then I'm not a sound judge of character."

Helen leaned back and covered her face with her hands. "Gabe Faulkner, you are insane. There isn't an adoption agency on earth that would let a couple our age adopt a child. Foster a child, maybe, but not adopt. We'd be setting ourselves up for nothing but heartbreak. We'd fall in love with that little girl, and our hearts would be shattered when she's given to a young couple who can raise her and do the things with her our ages won't permit."

"It won't come to that, Helen. E. J. will never give her child away."

Shaking her head, Helen reached for his hand. "You believe that much in her?"

He nodded. "I do. She isn't thinking straight right now, but given time, she will. Maybe we can't adopt the child, but Freeda will allow us to be foster parents. I've already talked to Freeda— she'll be bending every rule in the book and putting her job on the line, but she owes me a favor. I helped George find work when he was down-and-out many years ago, and Freeda hasn't forgotten. The law gives E. J. four months to change her mind, but Freeda isn't even filing it for six weeks. If E. J. doesn't change her mind at that time, Freeda will put the paperwork through and we'll hope for the best."

"Gabe, Gabe, Gabe." Helen shook her head.

He flashed her an embarrassed grin. "I know a woman deserves a better marriage proposal, but we're friends. Comfortable friends. We've both had the loves of our lives and lost them. Maybe we won't be wildly, madly in love, but this little girl will fill a void, Helen, and if it comes down to it, we'll fill a void for her. I'll be good to you; make you breakfast in bed on Saturday mornings . . ."

Helen smiled and bent to kiss his hand.

"What do you say? Think we can handle it?"

"Well, what red-blooded woman could ask for more?" She

smiled wanly. "This is a huge commitment, Gabe. I can't give you an answer right now, but I will pray about it. Maybe it isn't so crazy . . ."

He touched his lips to her fingers lightly.

"Thank you, Helen. E. J. will change her mind, but if she doesn't, I promise I'll make you happy."

"You already do." She smiled. "Abraham and Sarah, huh? How do you feel about changing dirty diapers?"

"I'll love it!" he said, glowing.

An hour later, Gabe left Helen's house, feeling lighter. He didn't know what was best for the baby, or what E. J. would do. But here was a chance to raise a child, with a woman whom he'd grown very fond of. Marriage with Helen would be safe, comfortable. Nell would approve of his choice. And E. J.'s little girl would have a father and a mother who loved and cared for her. Together he and Helen would give her everything a child needed: a stable home, her needs met, and the love of God and family.

He drove home, thinking of E. J. Who would have thought that the cinnamon-haired woman who'd moved in next door would make such a change in his life?

He'd thought his life was over. Oh, it had been a comfortable existence, settled. Lonely at times, but with a good circle of friends and people who cared. Now God had brought a new dimension to his life, and suddenly he was contemplating marriage and looking forward to raising a child.

"Thank you, Lord. I should never second-guess you," he conceded out loud.

Would his happiness be complete if E. J. stayed? He couldn't answer that question. She'd certainly filled a need in his life lately. Did he feel an attraction he could neither explain nor deny to the lost young woman?

He did.

But only God could change hearts, and God had his work cut out for him in the form of E. J. Roberts.

Forty-eight hours later, E. J. was feeling stronger in body but even weaker in spirit. Gabe had come to see her every day, and she'd talked to Grams twice. Neither Gabe nor Cora spoke directly of their wish that E. J. would rethink adoption plans, but she knew they were disappointed with her decision.

"I know you're faced with a difficult decision," Grams told her over the phone. "Giving up the baby is a valid decision if you feel in your heart that you can't give the child the love she deserves. I only wish you'd take more time to think about what you're doing—to make absolutely sure you're thinking clearly. Marlene might not have won Mother of the Year, E. J., but in her way she loved you."

"I've had nine months to think, Grams. I love this child— I want my daughter to have both a mother and a father, and I want this time in my life to be over."

On the day she was dismissed from the hospital, Gabe agreed to drive her to the airport for the trip back to LA. There was nothing left to do but leave. Leave her tiny sleeping infant in a nursery and walk away.

"Ready to go?"

E. J. turned to see Gabe silhouetted in the hospital doorway. "Just finishing up."

Helen and Maggie had both visited her during the brief recovery period. Even Lets Marley came with Reverend Matthewson. They stopped by that morning to wish her well. She didn't discuss her decision with any of them, though she knew Helen and Maggie would provide a willing ear. But she didn't want to talk. Or to think anymore. She'd made a decision and there was no turning back.

Freeda Williams brought papers by and she'd signed them, with a nurse witnessing. The papers said she had four months to change her mind. But she wouldn't be changing her mind. It was time to go back to LA and start over. She had a company to help run, a grieving friend to comfort. Perhaps together she

and Isabel could put the past behind them and find a reason
to live for the future.

Gabe put her suitcase in the back of his car and after seeing
her buckled in safely, got into the driver's seat.

"Maggie said she couldn't get everything in the suitcases
so we'll send the rest by mail."

"I appreciate that."

Tension hovered between them, and E. J. pretended interest
in the passing scenery. Both minds were on the baby, although
E. J. tried to block out her thoughts. The baby belonged to
someone else now.

"Think the plane will be on time?"

"Hope so."

Conversation was stilted. Eventually they gave up and rode
in silence to the airport.

Gabe parked at the loading ramp and set the brake. "Do you
want me to go in with you?"

"No, there's no need. I'll be fine."

"Leaving won't erase anything," he reminded softly.

She stared at the busy terminal—private cars and taxis coming and going, luggage being unloaded at the curb—and she was
afraid to look at him for fear of crying. "No, leaving won't erase
anything, but I have to go. You know that."

But how she wished leaving would change the awful hurt
in her heart.

Opening the passenger side, he helped her out. Their eyes
met. "I'll miss you." Gabe's bravado faltered. His voice broke,
and tears filled his eyes. Drawing her to him, he whispered
against her ear. "Please reconsider, E. J. You can, you know.
God can work miracles when we allow him to."

"I know he can, Gabe." Her voice failed her and tears blocked
her effort to speak. She laid one mittened hand against his
cheek. "Thank you for everything."

"I'm going to kiss you good-bye, Eva Jean Roberts. And
I haven't felt this way about a woman in years."

She nodded. His lips against hers were warm and firm, and
she cherished that ever so brief moment. Gabe Faulkner was

no longer just a friend or a neighbor. He was a man—a strong, compelling man whom E. J. could fall in love with.

"You're not a bad kisser, Gabe Faulkner," she whispered.

He cleared his throat softly. "There won't be a day I don't think about you."

Squeezing his hand, she turned and walked into the terminal, determined not to look back. If she did, she would never leave.

Isabel glanced up from the file she was holding to find E. J. standing in the doorway of her office. Her mouth opened and closed like a fish. "You're back."

"Isabel, I'm so sorry about Frank. I should have been here for the funeral."

E. J. was shocked by Isabel's appearance. For a moment she thought she had walked into the wrong office. The woman behind Isabel's desk looked a good twenty years older than when E. J. left. Dark circles shadowed her eyes, and her formerly lustrous gray hair lay limp and lifeless.

E. J. took a deep breath and walked behind the desk to embrace the older woman.

"Oh, E. J.," she cried. "It's been so difficult . . . first Jake, then Frank. My whole world has collapsed around me."

E. J. patted Isabel. What could she say without revealing the truth? She should have been with Isabel during these dark days, but then she'd been struggling with her own dark days.

The woman clung to E. J. as if she were the only life raft in the boundless ocean of misery Isabel lived in every day. "Oh, E. J., what's left to live for? All my dreams—of retiring with Frank, of having grandchildren—they're all gone. There's nothing left, no reason to go on."

Isabel's words renewed fresh guilt in E. J.'s heart. "Hush, now," she said soothingly. "The company is turning around, and things will be better. You'll get through this. I'm back now, and I'll help you."

"Yes, now things will be better." Isabel wept into E. J.'s collar. "Now you're back and I won't be so alone."

Brian's jaw dropped when E. J. appeared at his office door a few minutes later. He was behind his desk working on quarterly reports. Judging by his cool greeting, his defenses were up and running. So were hers. Both were anticipating a clash over the unauthorized marketing of the gel, and neither was prepared to budge.

E. J. sat down, and Brian instantly mentioned the reports. Nelly's Jelly was a hit, praised by the industry as the hottest new product in years.

"It doesn't make up for what you did," E. J. said.

Brian sighed. "I hoped we were past that."

"We're not. What were you thinking?"

Brian got up and put distance between them. Did he think she was going to swat him like a naughty child? She'd seriously thought about it.

"Your eight-month sabbatical put the bloom back in your cheeks."

"Answer my question."

Drawing a deep breath, he faced her. "I don't know, E. J. I overstepped my bounds. I wanted to get the gel to the public." He shrugged. "I don't know why, but it seemed the right thing to do at the time. I'm sorry. I should have followed your instructions to the letter. I had the company's best interest in mind; that's my only defense."

"There could have been serious repercussions for the company if Gabe had decided to sue."

"I understand. It won't happen again."

"I should hope not."

Relief shone in his boyish features. "I didn't do this for the glory."

"Maybe not," she answered. "Anyway, it's over now and we have Nell Faulkner's clinic to think about. Do you know any-thing about building a clinic?"

"I'm great with a hammer and nails," he joked.

"Good, because you're going to Cullen's Corner to help build it."

His face—and hopes for a Jamaican vacation—plummeted.

E. J. got up to leave. "We'll talk about the new ad campaign this afternoon. I trust you have some slicks to show me."

"Yes, ma'am." He saluted her.

E. J. took the reports to her office and tried to focus, but nothing caught her interest. Her daughter's face hovered over the figures and numbers. She shook her head to clear the picture, but it would not budge.

Reverend Matthewson would have been proud of the way she'd handled herself with Brian, not letting her anger take over. She'd given Brian a second chance, like the prodigal son. Gabe would also be proud, knowing how difficult it was for her to relinquish control.

Gabe. A thousand times a day she thought of something she wanted to tell him but couldn't. She'd closed the door on that part of her life. Gritting her teeth, she grimly settled into the life she thought she wanted.

Over the next two weeks, Brian and Isabel both looked at E. J. as if a change had occurred in her. Maybe it had. A gnawing guilt accompanied her these days. Isabel's grandchild was somewhere out there with her new adoptive parents. E. J. had given her away without ever telling Isabel she was a grandmother. How could she do that? She held the power to give Isabel part of her life back.

She poured another cup of coffee, a drink she'd become increasingly fond of since . . . she wouldn't think about the pregnancy anymore, or about Cullen's Corner.

Still, tears burned her eyes. Forgetting wasn't that easy. She couldn't just decide to forget. At the most unsuspecting times she would think about Gabe or Grams or Helen or Maggie, and she'd miss them terribly. She'd never been one for small talk, but in Cullen's Corner she'd become involved in people's lives . . . interested in the small things that make everyday life exciting.

Moving to the window, she looked out over Los Angeles. Smog was heavy. Smog didn't exist in Cullen's Corner. Suddenly she longed for the lush green landscape and the gentle hills. Even the occasional snow. She smiled, remembering childhood snowball fights, frosty noses, and stuffing cold hands into Grams's pockets for warmth.

A wistful smile hovered at the corners of her mouth. How about that? Maybe she did have memories. Good ones.

Gabe, true to his promise, had shipped the remains of her personal belongings to her office. Brian asked about the boxes, but she'd told him to have maintenance put them into storage. There was a note with the boxes that went unopened.

It was usually late when she'd finally drive home. The apartment felt like a mausoleum, cold and unfeeling. It had become a place to sleep, to forget for a few blissful hours the sight of a newborn's face . . .

Groceries. By the second week it hit her that there wasn't a thing in the house to eat. Not even cold cereal. What little she'd eaten lately had been bought in a drive-through window.

Grabbing the keys, she drove to the grocery store. Pushing her basket up and down the aisles, she gathered cereal, milk, bread, some spaghetti and sauce, and fresh fruit. At the end of one aisle she almost ran head-on into a young woman with a baby seat balanced on her cart. Before she could turn away, E. J. saw the small cherub face and the curious eyes of an infant swathed in pink.

"Sorry," E. J. murmured, darting around the young woman. The woman shielded a protective hand on her daughter's infant seat.

Suddenly overcome with the need to leave, E. J. abandoned the cart in an empty aisle and ran out of the store. In the car she rested her head against the steering wheel and sobbed until her stomach hurt.

Her daughter was about the same age as the child in the cart. She would have looked up with those curious eyes, and E. J. would have rushed to protect her.

Now someone else was caring for her, giving her kisses,

smoothing away tears, and laughing at her baby ways. Someone else would be there to see her first teeth, hear her first words, see her first steps, and take her to her first day of school.

Someone else would name her.

Turning the key in the ignition, E. J. drove home, tears streaming down her cheeks. Forgetting the shower that had sounded so good earlier, she stripped out of her clothes and fell into bed, sobbing into her pillow until sleep overcame her.

The next morning, she stared at her image in the mirror and groaned. Her hair was a mess, her face was puffy, her eyes red. If anything, she looked worse than she had a year ago.

By the time she'd salvaged herself, she was late getting to the office.

Brian was waiting in her chair, arms crossed. "Car accident?"

"Bad night."

She poured a cup of coffee, wishing she could mainline caffeine through an IV straight to her brain. "What's on the docket for today?"

"That new baby shampoo we're developing. Seems to be right on—" He sat up straighter, jostling his coffee. "E. J., what's the matter?"

"Nothing. I'm all right." She reached for a tissue.

"No, you're not. You haven't been all right since you got back. Talk to me, E. J. What's going on?"

She blew her nose, refusing to look at him. "It's nothing . . . allergies."

He didn't buy it. "Come on. It's more than an allergy. You tear up at everything, and that's not like you. What happened while you were away? Meet a guy and it didn't work out?"

E. J. looked away. "Where are the test results for the shampoo?"

Brian handed her a folder. For the next hour she made herself concentrate on the baby shampoo, closing her mind to her own child. Finally Brian left, and she leaned back in her chair, shutting her eyes. Her daughter's face appeared before her—corkscrewed, red, and crying. *Had* she met someone and it didn't work out?

"You might say that," she whispered.

E. J. threw herself on the couch, closing her eyes. When would this end? She'd been so certain that she could have an abortion. When she couldn't go through with it, she thought she could have the baby, sign the papers, and walk away. She hadn't counted on Grams, Gabe, Maggie, or Helen.

Or the child.

She hadn't counted on wanting—*needing*—her daughter. She hadn't counted on bringing memories back with her.

At the end of the day, she wasn't ready to go home. Home. The apartment would never be a home.

That night she chose a different route, one that took her past a chapel with a weathered wooden door. The neighborhood church sat in a section of the city she rarely drove through except on detour. She parked outside the church and was surprised to find it open.

Inside the chapel, chandeliers with flame-shaped bulbs gilded the walls with a soft glow. The pews were worn smooth by hundreds who had lifted up praying hands. Tonight, the chapel was empty. Her steps echoed on the wood floor. The quiet surroundings held a peace that she desperately sought. Tiptoeing down the aisle, she entered a middle pew and sat down, folding her hands on her lap.

God was here. She could feel him.

She sat for a long time, aware of nothing more than the quiet surrounding her. She longed for the same peace within.

Be still and know that I am God.

It was late when she finally left; she had been unaware of the time that passed. Darkness had overtaken the city by the time she reached home. She was tired but found she couldn't sleep. Every night had been the same. She closed her eyes and dreamed of her daughter. She woke with her heart pounding wildly and tears damp on her cheeks.

A month passed, then five weeks. Grams called to say that spring was bursting out all over. Los Angeles was warm, the smog thick, and E. J. was no closer to being her former self than when she'd first come back. She wasn't sleeping or eating. Brian commented on her weight loss, fussing over her.

Isabel sank deeper into depression and eventually turned the company over to E. J., shutting herself away in her home. Grieving, grieving, grieving.

Running the company alone took all of E. J.'s energy. Increasingly, she found herself in the pews of the tiny church, praying, searching.

"I can't stand it anymore," she whispered. "I can't do this alone anymore, Lord."

She who prided herself on her independence needed someone. Or some ones. She needed peace. She needed the Lord back in her life.

Slipping to her knees, she clasped her hands together beneath her chin like a child. "Help me, Father. I've made so many mistakes, made so many wrong decisions. I've gone against your will; I've tried to do it on my own. I've resented my mother for her mistakes, yet I've given my own child away. I've been harsh and unforgiving. My life is empty. I can't do it anymore. Forgive me. Take away the pain and give me peace. I'm so sorry. I'm so very, very sorry."

The litany continued as she poured her heart out, confessing everything that stood between her and God's forgiveness. It was surprisingly easy, and with each confession, her soul lifted and the muscles that had been tied in knots unraveled. The lines of worry left her face and when she was too empty to cry anymore, she dried the tears, experiencing a joy she couldn't explain.

That night she slept soundly for the first time in months. When she awoke, she looked forward to a new day.

"What happened?" Brian asked, handing her the latest Nelly's Jelly reports. "You look like a new woman."

"I *am* a new woman." *Forgiven by the grace of God.*

"You're not going to believe how well the gel is selling."

E. J. believed it. She was certain that Nelly's Jelly had phenomenal sales because God wanted Cullen's Corner to have that new medical clinic.

Another week passed while E. J. sorted her thoughts. Each

night she stopped by the chapel and stepped inside for prayer, sometimes for as little as fifteen minutes, sometimes for an hour or more. Down on her knees, in front of God, praying for guidance, she learned to speak her heart, talk to God like a friend, give over her fears, her hopes, and her pain to him. She had left God out of her decisions. That was the problem. She decided now to trust him with every aspect of her life, something she hadn't done in more than eighteen years.

Grams called to say that she was going on a cruise. To the Caribbean—two whole weeks in the sun. What could an old lady do on a cruise, Grams lamented. She couldn't dance because of her hip, and she didn't gamble or like those noisy floor shows. But friends had talked her into the adventure, and so she guessed she'd try anything once.

E. J. smiled, happy that Grams was getting on with life, still open to trying new things.

One evening at the market E. J. ran into the young mother with her daughter. The baby had grown and wore a pink dress and a ribbon in her dark hair. Her dark eyes were even wider with question, and pudgy fingers were stuffed in her rosebud mouth.

E. J. smiled, tenderness washing over her. Her daughter would be the same age by now, grinning, being wheeled around a supermarket.

"You're beautiful," she said, reaching out to touch the infant.

The new mother beamed. "Thank you."

Checking out, E. J. carried the groceries to the car. A moment later she reached for the phone and punched Brian's number. He answered on the second ring.

"Brian? This is E. J. I won't be in the office tomorrow. In fact, I'm taking a few weeks off. You're in charge."

"Is something wrong?"

"No. As a matter of fact, everything is very right."

"But weeks? E. J. . . ."

"You can handle it, Brian. I'll keep in touch."

Hanging up, she called the airline and booked a ticket to Raleigh on an early morning flight. She was going home for her daughter.

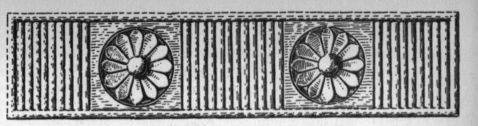

CHAPTER FIFTEEN

The wheels of the American Airlines 747 touched down at the Raleigh-Durham International Airport, shrieking down on the tarmac.

E. J. rented a car and loaded her luggage, anticipating the trip to Cullen's Corner with a mixture of apprehension and hope. Now that she'd made up her mind to regain custody of her daughter, she couldn't wait to begin the process. Her daughter. The thought sent a ripple of joy through her.

It was late afternoon when she arrived in Cullen's Corner. Martin Peabody sat in front of his store in the warm spring sunshine. He squinted as the car approached. Waving, she drove past Peabody's and straight to Freeda Williams's office.

Freeda's office sat in a corner of the small courtyard. Luck was with E. J. The social worker was in.

"E. J. How nice to see you," Freeda greeted her, getting up from the desk to clasp her hand.

"Freeda, I need to talk to you."

"E. J., please don't be concerned. Your daughter is in a good home. . . ."

"I can't do it, Freeda," E. J. blurted. "I made a mistake. I want my daughter back. Can you help me? Will you help me?"

Freeda frowned. "This isn't uncommon, but E. J. . . . you need to be absolutely certain. . . ."

"I'm certain. I have never been more certain of anything in my life. I know it won't be easy, and I know I haven't been making good decisions lately, but I'm thinking clearly now. I'll do anything to get my baby back."

Freeda sank back in her chair, contemplating E. J. "You were so sure you'd made the right decision before. What's changed your mind?"

E. J. tried to sort her feelings and thoughts into some sort of coherent order.

"I realized what a mistake I made. I wasn't trusting God to lead me. I was relying on myself. I want to give my daughter what I never had: a mother, a home, traditions, and Christmas trees, and . . . and butter molds, Freeda. I want to give her unconditional love, teach her the values I learned in life. Truth and honesty and God and family. I've wasted so many years, Freeda, done so many things I regret, but now I know who I am and what I want. God has forgiven me, and I want to ask my daughter to forgive me. I want to love her, care for her, see her first tooth, walk with her to school that first day. I want a chance, Freeda. Give me a chance to be a mother."

"Well," Freeda exhaled. "It may take a few days . . . I'll have to contact the foster parents. . . ."

"I'll wait forever if it means I get my daughter back."

"You'll be staying at Cora's?"

"Yes, but don't mention that I'm back to anyone else, not until this matter is settled." She thought of Gabe and Maggie and Helen. She wanted to go to them and introduce them to her daughter, personally.

"As you wish. I'll be in touch." She stood up, and the two women shook hands.

E. J. left Freeda's office with renewed hope. Maybe it wasn't too late to right a wrong.

This time she'd come prepared to stay. Brian could handle the business; she would stay as long as it took to get her daughter back.

She drove to Cora's house and located the key under the rose trellis.

Tired from the trip and emotionally drained, she opened the windows and put clean sheets on the bed. In a few days she would be meeting her daughter and begin being the best mother she could be.

Grams would be overjoyed when she returned to find a new great-granddaughter awaiting her.

Freeda's voice sounded anxious on the other end of the line. "E. J.'s back and she wants her daughter."

Gabe dumped hair out of his dustpan. "When did she get here?"

"She drove in this afternoon. Came directly to my office. She's different, Gabe. I think you're right."

"I know I am, Freeda. I'll close up and be over in a few minutes. We'll talk."

He locked the shop and walked across the square to Freeda's office. He'd expected E. J. back, but the six weeks without a word had worried him. He was encouraged, but with reservations. The baby belonged with her mother, but he had to be sure that E. J. wasn't acting out of guilt.

E. J. spent a restless, sleepless night back in Cullen's Corner. Up early, she stared out the window at Gabe's house. There he was, next door, but the short distance seemed unapproachable. How would she tell him she'd been a fool, that she'd asked for her baby back and now longed to raise her child? Grams would have known all along that she couldn't go through with the adoption, but Gabe? He wouldn't know.

Nor would he know that she'd decided to trust the Lord with all of her heart, soul, and being until she told him. She hadn't even told Grams yet. She wanted some time to get established in her renewed faith.

Gabe emerged out of his house on his way to the shop. Seven-thirty, right on the dot. He'd stop at the café, get a cup of coffee—sugar, heavy cream—and open the barbershop. He'd drink his coffee in the barber chair, waiting for the first customer of the day.

Predictable.

Wonderfully, hopelessly predictable.

E. J. passed the day puttering around the house. As much as she wanted to see Maggie and Helen, she wanted to wait. She wasn't sure at this point that she was ready to face Gabe, either. Her feelings were still so new. . . .

She'd put the rental car in the garage, and kept the lights out at night.

The long day passed, and E. J. was growing restless. She'd heard nothing from Freeda, but final adoption papers had not been signed. She'd been gone less than two months. She lay down for a fitful nap and woke to hear a baby crying. Each time, she opened her eyes and listened closely but couldn't locate the sound. She rubbed her temples, sure that the pressure was making her crazy.

Frustrated, she got up and paced the floor, blotting out the image of a tiny pink face with a prominent purple birthmark on her neck. The crying sound had been so real. Perhaps it was Maggie's twins. She dismissed the cries.

As five o'clock neared, she wore a path by the phone. Why hadn't Freeda gotten back to her? Was the foster family not cooperating? Finally she couldn't stand the suspense any longer and phoned Freeda's office.

"I'm sorry, she's not in at the moment. May I take a message?"

E. J. left her cell phone number.

Something was wrong. She was sure of it. But what could it be? She was still within the legal period to change her mind.

She made a pot of coffee and sat in the living room all night, turning on the television, but no lights. The cell phone sat by her side. She repeatedly checked the battery, and finally plugged it into the wall to ensure that it stayed on. Toward morning she nodded off.

Bright sun woke her, spreading warm rays across the lawn, touching first Gabe's house, then Grams's. Voices outside caught her attention. She sat up and peered out the window, hoping to catch a glimpse of Gabe.

But, no, the voice did not belong to Gabe. A female figure pushed back the curtains of the open window. She couldn't see who it was, but the figure was slim and moved with quick, efficient movements.

A girlfriend. Gabe had a girlfriend and it wasn't Helen!

E. J. sat back down, stunned. That Gabe would have a girlfriend hadn't occurred to her. That it wouldn't be Helen was more astounding.

"Why, the old *goat!*" she exclaimed.

E. J. could hardly believe her eyes. Gabe Faulkner sporting a young girlfriend. What was he thinking?

Looking down the barrel at fifty? Ha.

A girlfriend?

Poor Helen. What must she think? Everyone in Cullen's Corner believed Gabe and Helen would get married. They were so right for each other . . . comfortable together. Admitting the fit between Gabe and Helen was difficult for her. E. J. was drawn to Gabe despite their age difference. But he obviously hadn't noticed the attraction. What about what he said to her at the airport when he kissed her? Maybe he was going through a midlife crisis, being attracted to younger women—any younger woman, apparently.

E. J. fumed. If he was ready to move on, why wasn't it with her?

Suddenly the truth was blindingly clear. Gabe. Her daughter. That's what she'd wanted all along. Why hadn't she seen it earlier? It had taken an ugly rape to open her eyes and see that she needed God, and it had taken Gabe and his assurances, his unshakable faith, to convince her she needed family.

She wanted to rejoice for Gabe's newfound happiness, but couldn't. She had made yet another mistake, and this one could be permanent. Spurred by determination, E. J. decided to go down to Freeda's office. And if Freeda wasn't in, she'd wait. Even if it took all day.

But Freeda was in her office. She was clearly uncomfortable with E. J. in the doorway.

"Your secretary wasn't at her desk."

"That's fine. Come in . . ."

"I've been calling."

"I know. I'm sorry I haven't gotten back with you. I had an emergency come up yesterday, then a series of meetings. You know how government is—always red tape. . . ." Freeda shifted the papers on her desk.

"Have you contacted my daughter's foster parents?"

"Well, I'm working on it. They're . . . they're not available at the moment."

"They're away?" That hadn't occurred to her.

"They may be. At least, I haven't been able to discuss the situation with them. I'm sorry. It could be a few more days."

E. J. bit back tears. "But you will keep trying?"

"I'll keep trying."

"And you'll call the instant you talk to them? I want my baby back. Whatever it takes, I want her back." She got in Freeda's face. "I *want* my baby back!"

"Okay. Okay." Freeda gave her a sour look, stepping back. "You want your baby back."

Gabe was sweeping the floor of the shop when Helen came in, grinning.

"My goodness, that baby is growing like a weed. And happy! She's as cute as a button. Look at the darling jumper I picked up. Isn't it cute?"

"Real cute . . . hasn't she got enough jumpers?"

"A woman never has enough clothes. You know that!"

Gabe set the broom aside.

"She took almost three ounces of formula this morning," Helen continued.

The phone rang and Gabe picked up. "Barbershop."

"E. J.'s getting restless," Freeda said on the other end.

He grinned. "Good. Can you stall her a little longer? We want to make sure."

"I'll try, but she's pretty antsy. She yelled at me a minute ago."

"Yelled, huh?" His grin widened. "Now that doesn't sound like our E. J., does it?"

When he hung up, he sat for a moment lost in thought.

"What's wrong?" Helen asked, sitting in one of the straight chairs across from him.

"I didn't want to tell you, but E. J.'s back for the baby."

Helen sighed. "When did she get here?"

"Day before yesterday. She's been hiding out at Cora's, thinking that no one knows she's here. The only person she's talked to is Freeda."

Helen grinned. "Well, I guess you were right after all. Six weeks practically to the day."

Neither seemed eager to answer the question that was coming next, but folks, we know they had to.

"What now?" Helen asked.

"I don't know. What do you suggest?"

Helen was quiet for several minutes, her face solemn. Gabe knew her well enough to know something was on her mind, and he was pretty sure he knew what it was.

"If E. J. wants her daughter, I say praise God."

Gabe nodded. "That takes care of E. J.," he acknowledged.

"But you're worried about us?"

"Yes." He met her gaze. "I am."

"Don't be. We would be marrying because we care about each other, but we aren't passionately in love. And I don't know about you, Gabe Faulkner, but I'm a little too old and tired to care much about passion these days." She drew a deep breath, grinning. "I care about you very much. But if I marry again, I want it to be for love, the kind I had with Ed, the kind you had with Nell."

He closed the gap between two very good friends, drawing her into his arms.

"I do care about you, Helen . . ."

"Let me finish, Gabe. I need to say this, and you need to hear it." She leaned back, meeting his eyes. "I agreed to marry you because it was the thing to do. Everyone in town thought we'd marry eventually; the baby simply confirmed it. I knew that together we could give that baby a good life, but she needs her mother. E. J.'s coming back is an answered prayer."

She hugged him tightly, holding on for a long moment before letting go. They sat down again, facing each other in their chairs. "Besides," Helen continued, "what would a woman my age do with a baby? When she starts school, people will think I'm her grandmother. When she graduates, I'll be too old to go."

"What about me? We're the same age."

"It's not the same. E. J. is young and full of pep. She can devote the energy to the baby. And you'd make a wonderful father. Age is a matter of mind over matter: If you don't mind, it doesn't matter."

"Helen, are you suggesting—?" Color tinted his cheeks. "Are you saying that E. J. and I . . . why, that's crazy!"

Helen cocked her head. "I've seen the way you look at her. I've seen how careful you were with her, how you get all flushed when she's around. You were with her at the birth. I think you care about her more than you realize. And E. J. has a special glow when you're around. I've seen it—others have too."

"I'm too old for her."

"No, you're not. She's a professional woman, not a young ingenue. She's helped to build a company. If I know anything about business, I know that it takes maturity. You're two people who bring out the best in each other."

She reached out and rested a hand on his knee.

"You and I are friends. I hope we'll always remain so. E. J. and I will continue to be close; I love that girl. I can still be part of the baby's life. Aunt Helen sounds good, doesn't it?"

Gabe shook his head. "Helen, you never cease to amaze me. You know me too well."

She squeezed his hand. "And you know me. And more importantly, you know E. J. Tell her how you feel, Gabe. Give yourself a chance."

She reached over and kissed him on the forehead.

"I'll look like an old fool," Gabe argued.

"We are old fools, haven't you realized that yet? Take a chance for the first time in your life."

When the door closed behind her, Gabe remained in his barber chair. E. J. wanted her daughter, and Helen was right. He wanted E. J. It was foolish and everyone would say he was too old for her, but he knew that Nell would approve. And fiddle—fifty wasn't *that* old.

"Thank you, Nell, sweetheart," he murmured. "I guess there is no fool like an old fool."

E. J. let another day pass before she called Freeda's office again. Freeda was out, the secretary said.

Adding to E. J.'s frustration, she'd spent another sleepless night punctuated with the sound of a baby crying. Not loud or often, but there all the same. Every time she awoke to hear a cry, she convinced herself it was her imagination.

She paced the floor. Guilt. That was it. Any psychologist would tell her that. She wanted her child so badly she heard babies crying in the night. It seemed every television commercial had something to do with a baby. She ached for her child.

She was about to call Freeda the morning of her third day, when the cell phone rang. The noise startled her.

"Hello."

"E. J., it's Freeda."

"Thank God. Have you gotten in touch with the foster parents?"

"Yes, I have. I've been able to make arrangements for you to meet."

E. J. sank into a chair. "When?"

"Today."

"What time and where?"

"In my office. Two o'clock."

"I'll be there. Thank you, Freeda."

Breaking the connection, E. J. sat for a moment organizing her thoughts. In four hours, she would meet her daughter for the second time. She would meet the couple who had loved and cared for the little girl for the past six weeks. Nerves knotted her stomach.

She passed the rest of the morning praying for guidance. Every scenario flashed through her mind. The baby would cry. The baby would smile. The baby would throw up, and E. J. wouldn't know what to do.

The foster parents would not want to give her up. The foster parents would welcome her decision with support and encouragement.

By one-thirty, she'd worried herself into a frenzy. She was going to throw up. She changed clothes three times, hoping to make a good impression. She wanted the foster parents to realize she was a rational woman, even if she hadn't practiced the attribute lately.

She drove slowly to Freeda's office, parking around the corner from the complex. She walked the half block with shaking knees, carrying the teddy bear that Gabe had given her when her daughter was born. Still, she was twenty minutes early.

"E. J.," Freeda greeted. "How nice to see you. Please, have a seat."

"I'm early. I couldn't stand it."

"I understand. You're not the first nervous mother I've had in my office."

"You've done this before?"

"Oh, yes. These decisions are often recanted."

For the first time, E. J. felt Freeda was on her side. "I hope to undo this one. I want my daughter, Freeda."

Freeda smiled. "Before you choke me, I'll be right back."

E. J. tried to relax, but she couldn't. Every conversation in the hallway could be about her baby. Every footstep outside the door could be the parents bringing her child to her. When the door finally opened again, she expected Freeda, but Gabe appeared.

Gabe, holding an infant.

A precious tiny girl in a pink gingham dress. A little girl with bright blue eyes, fair skin, and a thatch of cinnamon hair just starting to curl.

A beautiful, God-given infant with a large birthmark on her neck.

E. J.'s gaze rested on the sight. The baby looked so soft, so huggable.

"Hello, E. J. . . ."

The baby's gaze slowly lifted to meet his.

"We've been calling her little E. J.," he admitted. "E. J., meet your mommy."

E. J. stared at the bundle, tears swelling. Gabe gently laid the child in her mother's arms.

"Hello, little E. J.," she whispered. She was transfixed by the sight of her daughter—her daughter in her arms.

"We haven't officially named her, of course—thought you'd like to do that, but I'm kind of partial to Nell and Jean. Nelly Jean. I like that—kind of old-fashioned, but let's face it. She's little E. J. no matter what the official document reads."

E. J. looked up. "Why are you here?"

"I'm the baby's foster parent, thanks to Freeda. I've been looking after your little girl until you were ready to return."

Tears sprang to E. J.'s eyes. "You thought I would come back?"

"No." He smiled. "I *knew* you would. Cora knew you would, too—that's why she went on the cruise with a clear conscience. And if you didn't—" he paused—"Helen and I would have raised her, with your permission. We wanted to make sure she was loved and with family until you came home."

Love flooded E. J.—love so strong she knew it could only come from God.

"You took my daughter? You were willing to change your life in order to take care of my daughter?" Her face clouded with confusion. "With Helen? But what about your girlfriend?"

Gabe frowned. "Girlfriend?"

"The girl at your house—the young girl."

Laughter rocked him. "Girlfriend! You must think I'm quite the Casanova. That's Mary Campbell, little E. J.'s nanny."

E. J. blushed. "I thought . . ."

"Well, you thought *wrong*." He eyed her sternly. "Again."

E. J. giggled, then turned back to the baby. "You would have had great parents, baby."

Early joy faded. Gabe had said he and Helen. Obviously they planned to get married.

"I knew you were here," Gabe continued, "but I wanted to make sure you were back for the right reasons. You can't raise a child out of guilt. It's love or nothing around these parts."

"I do love her."

"I know you do." He reached out to touch the baby. "She's a real blessing."

"What about you and Helen?"

"Me and Helen? Well, it seems I have lots of women friends these days." His eyes lingered on her. "Speaking of which, how about I take my two best girls to lunch? Hamburgers and malts at the café?"

E. J. nodded, eyes bright with tears, careful not to disturb the infant who had just fallen asleep. Holding the baby seemed foreign, but she'd get used to it. Oh, would she get used to it!

"Thank you so much for what you did," she whispered. "How am I ever going to repay you?"

"Well," he draped an arm around his two best girls and walked them to the doorway. "I imagine I'll think of something."

That evening, E. J. followed Gabe into Nelly's sewing room, which had been converted into a little girl's nursery with pale pink walls and ruffled curtains. In the corner sat a carved wooden cradle with white eyelet covers.

"Oh, it's beautiful!" E. J. murmured, cradling her sleeping daughter.

"I wanted something special for a special child. She's almost outgrown it already."

"You made this?"

He grinned. "I started it for my own child but put it away when Nell miscarried the second time. I finished it a few months back."

"It's lovely." That explained the hours she'd seen the attic light burning.

E. J. hesitantly laid the baby into the cradle and smiled when she gurgled and snuggled to one side.

"She is a special baby, isn't she?" She tenderly caressed her daughter's rosy cheek.

"Exactly like her mother," Gabe said softly, brushing E. J.'s cheek with his fingertips.

They left the room, lingering a moment at the door.

Gabe draped his arm around her trim waist. "I've got a fresh apple pie."

"You do? How lucky can I be?"

Gabe laughed. "When you give, you receive."

Now folks, Gabe Faulkner knew the instructions pertained to all sorts of giving, but right now all he could think about was love. Your gift will be returned to you in full measure, pressed down, shaken together to make room for more, and running over.

While Gabe cut the pie, E. J. poured mugs of coffee, carrying them out to the front porch. They sat in the swing, eating pie and drinking coffee. Everything was right in E. J.'s world for the first time in her life.

"Gabe? What about Helen? Surely she must be upset, knowing I've come back."

"She's delighted, and Helen and I are just friends. We were never meant to be anything more. She knows how I feel about you. In fact, she knew before I knew."

"Remind me to thank her." She snuggled closer to his warmth.

Resting her head on his shoulder, she breathed in the scent of his shaving lotion, that blend of spice and woody scent that was his alone. The swing swayed gently back and forth, and E. J. marveled at how perfect they were together. She realized God knew what he was doing all along.

"So, what is E. J. Roberts going to do now?"

E. J. smiled, recalling the response she would have given a year ago. Go back to LA and work. But not now.

"Stay right here in Cullen's Corner."

Gabe drew a deep breath. "What about your business?"

Her smile grew wider. God had taught her much these past few weeks. She'd learned that hard decisions could lead to love, as they did in her case. Or a wrong decision could be a tragic loss, as it could have been if she hadn't come back.

And sometimes love was imperfect, like the butter mold. It took God's love to make her see past the imperfections to the utter perfection within.

"I'll have all I can do here with Grams, Helen, Maggie, and my daughter. And if Isabel has no objection, we'll move Kilgore's Kosmetics to Raleigh. After all, *Money* magazine rated the Triangle the best place in America to live, and *Fortune* said it was the best city for business. Kilgore's Kosmetics and Nelly's Jelly couldn't do better. Oh, by the way, may I use your phone?"

"Who are you calling?"

"Don't be so nosy." She pinched his cheek affectionately.

In the kitchen, she picked up the receiver and dialed. It was three hours earlier in LA.

The phone rang four times before a woman picked up. "Hello?"

"Isabel?"

"Yes?"

"This is E. J. Are you going to be home on Saturday?"

"Saturday?" Isabel sounded confused, tongue thick with medication. "Yes, I suppose."

"Good." E. J. reached for Gabe's hand for support. His smile gave her everything she needed. "I have a very special young lady I want you to meet."

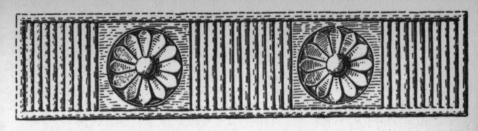

EPILOGUE

Oh, my goodness. Will you look at the time! I hear the baby stirring from her nap, so I have to go now. But it's been a joy sharing my story, my campfire with you.

I glance up as a cab pulls up in front of the house, and I see Momma and Grandma Isabel arrive, arms loaded with stuffed toys and sporting ear-to-ear grins found only in adoring grandparents. Oh . . . did you realize it was Momma's story I shared? I'm the child who might never have been, had it not been for God's intervention and Mom's decision to have me.

Getting up, I move to the railing, waving. It's good to see Mom again; I haven't seen her since Dad's—Gabe's—funeral last year. Cullen's Corner and the barbershop won't be the same without him.

Hugs and kisses exchanged, we wrap our arms around each other and move inside to view the main attraction, three-day-old Adrian Elise Morgan. But before we can climb the stairs to baby Adrian's bedroom, my husband, grinning like a Cheshire cat and brandishing the most glorious bouquet of yellow roses I've ever seen, pops out of the kitchen doorway.

It's easy to see a celebration is in order, but for whom I'm not sure.

Momma and Grandma Isabel giggle as if they were in on the surprise all along, but it's several minutes before they let me in on the fun.

Settling me comfortably on the sofa, my husband, John, hands the rose vase to Momma, then clearing his throat, ceremoniously and with great exaggeration begins to read from a slip of paper—a telegram, it looks to be.

I listen, first with interest and then with spreading warmth that reaches all the way to my toes. I catch snatches of my name, Ellen Jean Morgan . . . the name of the research lab I work for, but really I hear only one thing: ". . . Because of your exhaustive work in the development of a specific killer molecule that halts the metastasis of breast-cancer cells, the serum will be named Morgan's Vaccine."

My husband's eyes darken with pride as his gaze catches and holds mine. "Praise be to God, Dr. Morgan."

I look up and see Momma crying. Grandma Isabel pulls a tissue from her pocket and wipes her nose. And my John? He simply beams, eyes so full of love that I get a little weepy.

One step closer. Me, Ellen Jean Morgan, Momma's little baby girl, has found new hope for breast cancer—and maybe a link in the chain leading to a cure for all cancers.

Praise *be* to God.

&

Well, folks, that's the end of the story. I guess no one ever knows why bad things happen or why sometimes evil is rewarded. I suppose no one will ever know this side of heaven.

Someday, God willing, someone will unlock the cure for cancer. Who knows? Maybe that child is being born this minute, or carried in a mother's womb as we speak.

Maybe it's been conceived in love, or maybe it's a child of rape. Maybe it's conceived, but not convenient.

Every new life has a purpose, however conceived.

One thing I have learned from my story is that imperfect

beginnings can be God's masterpieces, and every life has worth—great worth in the eyes of the Lord.

That's the hard part, isn't it? Deciding who's God—him or us.

Like a wise old woman once said: Life is hard; it's our decisions that make the difference.

About the Author

Lori Copeland has published more than fifty novels and has won numerous awards for her books. Publishing with Tyndale House allows her the freedom to write stories that express her love of God and her personal convictions.

Lori lives with her wonderful husband, Lance, in Springfield, Missouri. She has three incredibly handsome grown sons, three absolutely gorgeous daughters-in-law, and three exceptionally bright grandchildren—but then, she freely admits to being partial when it comes to her family. Lori enjoys reading biographies, attending book discussion groups, participating in morning water-aerobic exercises at the local YMCA, and she is presently trying very hard to learn to play bridge. She loves to travel and is always thrilled to meet her readers.

When asked what one thing Lori would like others to know about her, she readily says, "I'm not perfect—just forgiven by the grace of God." Christianity to Lori means peace, joy, and the knowledge that she has a Friend, a Savior, who never leaves her side. Through her books, she hopes to share this wondrous assurance with others.

Lori welcomes letters written to her in care of Tyndale House Author Relations, P.O. Box 80, Wheaton, IL 60189-0080.

Books by Lori Copeland

Faith
June
Hope
Glory
With This Ring (anthology)